ONLY WALK SO FAR
CAROLINE LOPEZ

ONLY WALK SO FAR

Table of Contents

CHAPTER 1
Barenhohle

The dogs were howling, high and wild, on the day that Rennesson disappeared.

A war party was departing that morning, and Rennesson had stood frowning in the middle of a packed-dirt courtyard as he watched them, the men and women who had been selected to protect the safety of their home. Barenhohle – "The "Bear's Den" – was the seat of the Cimbrian Woods, and to defend it was to defend the honor of their country, Wendland, against the armies of neighboring Gaul, who periodically felt foolish enough to try and cross over the border.

The war hounds passed by him, all scrabbling claws and foaming teeth as they surged forward, straining against their chains towards the opening in the settlement's wooden gate that led to the shadows of the forest. The largest among them was a black and tan giant named Siegher, who pulled and whined against the hand of Linderic the Houndmaster, which held steady despite all the dog's height and muscle.

"Well, Renn, we're off. Wish us luck?" Linderic asked. His smiling eyes were belied by the dark warpaint smeared around them as he stopped in front of the boy.

Renn didn't match his smile, but muttered "I'd rather go *with* you. I still don't get why I can't."

"Come on now, your uncle isn't chief for nothing," Linderic said. "I'm sure he knows what's best for you. We'll just have to ask him again next time, but how about

I take you on the next boar hunt, to make up for it until then?"

"I've *been* on boar hunts. What good does that do me? A kid can do that, and I'm already fourteen," Renn sulked, absently reaching to touch the giant dog, but it snapped at him and he pulled his hand back. In his temper, he'd forgotten that the dog was on the warpath today. Though Renn was stuck at home, this was no ordinary day for Siegher, otherwise the dog would have licked his hand and rolled over. But today, the dogs sensed war in the air, and everybody not wearing Wendish warpaint was an enemy.

It had been on a day like this that Renn's cousin Jungbern, currently scowling at them as he stalked past with his battle axe slung over his lean shoulder, had gotten that scar on his face – a series of faded red jags running from his tanned cheekbone to his jaw.

"How many times do I have to tell you before you learn, Ranizone?" the young man said. "Leave my dog alone."

"Fewer times than it took *you* to learn," Renn shot back under his breath, eyeing the scar as Jungbern walked on.

"Watch it," Linderic warned, his voice low. "He might not have gotten your meaning, but he knows devil tongue when he hears it, and that's not going to help your case any."

"Fine," Renn said, using the Wendish words he was supposed to use in Barenhohle, rather than the Gallic language he'd used to insult Jungbern. He doubted Jungbern had heard him, anyway, with all the racket from the dogs.

"If he asks, I'll just tell him it was a compliment. He'll never know the difference."

"What are you on about, Ranizone?" a new voice boomed out behind him, suddenly evaporating all of Renn's confidence. His eyes darted to Linderic in alarm.

The voice belonged to Hagen – Jungbern's father and the chief of Barenhohle. Could Jungbern have told his father that Renn had been speaking devil tongue on the very day of a war party? That he was "probably bringing down curses on the warriors"? It wouldn't be the first time Jungbern had tried something of the sort.

"Stop chatting and let Linderic tend to his business. If we don't get these dogs – and these *animals* on the trail soon," he looked down at Siegher, smiling at his own joke, "they'll start eating us alive, and will have no appetite left for the Gauls."

"Yes, sir…" said Renn. It seemed Hagen didn't know about the brush with Jungbern. If he had, there would be no smiles, no jokes, no doubt of his anger.

"Good boy, Rani."

Hagen, like his son, only ever used the Wendish variant of Rennesson's name – "Ranizone", or "Rani", if he were in a good mood. Never mind the fact that "Renn", which was what the boy's parents had called him for short, was a perfectly good name in Wendish. The full name parents had bestowed on him – "Rennesson" – was a Gallic one, and Hagen scorned to speak the tongue of his great enemy. After the death of Renn's parents, he never encouraged the boy to speak it either. He had brought his young nephew up among the Cimbri and ignored the past so pointedly that many people forgot Renn had ever had a Gallic father, or at least pretended they did.

Hagen felt he owed it to his sister to take in her child, but he owed nothing to the wicked man who came from across the Bronze River to prey on her, tempting poor Adelhais to leave the protection of Barenhohle and degrade herself by becoming that demon's wife. When he'd learned of her decision, he'd banished both her and the Gaul to the farthest corner of the Cimbrian Woods.

She had cried when he'd done it, but she ought to have been grateful, for though Hagen would have nothing to do with her himself, she and her child were still his kin, and every person in the woods knew of the terrible punishment promised to any who took it on themselves to harass the little family living in isolation, and every person knew that Hagen, the huge and terrible chief who many believed was more bear than man, was fully capable of delivering on that promise. There was a reason the Gauls feared Cimbria more than anywhere else on the border, and there was a reason why Hagen was the ruler among all this fierce land.

The only person allowed to set foot near them was Linderic the Houndmaster, who had once been Adelhais's friend. Hagen sent him to check on them now and then, but the chieftan himself never saw his sister again, and he never saw her child until she and her husband had died of a wasting fever, and Linderic came back from one of his visits bringing the news and the boy back with him.

When, at the age of ten, Renn had first arrived at the home of his uncle, and trailing close behind Linderic, the only man he knew, and the only one who understood his father's language, he'd felt as if he would never fit into this strange place. But now, just four years later, he loved his mother's people as if he had always been with them. He'd even been learning to handle their war dogs under Linderic's guidance, though that still didn't seem to be enough for Hagen to let him join them on the war party.

His uncle still stood behind him. "Go ahead, back to barracks," he said when Renn still hadn't moved. "Come on, Linde."

Hagen swept forward through the quickly-emptying yard, the furs he wore brushing and rustling against Renn, and Siegher gave a hard pull on the chain, trying to follow.

"We'll see you later, then," said Linderic. "And don't worry, I'm sure he'll say yes next time. I could sure use some help controlling these monster dogs out there, and you're getting better at it every day. He'll see it soon."

With a whistle to Siegher, he and the dog were gone through the gate, and Renn stood watching them disappear into the gloom until his vision jumped with a shove from behind and he stumbled forward.

"Don't hold your breath, boy."

It was Jungbern who had knocked into his back, and Renn didn't believe such a supposedly great warrior would be so clumsy as to run into him by accident.

"Nobody's ever going to trust you squaring off against

the Gauls. Think about it. My father took me to battle when I was younger than you, yet he's leaving you behind. Again."

"I guess we can't all be as talented as you," said Renn, rolling his eyes.

"Talent's got nothing to do with it. The question is whether you wouldn't go running back to your people, those miserable pigs, the second you got them in your sights."

Some of the Cimbri might have forgotten Renn's father was a native of their enemy country across the river. The country whose army the war party was marching toward now.

Some wasn't all.

CHAPTER 2
Warrior

When the young chieftan had finally gone, and the last of the war party had disappeared into the trees, Renn turned and stalked towards the Houndsmen's barracks, glumly kicking a rock through the dirt as he went, dust and memories swirling up around him each kick. He kept his head down to avoid the curious gazes of the children who played outside their huts, most likely wondering why this boy who was so much bigger than them, was still left here, when most of the other men had gone, or were at least patrolling the perimeters.

Maybe Jungbern was right about Hagen's motives. But in the end, what did it matter where his father came from? His father was dead, and Renn hadn't so much as seen another Gaul since then. Why, he had never even *known* any other Gauls besides his father, and even that had only been for a handful of years, so it wasn't as if he had any real connection to those people.

It was true he had retained their language. It was the first one he ever knew, and Linderic still spoke it to him when they were alone, insisting that the boy not lose the memory of either of his parents. And it was true that he had loved the man named Guillame LeNotre, but he had always supposed that his father had been an unusual case. According to Hagen, Gauls were cruel and hateful, and Hagen ought to know, as he was constantly trying to drive them back from the border that Cimbria, by some ill fate, shared with them.

Yet his father had forsaken those people to come to Cimbri, to live with a Wendish wife and raise their half-Wendish son there, even after she had died. He'd stayed in Cimbria all the way up to his own death, and if his father had run *from* the other Gauls, why would Renn want to run *to* them?

Why would he want to be part of a people he didn't know except to hear how they fought and killed the friends and kinsmen who had taken him in when he was an orphan? Why would he turn his back on the Wends when he had lived and spoken and *been* one of them for a good quarter of his life? Couldn't Jungebern see that? Couldn't Hagen?

Renn gave the rock a final kick, and sent it skittering through the gate of the wide, empty enclosure that served as the dog's training pen. He lost it somewhere inside, and now had nothing left to do but drag his feet as he crossed the space where he had spent so much time working, training, and hoping alongside the other Houndsmen. But time after time, those efforts had come to nothing. Hagen had refused to let him into the war party again. He hadn't even let him be one of the perimeter guards.

Reaching the barracks on the other side of the enclosure, he ducked inside, and frowned to see that someone had left their warpaints scattered all over their cot. Pots of powder and grease lay out around a small, jagged piece of glass.

No doubt, those belonged to Keno, who was likely running late, as always. He was the only one who would leave his paint pots and mirror strewn everywhere when all the others had put theirs neatly away. Linderic would have yelled at him if he had seen it, for no set of warriors could work properly in the middle of disorder. Even Renn knew that, so why was Keno, who was habitually late, messy and irresponsible, allowed to go to war when Renn was not?

He picked up the broken bit of a mirror, with its array of smudged, colorful fingerprints around the edges. Black, red, and yellow – each color told something about the man who wore it. Black was always used to make the symbol of the Wendish nation. Red was for making the mark of your tribe. Yellow, to signify which unit you were part of; houndsmen, archers, axe-men, healers, and so on.

Frowning again, Renn dipped his fingers into the jar of red oil and dragged them across the bridge of his nose. Two horizontal lines under the eyes, broken by a long diagonal line under each, was the sign of the Cimbri tribe, his mother's tribe. He might be half-Gaul, but he was half-Cimbri, too, and he deserved to wear these marks as much as anybody.

Next was symbol for the Houndsmen, two yellow spikes meant to represent a dog's fangs, on either cheek. Last was the black, intertwined knot that was the symbol of Wendland, drawn on his forehead. Perhaps it wasn't perfectly done, but who was going to see it? Only his own reflection, peering back at him from Keno's fragment of a mirror.

Perfectly painted or not, he felt better when he saw himself in the glass. He looked like a real houndsman, and as a distant wailing howl reached his ear, a chill went through him. For the first time in his life, he was able to imagine himself out there. He could finally see beyond Renn, the boy who was always left behind. With the warpaint on his face and the cries of the dogs in his ears, he could see himself as a warrior.

The distant, muffled cracks of rifles followed the howl, and the children who'd been playing outside began to scream and scramble, as their mothers rushed to scoop them up and rush indoors. Renn felt as if he were the only one left in Barenhohle who felt no fear. How could he, with those proud marks representing his heritage and all the training he'd done over the years? He was ready to face the battle.

Even if he couldn't fight in it, he could at least watch it. He could follow the war party, couldn't he, and watch them from some safe spot – just to see what it was like? Hagen had never forbidden him that, and in all the commotion outside, no one would notice him leaving. He could go and come back before anyone knew he was gone, and next time, he would surprise them all by how much he knew about battle.

He ran back to the clearing where he'd said goodbye to Linderic, unnoticed, as expected, by those too busy running to take cover. He slipped behind the backs of the perimeter guards, and melted into the shadows of the trees beyond the border fence. Everyone was on the lookout for invaders coming into the settlement. No one noticed a boy going out of it.

Renn tried his best to track the footprints of the war party in the shade, but it was the sounds of the guns that gave him the best heading, for the Cimbri knew well how to step lightly and cover their tracks. It was how he'd so easily evaded the perimeter guards, for they were used to watching for loud, clumsy Gauls, not their own, silent kind.

He headed in the direction of the rolling cracks, knowing that the warriors would never let them get close enough to home to warrant all the panic he had seen there. He remembered the time that Henny, an archer two years older than him, had come back from his first war party excitedly showing Renn how he had smuggled home a weapon off a fallen Gallic soldier, They had gone outside the border fence, to the place where Henny had hidden what looked like a long wooden tube. He told of how it shot fire and could take an enemy down without even getting close to him, like an arrow, but with much more deadly results.

"This is how they use them...I think."

"Are you sure?" Renn asked, watching him fumble with the weapon, and how his arms and hands getting crossed and twisted while he tried to make it stay his shoulder.

"Of course. Now is how they make them go?"

Renn never saw how far the shot went. When it roared to unexpected life, he lost sense of anything but shock.

Henny had laughed to see him jump liked a rabbit, but

he looked scared enough himself when a scout named Cressido appeared suddenly through the trees, still fully equipped for battle, his face and voice thunderous.

"Are you out of your mind?" he demanded. "You've set everyone at home into a panic – they think the Gauls are going to ambush us on our own threshold. What's worse, you really could've killed yourself, which would have been bad enough. But to put *him* in danger, too," he glanced at Renn, "that would have been worse."

Henny's face grew redder as Cressido's voice grew harsher and louder.

"There's a reason Hagen outlawed those; they're the devil's work, and dangerous." He swiped it out of Henny's hands, though he held it loosely in his own, as if afraid it might contaminate him. "If this puts bad luck on me, it'll be your fault," he said darkly.

"I'll watch out for you next time, to make sure the bad luck doesn't get you," offered Henny meekly.

"Next time? We'll just see how many war parties you're allowed on after this."

No, remembering how quickly and how many of the warriors had shown up at the sound of just one gun, how fiercely Cressido had reacted, and how much trouble Henny had gotten in for even bringing it near Barenhohle, Renn was sure the warriors would never let the army get within firing distance, however far that was.

He knew he was getting close to *them*, though, by the burning smell – the same one Henny's stolen gun had given off – and the noise that grew ever louder. He could hear men's shouts now, but whose voices were they? He squinted, trying to see through the strange fog that crept through the thick trees.

If only the woods weren't so thick, maybe this fog would clear out and give him air to breathe. But the denseness of the forest was what made Cimbria so secure, even being on the border as it was. Shadowy at the best of times, only a native could navigate it, and no enemy arrows could penetrate it from the outside. Considering all this, it was a miracle that when his father had come walking in plain sight to the riverbank on the day his mother had been doing border patrol, she hadn't sent an arrow through him sooner than talk to him.

hadn't sent an arrow through him sooner than talk to him.

Renn tried climbing a tree for a clearer view, which let him see shapes in the distance – they were further away than he thought – dark forms grappling in darker shadows while lower ones darted in and out of the fog between them. Those would be the dogs, but he couldn't tell the difference between the men. How could he know who to cheer for when they were all just distant figures in the dark? How could he know which way the battle was going?

He would have to rely on the flashes of the guns. He counted them, one, two...three...four. They were coming slower now, and he guessed that meant the battle was ending? But was it ending because the Gauls were retreating, or simply because there were no Wends left to fight? There was still no way to tell without getting closer.

Surely it would be safe to move a little nearer now, just close enough to see what had happened. Then he would go straight home and wait for the warriors' return. His foot hadn't yet touched the ground when he felt a hand on his ankle.

"If blessings ain't just falling from trees. We've got one!"

At first he thought it was Jungbern, and he knew he would be in worse trouble than Henny had ever been. It wasn't until he looked down at the round, whiskery face and dingy, yellow teeth that he realized everything was

all wrong. Especially the fact that his cousin didn't speak Gallic.

"Dummy," said a second voice as another man approached – taller, leaner, his skin as sallow as the other man's teeth. "Does that look like a warrior to you? You're wastin' your time with nothin' but a lap baby. Come on down here, boy."

But Renn was too stunned to heed the command. These were Gauls. The only thing they did to Wends was kill them, and he was without any kind of weapon to defend himself. Or rather, any weapon *but one*.

"I'm not a warrior," he said in the tongue of his father, and still clung to the trunk halfway down the tree. "I was just watching. I followed the army…the Gallic army." If he could just convince them he'd come from the other side of the river, followed the other set of fighters…

"Ha, listen to that, comin' from the mouth the animal. Must think I'm dumb enough to believe it." The man reached up, grabbed the back of Renn's tunic, and pulled him down the remaining length of the tree to the ground. Renn's knees and fingers burned as they scraped the bark on the way down.

"You've got the sign for 'Wend' written clear across your face," the taller man growled into his ear. He pushed a rough hand across Renn's forehead and held his black-smudged palm in front of Renn's eyes.

The warpaint! Renn had forgotten about it. He had been so proud to put it on, but it meant he would never convince them now. Not with every detail about him spelled out in bright Wendish colors for anyone to see.

"See, I know some of your words, too," the man said. "Don't mean I'm one of you animals."

Renn couldn't stop himself. "I know you're not a Wend," he shot back. "I'm not sure about the animal part."

"You little…" the man growled again.

All hope of deception now being certainly gone thanks to Renn's outburst, there was only one thing left to do.

Renn ran. He easily broke free of the tall man's spindly fingers, but hit the ground like a rock when the fat man tackled him with unexpected speed. The scrapes on his knees stung with the impact, and he lay pinned by the weight, wheezing for breath, as the taller man, who leaning over them like a willow tree, his stringy hair hanging down around his face, pulled a pair of ropes from the knapsack on his back.

"I've changed my mind about this one," he said. "He might not fetch much, but he needs to be taught a lesson."

"That's what you keep me around for, eh?" smiled stocky one, whose badger-like whiskers shook when he laughed. "I caught him – both times!"

"Sure you did," Willow Tree muttered as he pulled the ropes hetight around Renn's wrists and feet. Renn tried to twist away but Badger just sat on him more heavily, and Willow only pulled the cords tighter. When they were sure he couldn't run, Badger rolled his weight off.

"Does this mean I get bigger cut of the money?" he asked as he rolled.

Money. So Renn was to be held for ransom. But what they didn't know was that the men from home would sooner kill them than pay them anything, so all Renn had to do was wait.

"We'll see when we get there. Time to head for the border, boys. "

"What about the money?" Renn asked. "You'll never get it if you cross the border."

"Heh, as if I'd want dirty Wendish money. It's not from them I'll be gettin' paid."

"*We'll* be gettin' paid," Badger corrected.

Was Renn going to be a prisoner of war, then? To be turned in for a bounty, and get the downside of battle without even getting the thrill of fighting in it?

"Then shouldn't you take me back to the rest of the soldiers? Shouldn't your..." he paused, unable to find the Gallic word he wanted. "...Your chief soldier handle trading prisoners?"

Willow rolled his eyes. "Don't think that band of fools would want *you*, young as you are. No, it's not to the soldiers you're goin.'"

"But then," Renn tried to keep the rising fear he felt from showing in his voice. "Who's paying you for me?"

"Enough talk," Willow snapped. "Get up."

Renn tried. He knew he had to move, to run, to escape back home and forget all about this day. He managed to push himself up his elbows and knees, but the ropes around his ankles meant he could only shuffle slowly and awkwardly. He couldn't run away like this.

"Have to loosen his feet if you want us to get there before next century," Badger said to Willow. "You tied it too tight 'cause you got mad at him insultin' you."

"I don't need you tellin' me my business," Willow glowered at him.

Renn looked into the shadows of the trees. Surely someone would come for him. Linderic would appear and send these men packing. Siegher would chase them away with his enormous teeth and claws. Cressido would come with his fierce eyes and scold Renn all the way home.

He listened. The guns still popped and the dogs still wailed somewhere beyond the shadows. But no one stepped out of those shadows, and Renn realized all at once that there was no reason anybody *would*. No one would even know he was missing. They had left him back at Barenhohle, and had no way of knowing he would be anywhere else.

Even worse than that, if he went with his captors, he would be long gone before anyone figured it out. Oh, there were trackers enough with the skill to find him, but how long would it be before the battle ended, before they went home and noticed him gone? The longer the trail, the harder it was the follow.

What if the trail went cold before they could find him? What if the Gauls did something awful to him before he was rescued?

"Think about runnin' and I'll kill you myself, without wastin' any more time on it." Willow pulled out a hunting knife with one hand and grabbed Renn by the back of the neck with his other.

Renn tested one step, slowly, and immediately felt the rope digging into his skin. Willow's knife looked pathetically small and thin compared to the knives Renn was used to, but he was sure any knife could kill if the prey was crippled like he was.

"What'll it be? Walk or die?"
There was only one choice with any hope in it all.
Renn walked.

CHAPTER 3
Miles

Through rough underbrush and countless trees, slowly and painfully, he walked.

They skirted around the route the army had taken, heading for the river that Renn had only heard about but never seen, and slid into the tiny dinghy that rocked and listed as the waters lapped around it.

Renn had never been to the river, much less been in a boat before, but even he could tell that this little vessel was barely holding together. He gripped its rotted wood with his two bound hands and prayed as they crossed to the other side, where his captors had to haul him up the bank.

With the river behind, he walked across streams whose water rushed into the holes that began to form in his thin leather shoes. If he'd ever been allowed his battle dress, he would have had better footwear for handling a long march.

But at least the water cooled his feet and washed away the grit which was grinding and scratching into the rope burns on his ankles. Badger hadn't lied – Willow really had tied it too tight.

He tried to be grateful for the cool water in the moments before he reached land, before new dirt settled into the now-bleeding marks, and into the newer ones he gained by the minute as thorns and brambles reached out for him, as if they were trying to pull him back home. Though this might be a good thing, as it could give the dogs the scent of blood to follow when they came after him. *If* they came.

When the first miserable night passed without sign of them, he woke with his ankles stiff and sore, and a shooting pain in his stomach. He'd been too unhappy to eat the hard tack they'd thrown him last night, but now he picked it off the ground, trying awkwardly to brush the dirt from it, for his wrists had still not been untied, and they, too, were turning red. He cringed at the crunch of grit between his teeth when he bit into it, and even though he was hungry, he could only force down one swallow.

He wondered if they might give him another for breakfast, and whether he could keep this one clean. Willow wasn't in any better mood this morning, and Badger was too busy eating his own biscuits to do more than toss Renn's single ration into the dirt again. Renn sighed and scooped it into his pocket, hoping that somehow the dust would fall off of it as he walked.

When Badger finally came to drag him upright, his wounds throbbed, for it was painful now to step, and he limped as their group began to move again. He looked over his shoulder, hoping for some sign that rescue had arrived, but the woods were still, save for the chirping of the early birds whose cheerfulness was jarring in the middle of this all-wrong morning.

How many more all-wrong mornings Renn suffered through, he lost count. The days began to shift and slide and swirl into each other, punctuated by moments of darkness that might have been nights, or might have been days lost from his memory. He remembered crossing the Bronze River, but he couldn't tell if three days or thirty had passed since then. Through it all, only two things were constant, infusing the days with haze and sorrow – the ever-worsening pain in his now-ragged wrists and gashed ankles, and the incessant question:

Where are they?

"The kid's barely movin,'" Badger's voice said at some point in the long journey. "Maybe we oughta take a break."

"Can't do that. We gotta reach Buron before he fills his quota."

"If we lame him, we sure ain't gonna make it. On top 'a that, he's just about sleepwalkin' most of the time, and I ain't seen him eat or drink hardly anythin' in I don't know how long. I think he's sick or something."

"Don't expect me to go running to get a doctor for your little darlin,'" snorted Willow. "If you're so concerned about it, you can pick him up and carry him yourself."

"Fine, but Buron ain't gonna give us nothin for bringin' a corpse. I'm serious...I don't think he's gonna make it if we don't do somethin'. That's lost profit for you, too, you know."

Willow considered this for few moments.. "Alright. Next town we get to, you get a mule from somewhere. I don't care where. And make it a mule, you got that? Not a horse. They're too fancy, and more likely to be missed."

At some point – Renn didn't know how much later – he felt himself being thrown roughly over the back of an animal. Too weak to care how its bristly hide scratched his face, he dipped into blackness again, dreaming of his cot in the houndsmen's barracks, and of Siegher laying his massive head next to him.

His next clear memory came – was it days later? weeks? – in the darkness of a night when the air carried a musty tang, and a bracing wind blew around him that helped clear a little of the fog from his brain. He lifted his head and saw moonlight rippling on wide, foaming water that spread out around the long pier they stood on. Further out in the water, was a boat so much taller and wider than the little river skiff. This must have been the ocean his father had told him about long ago.

"Get him off that beast, will you?" Willow hissed. "Buron's gonna think we brought him an invalid."

"We *did* bring him an invalid. That's what I've been ryin' to tell you," Badger grumbled as he yanked Renn from the back of the mule.

Renn winced when his feet hit the ground, expecting the familiar flood of pain to shoot up his legs, but found that he could at least stand without collapsing, if he kept a hand on the animal. He looked down and saw that his wounds had begun to scab over. When he looked up, a large, sinewy man whose bald head glistened with sweat was lumbering toward them. He was stocky like Badger, but looked stronger, with a build more like Hagen, though not as big. No one was as big or strong as his uncle.

"Let's see this peach of yours," the man said in a voice that sounded like dog claws scratching on gravel.

"Here he is, Wendish warrior straight from Cimbria." Willow showed a smile for the first time Renn could remember. It was ugly, and Renn looked away.

"Hah, this boy looks like he's never picked up a weapon in his life. You expect me to believe he's a warrior from the middle of the Wendish wilds?"

He bent over and grinned into Renn's face, but like Willow's, the smile held no comfort in it.

"That true, boy? You some kinda battle chief?" he asked, baring his teeth.

It occurred to Renn that if he hadn't chanced to have a Gallic father – if he had only known the Wendish world and nothing of the Gauls at all, he wouldn't even have been able to understand the question. It was that Gallic side that he would have to hold onto now. So far, the man didn't seem too inclined to believe Willow's claims. There might still be a chance if Renn could pass himself off as full Gaul to this man, and no Wend at all.

"I've never been to battle in my life," he said honestly. It was the first time he had ever been thankful for it.

"Besides, my name is Rennesson LeNotre, and I don't know since when a Wend could have such a name." That was true, too. His name had always stood out as different. It was the reason why so many called him Ranizone at home.

"Listen to that," Buron laughed. "If you're gonna tell a lie, you should at least know better than to tell one to me."

Renn's heart sank, thinking the man saw the truth he was hiding, until he saw Buron was looking up at Willow.

"You think a stupid Wend could answer me like that? If he was really what you say, how'd he learn to speak Gallic so nice and proper? I'd have thought it'd be nothin' but grunts and growls from a real Wend, but he speaks nicer'n you do."

Buron straightened, his smile gone. "If you'd been tellin' the truth, I'd have paid you good money for him, just so I could have the pleasure of tossin' him to the sharks myself. But I got no time or patience for your lies, so all you've done is get yourself a lower price for tryin' to cheat me. Not that you'd be in your right mind to expect any kind of payment for this one, anyway. This is just a sickly kid you picked up out of the street somewhere, and what good is that to me?"

Willow ignored the pointed look Badger gave him. "Your eyesight's goin', Buron, as well as your brain," he said. "I did get him from Cimbria, but if you're too ignorant to tell that, it's your own loss. Besides, this boy ain't so very young of a kid, and he ain't sick neither. Even if he were, the ocean air will do him good. That sort of medicine won't cost you nothin.'"

"I'm not in the business of nursing sick babies," said Buron. "What I need's workers."

"I believe that. As I understand it, your crew is lookin' mighty thinned out these days, 'specially after that last little tantrum you threw. I heard they were cleanin' blood off the deck for days."

Buron pulled back his lips in a laugh. "Made for good chum, though. You should've seen the catch we pulled in after."

Renn didn't know what "chum" meant – he couldn't remember his father ever using that word – but from the talk of blood and Buron's harsh laugh, it wasn't hard to put the pieces together, and he was reminded once more that he was in a country full of savages.

"But who was there to haul it?" Willow asked. "Did you

have enough men left to dress the sharks after half the crew went to feed 'em? 'Cause I also heard the mighty Buron had to go back to skinnin' fish himself, just like a common deckhand."

Buron's smile dropped into a scowl.

"Maybe you're right," Willow continued. "Maybe this merchandise ain't what you need. Maybe this boy is too valuable an item for the kinda ship you run." He pulled Renn to him by the shoulder. "You probably couldn't control him anyway. No warrior, not even a Wendish one, would ever follow orders from a captain stinkin' of fish guts." The edge of a smile crept into Willow's voice.

Renn knew this technique. When the dogs at home went after boars, they wouldn't attack them immediately, for the boars were too fierce to kill outright. Rather, the dogs were trained to lunge and bait and irritate the beasts first, working them into such a frenzy that they couldn't think straight. That way, it was easier to get around their defenses and strike the killing blow. Only this time, Renn was the bait.

"Follow orders, huh? We'll see if he don't do more than that by the time I'm through with him." Renn's teeth clacked together as Buron pulled him away from his captors.

"I dunno – can you *afford* to pay the money for him, just to find out?" asked Willow.

"'Course I can *afford* it," Buron snarled. "But you're not *gettin'* it. If you'd told the truth from the beginnin', I mighta given you half price for this half a man. But you tried to lie about it, so I'll take another half off for fraud."

"Sorry, but I can't accept that offer," said Willow, ignoring the fidgety protests of Badger behind him.

"Can't accept it? That's terrible bold for someone who can't catch anything better than little boys, and has to tell stories about 'em being Wends. You'd better take what you can get for him while you can get it. Two-twenty five, final offer. Nobody else would give you near that much."

"It's a deal!" Badger burst out abruptly, earning himself a murderous look from Willow.

Buron gave that fang-baring grin again, and handed Badger a few crumpled notes from his ratty pocket.

With a nervous glance toward Willow, Badger took off at a jog, the pier shaking with his heavy steps.

Willow cast only one last venomous glare at the both of them before turning to give chase, and suddenly, the two specters that had dragged Renn into a nightmare, whose angry hands had torn open his skin, and whose bickering voices had haunted his delirious days, were gone without even a final word, with nothing but the ropes and the scars to prove all they had done to him. He hadn't even known their real names.

He could have laughed at the sudden release, except for the knowledge that he hadn't been released at all. It hadn't even mattered that he'd passed himself off as Gaul in the end. He had been sold to a man who laughed about killing people and fed them to sharks when he was done.

"Guess I can go ahead and slaughter this animal," Buron said to himself.

Renn's knees buckled. It was only on the way down to the slippery boards that he realized Buron might have meant the stolen mule, which was still standing on the pier where the two slave traders had left it.

CHAPTER 4
St. Juste

It was strange to think that one of the last things Willow had done was tell the truth. For though Renn still stumbled through his first few days on Buron's ship, and slept hard through the first few nights, the salty sea air did do him good, as Willow had predicted. In spite of the poor conditions of the boat, and by the fourth morning, when Buron stomped below deck to demand his recent acquisition work harder or be cut up for fish bait, he found the hammock empty. Renn was already above deck, finally feeling strong enough to not be dragged up by one of the other crew members.

But those first mornings were some of the few times the other crewmen bothered with him at all. Most of them seemed too surly or too broken-spirited to give the new boy any extra help or attention. Not that Renn could blame them, for he didn't feel much like making friends either. It was hard to have the energy for it when you were a slave being worked to the bone, yelled at, or fed to the fishes at Buron's whim. But even had they not been prisoners on a dirty, stinking slaver ship, Renn had his own reason to keep to himself.

"*Never trust a Gaul,*" Hagen had always told him.

These men might be fellow prisoners, but every one of them spoke Gallic. And, Renn discovered from overheard scraps of conversation, half of them were here as punishment for real crimes they'd committed, and those who weren't pretended they were, for to say otherwise would earn a lashing from Buron.

Who knew what any of these men would do if they found out his secret? The men who'd been gang-pressed, like him, were already frightening enough. How much more so were the ones who'd already been proven dangerous criminals, even to their own people?

If he spoke too much, he risked giving himself away by accident. He might have been able to fool Buron, but how many others would that work on? The more he spoke, the more chances he gave them to question the things he said.

So he remained as silent as he could, not even joining in the groaning calls of "heave and pull" as they towed the lines to raise the ratty sails, or turned the wooden spokes of what he learned was called the capstan, to drop the rusted anchor. So the men did not talk to him, and he returned the favor.

The only group onboard who didn't seem entirely crushed by the weight of their work were the men called the harpooneers. On the day he'd bought Renn, Buron had spoken of catching sharks. This was Buron's ostensible trade, though Renn knew it was only one of them, and killing the animals was the job of the men who stood at the rails, hoisting thick spears with tow lines on one end, and huge, curving hooks on the other, and threw them overboard when they sighted one of the large grey fish that lurked in the waters. Though it was unsettling to see such weapons in the hands of Gauls, Renn couldn't help but enjoy watching them. Their spears looked a little like the ones the Cimbri used to hunt boars back home, and the way they shouted out to each other and to the dogs in clear, strong voices when a catch was made reminded him of the shouts when the hogs was brought to bay. So he couldn't help but stop and watch when a call went up, and the big creatures were pulled up the outsides of the boat, past faded paint spelling out in peeling letters the words:

ST. JUSTE.

He liked the way they would chatter excitedly when

they pulled the catches in, and how a few of them even sang as they carved out the pieces of the sharks' flesh – so similar to field-dressing a boar – to be sold at the next port, though they kept their voices low when they sang, to avoid incurring the wrath of Buron. In the captain's view, it was one thing to let the men do the work. It was another thing to let them enjoy it.

But Renn didn't mind it at all. For as much as he hated everything else on the ship, as much as he knew he had to mind his own business and no one else's if he wanted to survive, his was still a lonely existence, and the sound of a cheerful voice now and again buoyed up the young, frightened heart of a boy far from home.

But how was it these men seemed so much happier than all the others? Why did Buron allow them work that made them anything less than miserable? Why didn't they simply take their harpoons, stab Buron with them, and sail the St. Juste to freedom?

The secret, it seemed, lay with Mr. Fairinelle. The ship's tall first officer – its *only* officer besides Buron – seemed so different from his superior that Renn wondered how they had ever come to work together. Where the captain's heavy footfalls inevitably inspired
 dread and loathing, the men looked up eagerly when Fairinelle's boots moved lightly over the grimy planks. When he shouted orders, the men worked better than under the barking bluster of Buron. Fairinelle could be just as loud as his captain, his voice ringing out over the sounds of the sea and the gulls and the grumbling men, but the irrational meanness of Buron never seemed to find its way into Fairinelle's words, however loudly spoken, and the rapier with the elaborate hilt that he carried on him at all times had never yet had to come out of its sheath. The men never glowered threateningly at him the way they did the captain.

It was Fairinelle who had created the harpooneer crew, having convinced Buron that harvesting the natural resource that surrounded them every day was a smart business venture, as sharks could be used in everything from soups to face paint, and it was Fairinelle who had charge of them.

Renn was sure that it was his respect for Buron's authority, and his expectation that the crew do the same, was a good part of what kept them from staging a mutiny. They liked him too much, this officer who let them talk and sing and do something other than clean bilge, to go against his word.

Renn would have felt the same, had he been allowed on that crew. As it was, he was busy today with scraping the pock-marked deck, edging as close as he could to the rails as he could, trying to listen to the harpooneers' conversations.

A howling cry shot through the air that Renn, for one thrilling moment, thought was the hunting call of a Barenhohle hound. His head snapped up, but instead of a Wendish dog, he saw instead a man named Xavier flinging a spear overboard, his eyes wild.

The rope at the end of the harpoon spun out quickly, whipping and uncoiling out over the deck, and Renn could tell right away that something was wrong. Xavier lunged for it, and Renn realized it wasn't tied to the metal cleats on deck which kept the harpoons from being lost whenever the stuck sharks tried to swim away.

Xavier skidded on his feet, trying to hold it as other crewmen crowded around. Renn dropped his deck brush, moving closer to watch the scene. From below, there was the sound of thrashing water, and the rope bounced and jerked with weight of the shark. Did they normally struggle this much? Renn stood up, trying to see over the edge, and the crowd pressed around him, each of them having the same idea.

Xavier planted his feet against the base of the railing, grunting to the others who tried helping to stand back. This was his kill and he wasn't going to share it. The beads of sweat stood out on his forehead.

The line convulsed violently, and Xavier's legs went out

from under him. He fell backwards into the group and the line sped forwards over the rail. On instinct, Renn reached out for it, and felt the searing in his palms only a second before he felt the weight of the line dragging him off his own feet.

He tumbled towards the railing, and as his shoulder slammed into a rail post, a form bounded out of the group yelling "Let it go!"

Renn released his grip at the same time he saw a pair of hands yanking at the nearest deck cleat, making sure the rope there was tied tight, before launching another weapon over the edge.

The thrashing sounds in the water below went suddenly quiet, and the small bit of rope left onboard from Xavier's spear now snaked languidly over the rail, while the line on the second harpoon snapped taut, pulled by the suddenly still, dead weight of the shark.

Renn looked down at his burning hands. His palms were ragged and red where the rope had torn into his skin. They matched the scars he had gained on his wrists and ankles on the march from Barenhohle.

"Here," said the young man who had thrown the second spear. He fished a small metal tin from his pocket and handed it to Renn, who recognized him as one of the younger harpooneers. He looked close to Jungbern's age, which would make him about six or seven years older than Renn.

"Put that on your cuts. It'll help them heal," he said, and Redonnn gingerly untwisted the lid to find a sticky yellow salve inside. He dabbed his fingers in it, and found it cool to the touch. He was afraid it would sting his palms, but instead it quickly calmed the pain coursing there.

The harpooneer turned to Xavier, calling, "Come and help me pull in your catch, before the other beasts down there get a mind to snack on it. Unless you need this lad to pull it in for you, too?"

"Shut up, Badeau," the other man scowled as he got to

his feet, and bumping against Renn's sore shoulder, he moved to take hold of the taut line.

"Ha, no need for that," laughed the young man, lining up to grab the rope behind him. "All either of us did was try keep you from losing your spear, and spare you a chewing-out from Buron for it. Really, what were you thinking – tossing it over when it wasn't tied down properly?"

"Mind your own business," Xavier muttered, but the one called Badeau only laughed again. Renn watched as they heaved up on the line together, and how they had stop and catch their breath before much progress seemed to be made at all.

"You catch the leviathan or something?" Badeau huffed.

Renn wanted to ask what a leviathan was, but didn't.

"You did. It's not my kill anymore, it's yours," Xavier returned, wiping a hand across his forehead.

Renn wondered if he should offer to help, and whether his cuts would even let him hold the line, but the other harpooneers, who were still grouped around, fell into place behind them before he could ask, and together the bunch succeeded in hauling a shark more than twice Renn's length onto the deck.

Water rolled off its body and sloshed over Renn's feet as he peered down at its glassy eye, its gaping mouth, and the two harpoons stuck into its body. One of them – belonging to Xavier – had caught it behind the flipper. The other was lodged firmly in its eye.

With practiced speed, the men set to work dressing the fish. Someone hacked a thick blade through its tail, turning the water on the deck red, while another man curved a knife through its head, and down behind the gills. After a few short, bustling minutes, the rest of the shark was carved up into pieces, its torso being carried down to kitchen galley while the other pieces –the snout, the bones – were tossed back overboard to serve as bait for other sharks who would surely follow the scent of blood.

Watching them, Renn felt a twinge of what could almost be the called comfort. Not many would feel that way watching an animal being gutted, but it reminded Renn of learning how to dress the kills the hunting dogs made back home. This was messier, of course, with the water running everywhere, but it was the same concept.

Soon there was nothing left but the blood on the deck and the harpoons that had been removed from it, and both needed to be cleaned. Xavier snatched his up and took it elsewhere. Badeau sat down on a crate and began whistling under his breath as he wiped down his own weapon.

Because he didn't want to be caught idling, Renn ran to retrieve his deck brush and commenced scrubbing the splintery planks. It wasn't exactly a comfortable task with open wounds on both his palms, but the salve had at least stopped the burning. He veered close to the young harpooneer as he swiped his brush through the gore on the deck, cleared his throat, and timidly held out the tin he'd received.

"Um, thanks for this," he said.

"Ah, sure. The first catch is always the worst as far as hurts go, and you picked a devil of a one to get started on. But that should heal you up pretty quick," he nodded to the salve. "So go ahead and hold onto it for now. Once you get used to handling the spears, your skin'll toughen up a bit, and you won't have to use it quite so much."

Renn liked that. The way the young man talked as if Renn was already part of his crew, as if it were a given that he would handle more harpoon lines in the future. The way he didn't act like Renn was too young or weak or unworthy of the position, the way others did; from Jungbern to Willow to Buron.

"Your name's Badeau?" Renn asked, forgetting in his gratitude that he wasn't supposed to talk too much.

"Close. It's my last name, anyway. First name's Emile. And you?"

"Rennesson...LeNotre."

"You know," Èmile tipped his head. "Your accent's sorta different. Mind if I ask where you're from?"

Renn stiffened. This was exactly why he couldn't afford to get lazy, like he had just then. And maybe he was more out of practice with Gallic than he thought, having only had Linderic to talk to for so many years.

"Oh, you know, I come from the east – out by the, um, border," he said, more slowly than he wanted to, as he searched for an answer. Someone living close to the border with Wendland could reasonably have something resembling a Wendish accent, couldn't they?

"Hm," said Emile, and Renn prayed he wouldn't ask which *part* of the border, for Renn, never having been in a war party, hadn't actually been to it, excepting the trip that had earned him a place on this boat, meaning he had only the barest knowledge of the border's geography.

"How did you learn to aim like that?" he asked, trying to change the subject by pointing the spearhead Emile was cleaning – the one which had been stuck through the shark's eye.

"Oh, me?" Emile said. "I used to be in the army. Got the Eagle's Eye and everything."

"Eagle's Eye?"

"They give it to sharpshooters for accuracy. It's 'cause I got so handy with a rifle that picking off sharks comes easy to me now. Guns take a lot more skill and mental effort to aim true than a big spear does, 'cause the bullet is smaller, even if the spear is heavier."

Guns, like the one Henny had smuggled home off a dead soldier. That must be what 'sharpshooter' meant. So this Emile was one of those who would trespass into Wendland and kill Renn's people for profit.

He knew he shouldn't have been surprised, but it was still disappointing. Emile had seemed so friendly, but in the end he was just like the rest.

Renn looked down and gave the deck boards a hard scrub with his brush.

"Hey, if you want to heal right, you'll have to take it

easy on those hands. You're like to hurt yourself worse if you keep that up, and that'll put you out of commission for the next catch."

"If I don't get to work, Buron will put me out of commission right now," Renn countered, not looking up.

"Why don't you try asking Fairinelle to write you an injury reprieve? I'll bet he'd do it, even if Buron wouldn't."

"I'm not on his crew. It's not my place to ask."

"You're on the St. Juste crew, and he's got authority over that too, not just the harpoons. Besides, what you did today sorta counts as working for us, doesn't it? Haven't you got the proof of it right there in your palms?"

There it was again. Emile including him, acting as if Renn had actually done something useful. Renn was sure he wouldn't act that way if he knew the truth about who he was complimenting, but it was still gratifying for the moment, and more than he got from Hagen.

"You should ask him, 'cause you've done a good day's work here, Rennesson LeNotre," said Emile. He wiped his hand on his trouser leg and held it out to Renn.

Never trust a Gaul, Ranizone.

"I..." Renn offered lamely, holding up his hands up by way of excuse. "Like you said, I think I made it worse on them just now... They're hurting too badly to..."

"Ah, right," Emile's hand dropped. "Well, put some more of that medicine on 'em, and don't say anything to Buron about it until you get your note from Fairinelle."

"I wouldn't say anything to him anyway," said Renn.

I   shouldn't   say   anything   to   you,   either.

CHAPTER 5
Fairinelle

Renn's hands were healing much better than his first rope burns had, when Emile called to him a few days later, smiling broadly and waving a slip of paper.

"Here, Renn, I got it! Isn't it just like I said?" he asked as he crossed the deck. "I asked him to write it, and he did."

Renn could only look at him in silence. Emile had done him a favor, unasked, and even more surprising, Emile had called him "Renn." They hadn't even known each other a week, and Emile was already using the nickname Linderic and his father had always used, the name Renn called himself.

"See there?" he pointed at the gently sloping letters on the paper. "You won't have to work for a week, or at least not doing any heavy lifting, anyway. Lucky duck. How are you healing up, by the way?"

"Oh, um, fine," said Renn, turning up his palms. "But why wouldn't Buron just decide not to let me use this? Why wouldn't he just say he's captain and not Fairinelle, and tell me to get back to work?"

"Hm, hadn't thought about it," Emile scratched his head. "He just never has. He doesn't usually bother himself with Fairinelle's business."

Has he ever had someone like me onboard?

"So go on and take it, you ought to be alright."

I won't be alright until I get back home.

"I don't know. I'm not sure I want to take the risk," Renn still hesitated.

"Sakes alive, Renn," Emile tapped his knuckles on Renn's shoulder. "If you're that timid, how did you ever get in enough trouble to make it onto the St. Juste?"

"Don't say too much. He's a risk, too," was what he told himself silently.

"I disobeyed my uncle, that's how," was what came out of his mouth.

Well, he had to say *something*, and all of his built-up sadness and disappointment leapt at the opportunity to be released. And anyway, it wasn't as if he were just foolishly volunteering his story. He'd been asked, and it would look stranger not to answer than to simply be careful with the details.

"Your uncle sold you off for disobeying him? I guess your folks must be gone, huh?"

"He didn't sell me!" Renn protested. "I made a mistake on my own! He tried to warn me, but I thought I knew better. I'm sure he would feel awful if he knew I was here."

"Sounds about right, then, him not knowing. They didn't let me write home either, after I came on board." said Emile with a twitch of his mouth. "It was only 'cause Fairinelle got me some scraps of paper for me behind Buron's back that my folks know I'm here. Want me to ask him to get word home for you? He's about to go on furlough; he can do it then."

"No. Nobody else at home knows how to read."

Not Gallic words, anyway, except for Linderic.

They knew how to read their own language, and how to read the forest for signs of prey and approaching enemies. Skills Renn obviously lacked, or he never would've met Willow and Badger in the first place.

He was so angry at himself – angry that he could never be like those warriors, that he'd never get the chance now, all because he couldn't listen to good advice. Hot tears welled up and spilled over down his face, Embarrassed, he tried to look away.

But Emile reaction to his tears was even worse. His eyes grew wide and he reached a hand out to Renn's head, but paused in midair before actually touching him, his words alternating between tumbling out and trailing off awkwardly.

"Ah, hey, don't cry...Didn't mean to set you off. You don't have to write home if you don't want to. Come on..."

He was so busy trying to decide what to do with this tearful boy that he didn't notice Xavier, who had tried and failed to catch the shark, sauntering up behind him.

"What's the matter with this one? Not so strong after all?" the man asked.

Emile sighed and raised his eyes skyward but didn't turn around. "Leave it alone, Xavier."

"I always said he wasn't anything special."

"We *know*, you've told us all a thousand times. But *I* am telling you to leave it alone."

"What are you, his nurse?"

Emile did turn around then, all the awkwardness leaving his voice, and all the cheer, too. "*You'll* need a nurse if you don't mind your own business. Now shove off before I get Buron over here and tell him you're not working."

"Be stubborn like that, then," said Xavier, taking a step back. "But you're only dragging yourself down if you insist on sticking around with this kid. A blubberer like that'll be shark bait within a month for sure, and you'll go down with him," he said before turning and pounding off.

The lines of annoyance were already fading from Emile's face as he turned around towards Renn once more.

"Look," his voice had gone soft again. "I know it's hard to be away from home, but just – just don't cry, alright?"

Renn wiped ineffectually at the wet tracks on his cheeks. "I wish I hadn't been so stupid...I wish I weren't here…"

"Listen, ah, we all make mistakes," Emile hooked his

thumbs in his back trouser pockets. "Do you want to know how dumb I had to be to get here? I was the star of my division, and I went and broke rank one day in the middle of battle. My captain couldn't quite see the best strategy, but I figured I could, so I went for it my own. And what did I get for my trouble? Carted off here for insubordination – didn't even get to keep my Eagle's Eye, all because I thought I knew best. So there's stupid for you, huh?"

When he was satisfied that Renn had finally stopped crying, Emile asked with a note of relief in his voice, "Alright, then?"

Renn nodded, managing a small smile. "Thanks," he sniffed, and Emile was back to beaming again.

Maybe Hagen would say it was no accomplishment to be equally as stupid as a Gaul had once been, but Hagen wasn't here, and Renn had to hold on to something.

It was Xavier he held onto next, and neither of them was happy with the arrangement.

"It's barnacle duty for you, Xavier. Thank your friend there for the privilege, and make sure you tie your line *before* going overboard."

Xavier glared at Renn for the whole of the time it took to untie a harpoon from its line, then knot that loose end around his waist, making sure, as Buron had said, that the other end was secured to a ring.

Barnacle duty involved hanging off the side of the ship by a harpoon rope, picking at the sharp-edged crustaceans that had attached themselves there, and hoping the rope wouldn't give way to drop you down to the sharks. Cleaning barnacles wasn't even the real point, as there was no way to remove them by hand anyway. You'd cut your skin to ribbons before getting even one of them off, and likely die of the infection with a thousand still left to go. No, the real point of it was for Buron to vent his anger on somebody, anybody. It didn't matter if you were the one who had made him angry or not; you only had slightly less chance of being sent over on the rope if you were innocent than if you were guilty.

In this particular case, Renn had muttered under his breath during one of the jailer's rants, but Xavier had been the one to pay for it when Buron overheard. Renn had been set as the hauler, who was to bring the cleaner back up.

Had Buron really wanted to clean the hull, a man could have easily gone up and down the hanging ladders meant for that purpose, but Buron disallowed it. Barnacle duty was a strictly convenience-free affair, so it was hang and haul each time.

Renn was getting stronger from the physical labor he'd had to do since arriving onboard – he still hadn't used the injury note – but not having hauled another shark after his first one, he still wasn't strong enough to pull in a full-grown man by himself, or at least not without a lot of difficulty. Buron knew this, and he knew how Xavier had spent the last three weeks holding a grudge against the boy. He didn't pick his barnacle partners at random.

The result was that when it was time to haul Xavier in, it took Renn a good many tries, setting and resetting his grip on the rope, losing the grip, and trying again, before he was finally able to get the man back on board by planting his feet against the rails as Xavier himself had done that day with the giant shark. He wished someone could have helped him, and looked around for Emile, but it wouldn't have mattered even if Emile had been there, for they both knew nobody was allowed to interfere with the punishment, so Renn tried to pretend he was hauling in a shark and wondered if this could count as his audition for the harpoon crew.

By the time Xavier had made it back over the rails, he'd

been swung back and forth, up and down so much that he crawled over the rail and fell, spluttering and flailing, to the rotten boards of the deck.

Renn smiled at the sight of the hard-bitten harpooneer looking so helpless and undignified.

"You think this is funny?" the man asked angrily, raising himself up on his hands.

Renn bit his lip and shook his head, but Xavier ranted on.

"You know what *I* think would be funny? Feeding you to the fishes right now. Toss you over and use your guts to attract a nice, big one. Make up for the kill you cost me last time."

"Emile told you about that himself, remember? It was your own fault because you didn't tie your rope."

"Like I care what that Wend-lover says," Xavier spat seawater. "I'll send him overboard, too."

Renn felt the blood drain from his face. *Wend-lover*? How could Xavier have possibly figured out that truth? Renn was sure he hadn't said a word about it, not even to Emile. He swallowed, trying to hide his fear. He couldn't let Xavier know he was right.

"Forget about him," Renn said. "Why don't you just throw Buron overboard and take control of the ship yourself?" Maybe he could distract Xavier by diverting his anger to a common enemy.

"Don't tell me my business, little boy," Xavier snarled.

Renn instantly felt the heat rise back into his pale skin. He'd heard that line too many times before. When Jungbern would bully him, then mistreat him even more if Renn complained about it. When he'd try to argue for a place in the war parties, to be denied over and over again, and be chastised by Hagen for questioning the decision. When he'd had to stay at home, with the very young children, embarrassed to be seen, as everyone else got to go to battle.

Anger flared up in him as he remembered it, crowding any thought of caution out of his mind. He would show this Gaul that he wasn't a pushover; that he wasn't some useless child to be dismissed and ignored.

"I'll tell you your business whenever I please," he heard himself saying. "Since you can't seem to manage it yourself...can't even remember not to throw your own spear away into the ocean. Some harpooneer you are. Seems like cleaning barnacles is all you're *fit* for."

Xavier was up from the deck quicker than Renn expected from a man in his state, and had his arm locked around Renn's neck before the boy could react.

Renn struggled at first, as he'd do with Jungbern, but Xavier was not letting go. He clinched his arm tighter and tighter, until black spots began to bloom in the center of Renn's vision, and a ringing grew louder and louder in his ears.

Dimly, there came a shout that sounded miles away, and suddenly he could breathe again. He gulped down a breath, only to have the little air he'd regained forced back out of him by the Xavier's ribcage knocking into his backbone as they both fell to the deck.

Somebody was pulling Renn up by his arm. He twisted as he was lifted to his feet and saw his attacker with lip curled, bristling up Dumoulin, the head harpooneer, who crouched over him, harpoon in one hand, Xavier's collar in the other.

With his ears still ringing and his heart still pounding, Renn couldn't hear what Dumoulin was saying, but he saw how Xavier fought him, struggling to throw him off. He looked like a cornered boar, panting for breath, his head whipping side to side as he clawed to get free.

Dumoulin was knocked off balance, and the two of them struggled for control of the harpoon. Xavier climbing to his feet, trying to turn the spear end on Dumoulin, who rolled and kicked up into the other man's gut. But Xavier only went down for a moment before he sprang again, and his target swung the harpoon around in an instant.

Renn knew his hearing had come back when he registered the cracks, then the splatters – the sound of

Xavier's ribs breaking, and the blood squirting and splashing onto the planks – and Xavier sank down, his snarl gone slack, and a shark hunter's spear in his chest.

"Stupid," Dumoulin said, climbing to his feet. "He only had a few months left." He looked down at the body, shaking his head, then reached to pull the harpoon out of the dead man's chest.

Renn winced as the body was lifted briefly off the deck before it thudded back when the spearhead pulled free of the flesh, accompanied by another series of crunches. The anger that had so quickly filled Renn drained away as he watched the life drain out of Xavier. Now he only felt numb and sick.

Others were crowding around, the same way they had with the giant shark Xavier had tried to catch. As if he were now just another animal, another trophy to be gawked at. One day the hunter, one day the kill. It seemed not to matter to these Gauls, so long as there was blood involved. The red pool leached its way toward Renn's feet, and his stomach gave a twist.

Through the group of men bunched around, a tall figure waded. It was First Officer Fairinelle, who scanned the scene, his high black boots coming to a stop just short of the puddle of gore. Renn saw him grip the center him of his red woolen coat, white-gloved knuckles tightening around the brass buttons, and heard him let out a long, controlled breath.

"He finally snapped," Dumoulin gestured to the body defensively. "You know how he was always holding grudges...tried to choke the kid...tried to stab me…"

"Are you hurt, Mr. Dumoulin? Mr. LeNotre?" Fairinelle's voice was almost jarringly serene

.   "Um, no...sir." In his shock at what had happened to Xavier, Renn had nearly forgotten that he'd almost been a victim himself.

"Then I shall meet you in my quarters for a full report in half an hour's time." He turned to leave, having been there for what couldn't have been more than ninety seconds.

Wasn't the death of a man worth more than ninety seconds' consideration?

*"*Well, you going to get to help me or what?" Renn realized Dumoulin was speaking to him.

"Grab his feet and help me throw him over. You've got just as much share in this as me, seeing as it was you I had to take him out for."

Only a few minutes ago, he had been struggling to pull Xavier up from the water. Now he was having to throw his dead body down. Was this what would have happened to him had Xavier succeeded?

"Come on, boy. Don't act like you've never seen blood before."

Renn had seen animal blood before, but human blood was different. Not least in its thick, heavy smell. There was no way he was going to be able to do this.

"Allow me to assist you this time, Mr. Dumoulin."

Fairinelle had come back, slowly and deliberately removing his gloves and his overcoat. "Mr. LeNotre, would you be so kind as to hold my things?"

He was giving Renn an excuse not to touch the body without seeming weak, and the rush of gratitude Renn felt made him understand why wild men like Xavier and Dumoulin worked for the officer without complaint.

Fairinelle's calmness in the face of the grisly scene, that had so bothered Renn before, was now a welcome relief, and he stood wondering what sort of man cared about the feelings of a young slave, sparing him from something he was clearly uncomfortable with, yet was willing to command a miserable slave ship like the St. Juste, where the point of every day was to be as uncomfortable and unhappy as possible?

Some of the men brought over ballast bags, which Fairinelle and Dumoulin tied around Xavier for weight, and Renn watched as the two of them lifted the body. He saw how Fairinelle, willowy though he was, his white linen shirt fluttering against him in the ocean breeze, easily hoisted the torso of corpse and the extra weight of the ballast above the railing while Dumoulin shoved the feet over.

Renn vaguely felt that it ought to have been wrapped up in something – an old sheet or sail, maybe – to give it *some* dignity, some final protection from the jaws of the fish in the deep. In Cimbria, warriors were given elaborate burial rituals and sent off to the afterlife in honor.

But the St. Juste afforded respect to its crewmen neither in life nor in death. The body was dropped as it was, its arms rising above its head as it fell, like some giant, deformed seabird diving into the waves.

When the job was done, and Xavier had sunk below the murky water, large blotches of red stained Fairnelle's shirt where the dead man had touched him. He rubbed the back of his hand across his face, accidentally leaving a streak of color smeared under his eyes, running from one cheekbone to the other.

His white sleeves were matted against his arms, leaving his skin visible through the bloody wetness, and beneath one of them, Renn could see something dark on Fairinelle's skin.

There, just below the right elbow, was the same black Wend symbol Renn had drawn on his forehead at Barenhohle. But on Fairinelle's arm, the shape was crossed through with two daggers.

Renn's mouth fell open. He knew those marks. The men at home told of Gauls who were fiercer and more dangerous than any others of their kind, who were known for killing Wends with particular brutality. As a way to taunt their adversaries, these Gauls etched the symbol of their enemy on themselves, marking through it each time they made another important kill. The man who had killed the famous warrior Ottokar was said to have been covered from head to toe with dagger tattoos.

Fairinelle wore only two. It was enough.

Above the red line on his cheeks that suddenly looked like warpaint, his blue eyes settled on Renn, who clutched the overcoat against his chest like a shield.

"Are you quite alright?" he asked. The words were as elegant as ever, but to Renn, the sound rang false. The man was a killer, beyond even the common level of the murdering Gauls, and no amount of genteel behavior could hide that now.

"That's enough!" came Buron's voice as he stomped his way to the group. Apparently, he was bothered more by men who were not working than by men who were killing each other. "Start cleaning up or clearing out!" he said, and began calling names for cleanup duty.

Renn's name was among them, but he didn't move.

"Mr. LeNotre?" Fairinelle took a step toward him.

"Right, sorry, I'll go right away," Renn stuttered and fled, dropping the coat and gloves into the blood on the deck.

Whose blood had they been covered with when he had earned his tattoos?

CHAPTER 6
Celine

Renn let Dumoulin do most of the talking during the report on Xavier's death, and in the days and weeks that followed, Renn gave Fairinelle as wide a berth as possible. He spoke to Emile as much as he dared, but given which of the two officers oversaw the harpoon crew, it wasn't always easy.

He knew he shouldn't be talking to Emile this much, but if somehow he had let his true self show enough that Xavier had figured it out, he was in danger of it happening again, and it might be useful to have a friend on his side if that day ever came. As risky a hope as it was, it was better than having no options at all. And at least Emile didn't have any killers' tattoos – or not that Renn could see, anyway.

Unlike Fairinelle, Emile wore no coat, and one of his shirt sleeves was torn off above the forearm, while the other was perpetually rolled up to the elbow to avoid the constant mess of blood and water in his harpooning work. The skin visible there was mercifully unmarked. Emile might have gotten the Eagle's Eye, but whatever he had done to earn it, it was at least not enough to earn the kind of marks Fairinelle had.

"Was Fairinelle ever in the army?" he asked Emile one day. If anybody knew the answer, it might be him.

"Hmm, don't think so," Emile scratched his head. "Haven't heard anything about that."

"Do you know how he got his kill marks, then?"

"Oh, so he's got some? Wouldn't have guessed that of him. How did you find out? It's hard to tell, you know, with his coat on all the time. I wonder why he does it, 'cause I can tell you wearing a wool thing like that in the midday sun isn't exactly a picnic. We used to sweat our weight in water in our army coats."

"Um, the tattoos?" Renn interrupted, hoping to draw Emile's attention back to the point.

"Well, if he *was* in the army before, I'd guarantee you he didn't get his marks there."

"Don't soldiers get them?" A flicker of hope rose in Renn's chest. If Emile didn't have any on his arms, maybe he didn't have any anywhere else.

"Nah, if we got marked for every man we took out on the field, we'd be so covered we wouldn't have room for our own natural skin. That's what the medals are for."

"I guess you took out a lot of men, then?" asked Renn, the brightness of his hope dimming just a little as he remembered Emile's lost Eagle's Eye.

"Well, sharpshooters don't work like your average artilleryman. We get fewer hits, but that's because we focus on accuracy. It takes time to line up those shots, so we'd usually be sent out when a specific person needed to be, ah...handled. Otherwise, we tended to stay in the back and provide cover when needed. It wasn't all melee for us."

Despite the grim reference, especially as Renn could recall several people throughout the years who had been "handled" by Gauls, it made him feel better, once he worked his way through all the military terms, to know that Emile hadn't been indiscriminately mowing people down during his time in the service.

Even better, it was sure now that he didn't carry any kill marks. At least a medal could be separated from who you were, it could be taken away like Emile's medal had been. A tattoo became part of you. Forever. The killing of Wends was something Fairinelle had chosen to etch, forever, into his being.

And Renn couldn't escape him. His only choices were live in fear of him every day for the rest of his life, or have that life shortly ended when the truth came out. For with each day that passed, his hope of being rescued grew fainter and fainter. The chance that any of his people would cross the border was never very high, though he'd hoped they would make an exception for him. But now, even had they wanted to track him all the way to…wherever in the country this was, how could they find him in the middle of the water?

Though the St. Juste did, in fact, come to port once a week, the chances of anybody making an escape were slim, thanks to the fact that the ship dropped anchor a mile out from land, and either Buron or Fairinelle would take the week's catch on a dinghy to sell, leaving the other to guard the prisoners, and the sharks below kept anyone from attempting to swim for land.

Making it all worse was the knowledge that had none of these other circumstances been true, had he been able to walk right onto land with nobody stopping him, he still had no idea at all where he was, nor which was the way home.

He was utterly lost whether he got off the boat or not.

This thought circled in his mind as he went through the motions of the morning deck-swabbing several weeks later, splashing more water than was necessary but succeeding in cleaning very little. The grime in the cracks never seemed to get any cleaner.

A few paces away, Buron was yelling at someone, but Renn paid it little attention. He had been yelling more than usual this week because Fairinelle had been off on leave, and while it made Renn feel better, it only made Buron crankier to have to take both of their duties on himself.

Under his hands, Renn felt the vibrations of footfalls approaching, quick and staccato, tapping importantly, and a pair of muddy boots and the fraying hem of a woolen skirt swishing above boot tops went past him.

Renn was not the only one staring at the woman they

belonged to, who had appeared as if out of thin air. None of them had never seen her before, and she was most certainly not a prisoner, but how had she gotten onboard, when they were a mile out from land? From the scrapes and scratches on her face, and the hair that was a bird's nest of messy curls, she looked as if she had been dragged here the same way Renn had. But the proud tilt of her chin and the straightness of her back as she marched directly up to the bawling captain didn't seem to belong to a slave or a prisoner.

"Are you Buron?" she asked curtly, with no other word of introduction or explanation.

Renn had never seen Buron at a loss for words, but when the jailer turned, having been too busy shouting to notice her before, his voice completely dropped out, and he stared in shock, his eyes bulging and his mouth hanging open, before his expressions returned to its usual scorn, and he recovered himself.

"I might be," he said. "Mind tellin' me who *you* are, and how you got on this boat?"

"I rowed. Then I climbed." She shrugged, pointing to the place where the stairs went down the side of the hull. The stairs Buron never let them use for barnacle duty.

"If you're not Buron, you must tell him it needs a good dry docking," she finished dismissively.

"This ain't a pleasure cruise, lady. You can't come waltzing on here whenever you please."

"Pity. I heard you were a man who didn't mind making a profit."

"Our haul of sharks went out to town this morning. Get off my boat and go find 'em there."

"It's not the seafood I'm after. I'm interested in the other merchandise."

"Shut up with that talk!" Buron hissed at her.

Renn scooted closer to hear what he said next.

"Whoever you got your information from shoulda told you that sorta business don't exist in broad daylight. Come back after dark and I might decide to let you pick some out."

"Sorry, but I don't have time to accommodate slavers who are too afraid to actually sell slaves. It'll be now or you lose my business."

"Who said I have any business with you in the first place? I only sell to customers as have brought me something first, to fill up the holes they put in my crew."

Though Renn knew firsthand that human goods were what Buron dealt in when he wasn't selling shark meat, it was strange to hear it being spoken of out loud. Buron growled in quiet tones, but the woman didn't bother lowering her voice at all.

"If I could find a specimen worth selling, do you think I would bother bringing them to this two-bit rig instead of using them myself?" she asked. "But as it is, I cannot find two free men together who are unafraid to do the work I need, so I must make use of those who have no choice. Believe me, I wouldn't have come within fifteen miles of this stinking hulk otherwise. I will pay you five hundred for two of your best brutes, which is plenty more than what they're worth," she finished, eyeing the dirty, ragged men toiling across the deck.

"You think I need such measly kind of cash? Get out of here before I throw you overboard for that insult."

"You obviously can't afford any better," she gave the crew another sweeping, disdainful look. "Learn to take a good offer when it's given, and you might be able to pay for better quality products next time."

Redness rushed to Buron's face and spittle sprayed from his mouth. " I do business with so many people, who pay so much more than you, you couldn't even count 'em. If they don't mind my quality, neither should a poor first-timer like yourself."

"Good," the woman said. "Then it won't damage your finances if I only give you five hundred. I'm only a poor, pathetic, first-time customer, but surely your richer clients can more than amply make up for what I lack." She smiled sweetly at him.

Renn put his head down to hide his laughter at the way Buron fumed. He understood now why Willow had laughed all those weeks ago when he'd suckered Buron into buying a young, stupid boy for his crew. For all his pompousness and arrogance, he really was just an unintelligent, easily enraged animal.

"But you still ain't gettin' one man for that price, much less two." He growled menacingly, stepping toward the visitor, but she did not step back.

"Oh well, then, if I can't get up my hunting party, I guess I may as well amuse myself by visiting the provost. He loves to gossip, you know, and I heard something very interesting about them tightening the noose on illegal trading the other day," she looked sideways at him.

Renn didn't know what a "noose" was, but it sounded painful. Buron's face, where wariness was now mixed with anger, seemed to confirm that.

"Yeah, and what's to stop me from sharin' what I know about you?" The bite in Buron's voice was wavering.

"Two things, actually. One, you don't know me. In case you hadn't noticed, I haven't given you my name. How would you describe me to the provost? As the person who ran intellectual circles around you and exposed the ridiculous prices in your *illegal* trade? Two, I do have *your* name, and were your mind somehow capable enough to correctly identify me, I will first let the provost have his way with you, and afterwards, I swear I will find you myself, and it will not be in the broad daylight."

The woman's voice was hard as she leaned in to Buron's face, her hands on her hips and her eyes slitted like a cat's.

Renn didn't understand all of her words, but it was clear she was threatening him, and Renn wondered why Buron was taking it from her without a fight, until he noticed how her hands didn't rest idly. Her fingers were curling around a double holster strapped across her waist, which held what looked like a pair of smaller, more curving versions of Henny's stolen gun. Emile had said soldiers most often carried the long ones – rifles, he'd called them – but apparently some Gauls carried these smaller versions, which he called pistols.

He'd said they could shoot, too, only not as far, and the men back home had told him the same thing before, describing how the Gauls carrying them had to get closer to the enemy than the rest of soldiers before they could be of any use – and that wasn't much, for the closer they got, the easier it was for their enemy, the Wends, to eliminate them.

But this woman was plenty close to do damage to Buron, and he seemed to know it.

"You were too dense to notice me until I was right on your deck in the noonday sun," she said. "What chance will you have when I come for you under cover of darkness? Just give me two men, and you won't have to worry about any of it."

"Fine, sold," said Buron, just as quickly as Badger had when Renn was sold. He stuck out a dirty hand, and the woman, after a moment spent disdainfully eyeing it, took it in hers, though her own fingers were not much cleaner than his.

Buron's eyes landed on Renn, noticing him watching. "For five hundred, you get Renny-boy here." He turned, regaining his confidence as he strode over, and yanked Renn up. The scrub brush fell from Renn's hand as he was pulled to his feet.

"I need men, not cabin boys," she said, her fingers running lightly over one of her guns.

"This one's ain't no cabin boy, he's killed a thousand men, can't you tell?" Buron pulled Renn's head back by his hair., as if to show off his prize wares.

The woman came to stand before him, looking down her nose and taking his chin in her hand. "You look awfully tender to be here, child."

Renn's pulse began to pound. He didn't know what she

was planning to do with her slaves, but whatever it was, she was leaving the boat with them, and suddenly, it made very much difference whether he was off the boat or on it. But she needed someone who was unafraid.

She'd never take him if she thought he was soft, not even for five hundred coins, which Renn supposed was not much, based on Buron's reaction. He was going to have to bluff his way through this.

He stuck out his jaw and tried to strike the kind of careless pose Jungbern always adopted when he bragged about his feats in battle, despite the fact that Buron still held his head back.

"Looks aren't everything," he said, looking straight and (he hoped) confidently into the woman's cat eyes.

"Is that so? Then tell me, how came you to be on this boat?" She wasn't immediately dismissing him. That was a good sign.

He shrugged. "Might've killed a man or two." He hoped his weeks of covering up the truth had made him a capable liar.

"But there are more than mere men in Cimbria, my boy."

Cimbria! Renn's act almost fell apart right there. Of all the places in the world, this woman was going straight to his own home! He stumbled for words, and the woman frowned again.

He had to say something. It was more important now than ever. A minute ago he was simply trying to get off the boat. Now he was playing for a ride home.

The woman's mouth was moving. He made himself focus on the words.

"Anyone can kill a man," she was saying. "Are you strong enough to face demon dogs the size of men, and demon men the size of bears?"

Renn thought of Siegher, Jungbern's warhound in name only, and how the dog, so fierce in battle, would bound up to him like an excited lamb after the smallest time spent apart, and sleep with his giant head in Renn's lap at nights.

"They're not so very frightening," he said with perfect confidence. This, at least, was something he didn't have to bluff about. "Not if you know how to handle them."

"Oh?" she raised an eyebrow. "And how would you know?"

What would Jungbern say in a situation like this? What would Hagen say?

"I've dealt with them tons of times. Their dogs are just like their men. Show them you're in charge and they'll roll over and lick your shoes before putting up any real fight." For good measure, he added. "Though I think the dogs would deserve it less."

"Well, well. You've got the right spirit, at least."

"I've got more than that."

Now was the time for the finishing blow. "I've lived near Cimbria all my life, and I've seen enough of them to make me sick for the rest of it. I can tell you all about them – how they work, who their leaders are, where they like to hide. I can even show you around the other side of the border."

It was risky to come so close to revealing himself, to give so many specifics, but he had to try. Of course he had no real intention of telling her anything. He had already half-formed a plan to skip out on her as soon as they got close to home, but he had to *get* there first, and he needed her to take him there.

"Are you telling me the truth?" she asked, her voice was still cold though her eyes had lit up.

"Nothing but," said Renn. He *could* tell her what he knew. He just wasn't *going* to.

Near the prow of the boat, Emile stood up from the harpoon line he was mending, rubbing his neck to relieve the strain of hunching over it. He tilted his head and it was then he saw the strange, hard-looking woman peering down at his friend at the other end of the deck, while Buron held his head back by the hair. He could not hear their exchange, but he quickly understood what he saw.

Although a beating awaited anyone who mentioned it

aloud, it was no secret that half the crew was comprised of men who had been in a bad place at a bad time, and had run into kidnappers and desperate men looking to make a profit in the slave trade. He almost envied them, after a fashion. At least someone had thought these men were worth something. Quite the opposite of the reason he was here.

And then, of course, there were the disappearances. Men who had been sent to work here as punishment for crimes suddenly "worked off their debt to society" overnight, without any word of warning, except glimpses caught in the dead of night of "court officials" who just happened to pay Buron his jailer's salary at the moment the "freed men" were handed over.

Emile watched the woman's hand closing on Renn's shoulder like the claw of a hawk grasping its prey, and saw the way her grin grew ever wider. He dropped his rope half-mended, and moved toward them.

"I'll take him," he heard the woman say as he drew closer, confirming his fears.

"Glad to hear it," said Buron. "You'll sure go far with this one. Cimbria's just the place for him."

"Cimbria!" gasped Emile. There had been more casualties in Cimbria than anywhere else on the border. The warriors there – men and women both – were fiercer than in any other place Emile had fought, and that was where this boy, who was scared even of kindly Mr. Fairinelle, was getting shipped off to? What were Buron and this woman after? What good would such a slave do in that place? How could he survive it, if he even survived long enough to get there?

"That's one man down. A scout is a fine thing, but who shall I have for my watchman?" the woman straightened, scanning the deck.

"I'll go!" Emile called out, and he ran to close the distance between them. The way to save Renn had struck him in a flash. "If your aim is a pair of sharp eyes, there's none better than me."

"You'll do no such thing, Badeau," Buron answered him. Aside from having the nerve to eavesdrop, he knew that what this bold harpooner had said was true. Emile consistently brought in the most catches, therefore the most money, and Buron had no desire to lose him.

"I was in the army. They gave me the Eagle's Eye," Emile continued, ignoring Buron and speaking directly to the woman, though his eyes flicked between her and the boy whose shoulder she gripped.

"They did not," Buron said flatly. He had no idea if Emile had really gotten a medal – reading prisoner reports was Fairinelle's job – but he wasn't going to let anyone *believe* it was true.

"I'll prove it," Emile returned just as quickly, then turned and headed back toward the rails, near his harpooning equipment. "You see that line of foam out there, about twenty yards off? That's the wake made by a shark, and it'll be dead a few seconds from now."

He hoisted his spear.

"Not with the property of the St. Juste, it won't!" cried Buron "That harpoon belongs to me, and I say you're banned from using it!" His voice was gaining an edge of panic now, but Emile was as much at ease as ever. He set the weapon down with a shrug and walked back to the group.

"Let me borrow one of those squirrel-shooters, then," he said as he motioned to the small guns the stranger wore strapped on either hip.

"You ain't seriously gonna let this criminal get his hands on a firearm, are ya?" the captain sputtered at her. "We'll all be killed."

"Is the lord and master of a mighty warship really frightened of a lowly slave?" she asked, laughter in her voice, and handed one of her pistols to Emile. "Here. If you're going to shoot someone, please let it be him, just to shut him up."

Renn expected something exciting. Maybe Emile would actually shoot Buron, who was currently hovering in indecision over whether he should attempt to grab the gun Emile was inspecting or run to take cover from it.

"I can assure you it's real," the woman rolled her eyes.

Emile shrugged a second time. "Just checkin' for defects," he said, but he did clock the cartridge back into place, and lifted his head towards the water. "Now where did it go…" he muttered, and after a moment, looked back down at the gun. "Too far for this thing to reach now."

He raised his head again, this time searching the skies, then threw his shoulders back, sucked in a breath, held it, and with a crack, brought a mutilated fish falling down to the deck from the sky, followed by the seagull that had been carrying it.

Three cracks more, and three tiny brown birds joined them, their spindly legs splaying out behind as they fell away from the dark flock flying far above. There was no excess of feathers, no unnecessary wounds, no convulsions. Each animal had each been shot cleanly through the head.

As impressive as it was to make such clean work of even the smallest of the birds, Renn felt sorry for them. They had only been minding their own business when they'd been shot down, just as he'd been minding his when he'd been taken from his home. He could almost hear Hagen telling him that was the way of the Gauls – hurting and killing anything that happened to be convenient, but he tried to comfort himself with the fact that at least these animals had died quickly. That Emile had given them a quick and, Renn hoped, painless death. Well, except for the fish. There was no guarantee of what the seagull had done to it beforehand.

"Hmm, at least you had sense not to shoot an albatross," was the woman's only remark as she looked over the offering at her feet.

"That's exactly why I ain't givin' him to you for five hundred," Buron had regained enough nerve to grumble. "You'll have to cough up more than that if you want my best shot."

"I didn't say I wanted him. He volunteered, and if I were you, I would let the matter rest, lest he *does* decide to shoot you. In case you hadn't noticed, there are only five dead creatures here. He has a bullet left for one more."

"He wouldn't if you'd get your pistol out of his hand."

"Oh, I couldn't do that. Accosting a dangerous criminal in possession of a firearm? I'd be too afraid of what might happen to me."

A smile twisted her mouth as she echoed his words and threw down a small bag tied with twine, which jingled dully as it hit the deck.

"Five hundred or I go to the provost, and not only will you be removed from heading this miserable crew, you'll be a prisoner yourself." Then, when he gave her no response; "We're all waiting, especially Provost Leblond."

At the repetition of that name, Buron grudgingly waved his hand. "Then get out of here, already," he said, and squatted down to grab the bag of coins.

"Don't expect me to let you get your things, if you've got any," he added, looking at his former slaves.

Neither of them minded. There was no part of the St. Juste they wished to keep.

CHAPTER 7
Sea Legs

The first thing Renn noticed was that the ground was moving. It swayed as if it, too, were a boat on the water, making it hard for Renn to keep steady as he and Emile followed their new owner.

But why should this be? He had been perfectly steady on the boat itself, or at least he had been after those first few half-conscious days. In fact, he rather felt now like he had then, when the trip out of Cimbria had made him so sick and dizzy that even now he didn't know exactly how long or far it had been from the Cimbrian border to the shore. If it was going to be like this every time he tried to walk on Gallic land, he didn't know how he would last through the trip back home.

He tried to distract himself by whispering questions to Emile behind their new mistress's back. "Is this even allowed? For her to just come and take us off like that?" he asked.

"Who cares? You know it wasn't legal how half of us got onboard to start with," Emile whispered. "If that's how Buron works, might as well play by his rules to get ourselves off, right?"

"If you're worried about it," the woman called over her shoulder. "I can return you to your ship when we get through."

"*You can try*," thought Renn, "*but I'll already be gone, once we cross the border.*"

"No thanks, Ms…" he said instead, but trailed off. What were they supposed to call her? Their master? Their boss? The only thing Renn cared to call her was his way home, but he couldn't say that to her face.

"You may address me by my first name; Celine," she said. "I don't think I'll trust you with my last just yet. Not before you've proven yourselves. You are still criminals, after all."

"Being a prisoner doesn't make you a criminal," Emile said, but Renn didn't voice his agreement. It was only because he'd made Celine think he was tough enough to be a criminal that she had taken him along. Emile could earn his keep with his sharpshooting talent, but what talent did Renn – the real Renn – have that would make Celine want to keep him around? He could work with dogs, but there were none of those around here, and he didn't think the Gauls used them for battle, anyway

. "Prisoners, criminals, I don't care what you called yourselves before. You're my property now, so see that you behave like it. You, my knowledgeable child," she said, addressing Renn, "can start by telling me what you know about Cimbria, and I don't want to hear that it's a stinking, blighted place full of stinking, blighted people. That's no information I couldn't tell you myself, and it's more than common knowledge about those brutes I'm after."

"What should I tell you?" Renn grumbled, with a sudden rush of offended pride streaking through him. "Would you like to know how they could kill you with their bare hands if you met them? How they can track in you total silence, and you won't know a thing about it until they're right on you? How their homes are hidden away in the deeps of the woods, and how you will never find them even if you look for a hundred years?"

"That's why I have you, isn't it? To find them for me?"

"Of course it is." *But that's not what you'll get.* "You don't know anything like what I know." *And you never will.*

"I know how much bounty money I'm *not* going to share with you, thanks to that tongue of yours," she said.

"Would she have shared any of it anyway?" Emile whispered.

"Bounty money?" Renn asked Celine.

"You know so much," she said, "but you don't know what kind of prize currently sits on the heads of the Cimbrian warlords? The army isn't faring so well against them these days, so they've taken to calling in outside help. Anyone who can take out a chief gets paid five thousand livres in gold."

Was that why Willow and Badger had been there that day? Had they been looking to capture someone important, and ended up with him instead? Thinking back over their words, it seemed Willow knew they couldn't earn any bounty off of him (and the thought of that stung him), so they had sold him to Buron to regain their profit. How fitting then, that it was also a bounty hunter who would bring him back home.

But as lucky as it was for him, he couldn't see why there should be these bounties at all. What had any of the Cimbri ever done except fight back against people who threatened their land? Why should they have a price on their heads when it was the Gauls who were always on the attack?

"No, I don't know anything about bounties," he said angrily. "Where I come from, we mind our business instead of bothering other people, and we don't need rewards to make us do our work."

"We're in agreement, then. You don't want the money, and I don't want to give it to you. Sounds like you and I will get along just fine."

Renn had nothing to say to that, so he focused instead on avoiding collisions with the growing number of people who had begun to appear in their path, though it was hard with the world still rocking around him.

Buildings began to appear behind the sand dunes, first small, square, windswept little cottages, which gave way to taller, bigger buildings as the road widened and the sounds of the gulls and the waves gave way to growing clatter and chatter. More people than Renn had ever seen in one place were moving about, calling to each other while big horses pulled giant metal wagons over stony paths, and tiny dogs and hissing cats, ran about underfoot.

Lanterns glowed in doorways against the purple sky, and men in tall hats lit tall lamps on corners. While a few passersby gave curious glances at the ragged, dirty clothes sported by Renn and Emile, most barely looked their way.

How was this possible? People were smiling and laughing, without seeming to have a worry in the world, and all within a day's walk of the misery that was the St. Juste. Did these people have no notion that men were suffering and dying on a ship docked just off their shore? Or did they just not care so long as they could go about their own lives undisturbed? Was this how normal Gauls lived – all noise and action and indifference? The only Gauls he knew besides his father were those on the boat, and he didn't think those counted as normal.

He had a few fuzzy recollections of hurried, silent movements through places that looked something like this, when Willow and Badger passed through them in the nights, dragging Renn behind them. But at those times, the cities had been dark and empty, and they hadn't seemed quite so large, unlike the crowds and looming buildings he faced now.

He tried not to show how foreign it felt, and he combed his memory for anything his father might have told him about such places. But his father had been dead for years, and if there had ever been a story about cities in the time Renn had spent with him, the memory of it had faded. He'd have to figure this out on his own.

Watching Emile and Celine, he tried to imitate their actions, to pretend as if he were as used to this civilization as any other Gaul. When carts raced down the narrow foot paths between too-closely-crowded buildings, he tried not to fling himself against the walls, though he was sure he was going to be run down in the cramped space, for Celine didn't even flinch, and Emile did so only moderately, as they stepped out of its path.

He hung close in their shadows when, heedless of the danger, Celine led them confidently out to cross the roads, and he tried not wonder at the way she exchanged angry shouts with drivers who barely avoided hitting her. None of this was at all helped by the continued rolling of his vision, which would have made it hard to keep his feet even in calmer surroundings.

"The first thing we need to do is get you some weapons," Celine said as soon as she had finished insulting the most recent cart-driver to nearly kill them.

"Can't we rest first?," asked Renn wearily. "I don't even see any smithies nearby."

"Smithies? You really are a rustic, aren't you, child? There are no smithies in the middle of town. Most city folk are blissfully unaware the need for such a thing even exists, and those who aren't think themselves too sophisticated to do use them, believing only those of lesser moral status would choose to carry something so 'barbaric'. So they exile all that sort of trade, such as it is, to the outskirts of the city, where they don't have to see it. Of course, they don't mind when their economy benefits from the hunters who come seeking it."

Import, status, barbaric, exile, outskirts, economy. Renn would have to start writing these words down.

"It's just as well, I suppose," she continued. "I've always preferred the untamed places to these stuffy streets, though it would be nice to get some recognition for the fact that it's only the work we do out there which keeps them safe within their precious little walls."

Renn thought how much like Hagen she sounded. He, too, hated those who thought themselves above others, particularly 'those uppity Gauls.'

"Though now I suppose I am doing the very thing they're worried about," Celine mused. "Buying weapons for criminals...whatever will it do to my reputation?"

Renn was only too glad when they reached the little rows of smaller shops and quieter streets on the far side of the city, which he'd deduced was called Concertine, based on the number of signs and storefronts bearing that name. Though the people in this area looked rougher than those he had seen in the town's center, there were fewer of them, which meant a little peace for his throbbing head, and its humble, wood and thatch buildings reminded him more of Barenhohle than the straight, imposing ones of brick and stone at the city's center.

He remembered the first time he had ever come to that shady grove where his mother had been born, and how strange it had all seemed as he crept quietly beside Linderic towards his uncle's lodging. He had been so frightened then, knowing he was going to live with people he had never met, whose way of life he did not know.

He had been more frightened yet when he was introduced to his giant of an uncle, with that booming voice and that wild expression. But Linde had put a hand on his head when he felt Renn shrinking against him, to give him comfort and courage.

He was following a completely different type of person now, as he trailed behind Celine through a doorway over which a sign painted with the symbol of an axe hung, but he still couldn't help finding a little relief in the fact that this shop was quiet, even as the unsettling sight of Gallic weapons surrounded him.

He looked at them glittering faintly on the walls. Thin swords much daintier than anything used back home, lances with delicate designs carved into their polished wood poles. Whoever the weapon-maker was, it seemed they were more concerned with form than function.

In Cimbria, little thought was given to the appearance of a weapon as long as it did its job. That was ensured by custom-making them for each person. The smiths would work with the warriors to design with an item that matched their strengths and compensated for their weaknesses.

Renn wondered how someone could fight effectively with a weapon merely picked up off a rack.

"Well, what weapon do you take, boy?" the shopkeeper asked in an unfriendly voice. No wonder Celine had chosen to come here. He sounded just like her.

"I– " Renn hesitated. Linde had trained him on boar spears and hunting knives, which worked just as well on Gauls as they did on boars, but he didn't see anything that looked like that here. Everything looked like it would break the first time it touched anything.

He looked at the axes. They might be sturdy enough. After all, both Hagen and Jungbern carried them. But, Renn realized, it was for that same reason he couldn't choose them. Axes were hard to handle; only celebrated warriors like his uncle could use them effectively, and it was crucial that Renn not look like a beginner with such a weapon in front of Celine. He had no idea how young Gauls started their training, if they even did any outside of their army, but he'd promised her he knew how to fight, so he had to show her something to prove it.

He glanced around the room, searching for something that might work, but everything seemed either too small and ineffective, or too large and too hard to use.

"What did you use when you lived in the borderlands?" Emile suggested. "I think I heard Celine say something about you fighting Wends out there."

But this only made Renn's choice more difficult. The lie about the borderlands had covered the truth about his accent and had convinced Celine to take him out of prison, but now the payment for it was coming due. He'd said he had dealt with Wends, and he had. He had just never fought *against* them.

The only thing that might save him at this moment was the fact that Celine had wandered off to the other side of the room, restlessly picking up one item after another, and setting each of them down without really looking at them. If he could find an excuse to give Emile quick enough, Celine might never have to know.

He could only hope Emile would take pity on the truth.

"I hunted boars, mostly," he admitted. "Not people."

"Oh!" said Emile brightly. "If you're a hunter, then why didn't you ever go out for the harpooners?"

Renn had wanted to, but then he had seen Fairinelle's tattoos.

"So I guess you'll be needing a lance, then?" Emile asked when Renn didn't answer.

"But none of these look strong enough," Renn said.

"That's 'cause you're used to killing animals. These probably wouldn't hold a shark's weight either, but people go down a bit easier, you know. No need to carry a heavy thing when a lighter one will do the job," Emile chattered on. "Trust me, on the long marches, everything you carry weighs twice as much by the end. Besides, something this light – I bet it would be a breeze to maneuver it."

He picked up a slender, ash-colored pole, stepped to the open center of the room, holding it horizontally in front of him, and crossed one foot over the other until he had made a full circle.

"Yep, you'll move quick enough with one of these. Not like those big old shark spears. That'll help when you face off against people who can hit back, 'cause deflecting is just as much a part of survival as striking."

"See, if you hold it like this," he held at his side so that it extended as far behind him as it did in front, "you get coverage in both directions. No matter which way someone comes from, all you have to do is swing yourself around like this, and nobody can touch you."

He touched his fingers to the spear tip. "Oh, but you won't want one with the winged blades on the tip like this. This is how harpoons have 'em, 'cause those are made for sticking once and holding fast."

"Boar spears are the same," Renn said before he could stop himself. He ached to say something about home after all this time, and it wasn't as if he was giving anything away by saying this. He had already told Emile he was a hunter. He would just make sure not to give away the exact details of where or with whom he had done it.

"Without the wings, the hogs can run right through them and reach you."

"Yeah?" Emile's eyebrows went up as he broke into a grin. For this sad, skittish boy who cried when asked about the past to volunteer something about himself was definite progress.

"With sharks we had the reverse problem." Emile said. "Had to worry about 'em slipping off the other way, back into the water."

"And pulling you with them," Renn smiled back, turning his palms out in memory of when he'd almost been pulled over himself. It felt good to have a normal conversation for once, without having to spin lies at every turn.

"That's why they're not so good for when you need to get away quick and strike again," explained Emile, as he swished and jabbed and pulled back with the lance he still held. "You don't want to get stuck on them after the first hit."

He looked back over his shoulder but was dismayed to see Renn's smile had faded again without warning.

Renn was thinking how much Emile had looked like Dumoulin, swinging his harpoon around to kill Xavier, and how it had been the wings of the spear which had stuck in Xavier's ribcage, pulling his corpse off the deck. The wings helped stick once and hold fast, indeed.

"No, I definitely don't want that," he said.

Emile picked up a different lance. "Give this one a try." He held it out to Renn.

"Are you sure you wouldn't rather use it yourself?" Renn asked doubtfully.

"Law, no. Give me a rifle any day."

"But you're so good with it."

Emile gave a short chuckle. "That's 'cause I had to be. You saw yourself how much more freedom a man could get if he was handy with a spear back on the St. Juste."

"You never used *those* moves catching sharks."

"Not on sharks," Emile admitted. "Had to learn how to defend myself pretty quick on the St. Juste. You remember what it was like. The boys got sort of riled up sometimes."

Renn did remember. It was the reason why Xavier was dead; because Renn had "riled him up." Because somehow, he had let Xavier figure out that he was a Wend.

What had he been thinking now, sharing as much he had about the boar-hunting? Even having spoken barely five sentences to Xavier, the man had realized the truth. He couldn't just go around opening his mouth about home like this and assuming it would be alright, no matter how nice it felt to share things, however ambiguously phrased.

But on the other hand, his past was the whole reason Celine had brought him here. She was bound to ask about it, and he would have to tell her something.

So what was he supposed to do, then? On one side, silence was the way to survival, and on the other side, silence would do him in. What were his options?

"Well, what do you say? Think you can learn to fight with a lance?" Emile asked him.

And there it was – an answer. If he could learn to defend himself, learn how the Gauls fought, he would have something to show Celine, something to show that he was as tough as she wanted him to be. If he could fight well enough, he could forestall her questions for a little while, at least.

"I can do it," Renn nodded. "Would you show me that move again?"

They stayed in the enclosure out back of the shop for the rest of the day, claiming they needed time to break in their new weapons, and Celine had left them under the eye of the shopkeeper, saying she would return for them at dusk.

They spent hours going over thrusts, parries, hand positions, and footwork, Emile using his new rifle as a substitute staff for demonstration, and they practiced move after move, spin after spin together, until the rocking in Renn's head that had plagued him all day became crash after crash of painful waves against the inside of his skull. His temples pounded and his vision swam, but he couldn't afford to give into such weakness now. Not when his life was on the line and he had so much to learn.

"Once more, and we'll call it quits for the day," Emile said, wiping the sweat from his brow as he looked up at the darkening sky. "Go ahead and show me Badeau Number Four."

Renn closed his eyes to shut out the dizziness, and launched into the one of the moves he'd spent all evening learning.

"There you go!" Emile cheered. "If you can do it with your eyes closed, you've got it mastered."

As ill as he felt, Renn wasn't insensible to the praise. For once in his life, someone other than Linderic thought he was capable of being a warrior. But this happiness was short-lived, for his stomach was now as unsteady as his head.

Dazedly, he followed Emile's instructions on rubbing down the wooden shaft of his lance ("Have to make sure the sweat and dirt don't eat into it,") and cleaning the metal blade. ("Never mind that you haven't cut anything yet. It's good to get in the habit now.")

On the way back into the shop, the world in front of him took a dip as another throb rolled through his head, and he lost his footing, stumbling into Emile's back.

"Tiring work, huh?" Emile asked as he turned around. "If you'd been in the army with me, you'd have gotten your endurance up soon enough. Nothing but drilling and marches all the time, trying to get from one base to another a hundred miles away, and sometimes even going straight into battle after. But as it is, I suppose I could take you to the cothouse now. Celine said to watch out for her here, but you don't look like you can wait."

He turned to the shopkeeper and called " 'Scuse me, do

you know which way's...The Bashful Swain, I think she called it?", but the shopkeeper answered with a frown and repeated Celine's warning that he should not let them out of his sight.

"My friend needs a rest," said Emile. "We're just going straight to the place she was taking us anyway, so he can lay down for a bit."

"Can't do it. Who's to say you wouldn't cut and run?"

"Come on, how far would I get with this one in such a state?" Emile put his hand on Renn's shoulder, and even he seemed surprised at how much Renn was swaying. His brows drew together, and when next he spoke to the man, his words were faster, his tone darker.

Once again, memories of Xavier swam through Renn's head, and how Emile had threatened him. Only this time, Xavier did not back down. He advanced toward Emile, his voice getting harsher and louder, the noise seeming to slam into Renn's ears and reverberate through his brain. If he could just get out of this room, maybe the pain would go away. Maybe Xavier would stay alive this time. Renn didn't remember that the day the harpooner had been threatened and the day he died weren't one and the same.

He stumbled towards the cool air of the open doorway, and the slice of gloaming sky he saw beyond it, desperate to get away from the scene of oncoming death. The rooftops that had moments ago been so comforting now swooped and rocked as if they would fall on top of him, and the space behind his lower ribs began to churn.

He stretched out his hand, shakily feeling for the doorpost, not realizing that crash that clattered behind him was the new lance he had let fall from his grip as he turned.

"Law, Renn!" cried Emile, moving after him, but before Emile could reach him, Renn staggered into the path of a man in the doorway, who peered bewilderedly down into his pale face.

"Rennesson LeNotre, whatever are you doing here?"

Emile saw the boy look up at the man with languid, unfocused eyes.

"I didn't kill Xavier," Renn mumbled weakly.

"Rennesson, I know," came the soft reply. "It's me, Fairinelle.

CHAPTER 8
Strange Fellows

Renn was perpetually waking up in strange places without knowing how he had gotten into them. Or at least that's how it felt as he fought to focus in his new surroundings. His head felt like an axe blade had been firmly planted in the middle of it, but beyond the edge of the strange cot he lay on, he could see Emile sitting at a small, round table, hunched over a steaming mug and speaking seriously to another man. Behind them, windows set high in a wooden wall showed an inky sky darker than the one which Renn remembered rocking so disturbingly.

"I certainly do believe bad luck follows certain people," said the man whose back was to him.

"That's true enough, Mr. Fairinelle, but I think – "

Fairinelle! The first officer of the St. Juste, who had perfect manners and the marks of a murderer. Renn didn't hear the rest of Emile's sentence, for he instantly threw the blanket off of himself and swung his legs over the edge, but the axe blade dug deeper into his brain with the sudden movement, forcing him back down.

"Steady now," said Fairinelle, rising from his seat and approaching the cot. "You don't want to put yourself out of consciousness again. What has Buron been doing to you while I've been away that makes you show up fainting on the doorstep of a bounty hunters' den?"

"It wasn't Buron," Renn said. "I just haven't been walking straight since we, um…. left the St. Juste." He hesitated to speak the name of the barge, fearing that even mentioning it might remind Fairinelle to take them back there. After all, he hadn't been onboard to witness Celine's purchase, and probably thought they were trying to escape.

"It's alright, I laid the situation all out for him," said Emile, guessing Renn's thoughts as he joined Fairinelle at the bedside.

"I guess something's wrong with my legs," said Renn.

"Do you feel like the world is rocking around you?" asked the officer.

"Yes…sir."

"Not to worry, then. It isn't your legs, it's your head. You've been on the boat so long you've forgotten how to stand on dry land. You keep trying to adjust for waves that aren't there. That's why the world is moving – because your inner balance has gotten misaligned."

"Why didn't it happen to Emile?"

"It did," Emile admitted, scratching the back of his head with a shrug. "Just sort of tried to roll with it, though. But why in the world did you keep practicing for so long if you felt that bad?"

Renn didn't have an answer. He couldn't tell the real reason why, and was glad when a sharp rapping on the door was heard, even though it hurt his head.

Emile got up to answer it, and found Celine standing on the other side. She swept into the room without waiting to be invited, and bore down on Renn's little bed like a dog on the hunt.

"Child, I swear you are causing me more trouble than you are worth. I was informed that I am to pay for a room I didn't request, and I come here to find you lying in repose like the king himself. Would you mind explaining why you decided all this without my permission?"

"Nobody decided it, boss. He's sick, is all," said Emile. "He needs somewhere quiet to get his strength back up."

"Up out of that bed is all this boy will get," Celine said.

"He has a name, you know," Emile protested.

She ignored him, but she could not ignore the tall figure which rose behind them, casting his long shadow over her.

"Celine Lauvin. So it *is* you."

She spun to face him.

"I have settled the payment for this room, which, I believe, makes it mine. Now, seeing as it *is* my room, if you have you have business with me, kindly inform me of it or else get out."

Her back was to Renn, and he couldn't see how her mouth fell open when she realized who spoke to her. He wouldn't have seen anyway, for he had already blacked out again in another wave of pain.

Emile told him the next morning how Celine had tried to insist she was staying until she recovered her property, and how Fairinelle had kicked her out anyway.

Fairinelle was no longer present by the time Renn woke up to see Emile leaning over a washbasin, with a thin metal blade in one hand and a small mirror in the other. Renn abruptly remembered the last time he had held a mirror, when his warpaint had been fresh and his heart had been filled with pride.

"You should have heard him," Emile said, and began to imitate the first officer's serious tones. "'Don't make the mistake of thinking the whole world bows at your command." Then, in his own voice, he recounted "He just took her by the arm, yanked her right along to the hall like she was any of the men from the St. Juste, and locked the door behind her."

The thought of having been locked in a room with Fairinelle made Renn shiver, but he said nothing.

"If it doesn't feel good to get a close shave," Emile said into the silence, running a hand over his chin and inspecting his handiwork in the mirror. "Never could get a very good one with those dull things Buron used to give us. Guess Fairinelle can give us whatever he wants when old Bossy Buron isn't here to see."

Renn tried sitting up, and this time, his head was mercifully clear of pain. When he tried standing, he found that his legs supported him as well as ever.

"Feeling better, I guess?" Emile asked, looking pleased,

then held a hand out. "Here, let me see your shirt. We've got to wash the seawater out of it. You might not have noticed, being asleep and all, but it's not 'til you get away from the water that you realize how much the brine gets in your clothes, and how much it stinks. Already washed mine, not that it's not poor sight anyway," he tugged at his torn, mismatched sleeves. "But at least I got the salt out of it. Make a clean break from the old sailor's life, huh?"

"No need for that," Fairinelle announced as he walked in with a pile of clothing in his arms. "You'll have to forgive me if they don't fit properly. I didn't know your sizes. He handed a set of shirt and trousers to Emile, and another, along with a pair of leather shoes, to Renn.

"Mr. Badeau, you'll forgive me, but your shoes will last for a while. His have holes," Fairinelle motioned to the thin soles Renn had torn up on the way down from Cimbria."

"Heh, army issue. Meant for marching," Emile tapped his own brown boots. "But as for the rest, you didn't have to, at least not for me. I could've made do."

"You won't get any protection from tattered rags out there on a bounty hunt, and as I very much doubt Celine will go to the trouble of buying you any herself, please put them on."

Renn went to the basin to wash away the filth from his skin ("I'm telling you, clean clothes won't do a thing if you're still carrying that old dirt around," Emile insisted), and slipped into the new clothes. The fabric was twice as fine as anything he'd worn before, and he could only guess how much Fairinelle had paid for them, or how much he would expect in return.

When they were both dressed, Fairinelle led them out into the hall, where they could see Celine at the foot of the stairs, leaning against a newell post and staring up at them with arms crossed. As he moved down the steps, Renn felt as if he were a bird flying into a lion's mouth.

"I'm honored that your highnesses deigned to join me this morning," she said with a mock curtsey.

"Walk on, gentlemen," said the officer, with a hand on each of their shoulders. Renn resisted the urge to shake it off as he and Emile were steered past Celine, and on towards the open space scattered with wooden tables of various sizes, which served as *The Bashful Swain*'s dining room and common meeting space.

She followed them all the way to their seats, and stood glowering as Fairinelle, seeming not to notice her presence, handed them biscuits out of the wicker basket placed there by the cook that morning.

"Get up from there this instant," she hissed.

Renn wondered whether he really ought not get up. After all, for as brusque as she was, she *had* brought him out of the misery of the St. Juste. Didn't he owe her more than he owed a man who had served to keep him on it? He was just on the verge of rising from his chair when the officer acknowledged her for the first time that morning.

"Celine, surely someone with as *excellent* judgement as yourself would realize it's in bad taste to accost people before they have finished their breakfast."

She huffed at him. "Surely *you'd* know, Adrien, that it's in bad taste to keep someone's property from them. I bought these men," she stopped to give an unimpressed flick of her eyes toward the former prisoners, "With legal tender, and I intend to do whatever I see fit with them."

"Your tender might be legal but your business is not. In case you were unaware, owning slaves is against the law in this country. No matter what Mr. Buron might have told you, these gentlemen can at best serve you as contractors, as part of the penal work program. At worst, I, as a correctional officer, would be within my rights to arrest *you* for illegal human trading."

She gaped at him, and she was not the only one.

Renn, after a few quick questions to Emile as to the meaning of certain words, also stared in surprise, not believing for one second that Fairinelle minded whether slave trading was legal or not. Not after serving as an officer in a slaver ship. Renn didn't care if it was technically supposed to be prison barge. He himself was living proof that you didn't have to commit a crime to earn your way onto it. Well, at least not any other crime than daring to be a Wend.

"I will not arrest you, but you may consider yourself on parole, as it were. You may continue on your way, but you will have to have an officer of the law with you to make sure you don't overstep your bounds as a contractor. Luckily for you, I have the capacity to serve as such an officer."

She gave the loudest, most indignant huff yet, and again, Renn found he couldn't disagree with it. For all this talk of legality, was it even legal for someone just to decide on their own what someone else's punishment would be? There was Gallic hypocrisy for you.

Celine pressed her lips into a thin line, flopped down into the last empty chair at their table, and began buttering a biscuit, glaring at each of them in turn. But for all her "parole officer" reacted, she may as well have disappeared. He didn't even display single smirk, just went on serenely drinking from a chipped mug of coffee the serving girl had brought him.

Why wasn't Celine threatening Fairinelle the way she had Buron?

That's a silly question. The answer was obviously under the officer's sleeve. She knew his first name, and he knew her last, which meant they must have known each other from before, and she, no doubt, knew what he was.

"Well, there goes my hope of getting away from shark fishing," Emile whispered. "I kinda thought if I was legally bought off Buron, I'd have an excuse never to go back. For as much as I like Fairinelle, I think he's too decent not to take us back after it's over. Not after *that* whole speech."

Renn didn't think the man was too decent for anything, but he didn't care if even if he was. No matter *what* Fairinelle intended, Renn's intent was to get home and stay there.

"Say, Fairinelle," Emile was leaning on his other elbow now, speaking around a bite of biscuit. "Can't say I'll be sorry to have you along, but how are you going to work it out with Buron? Won't he be sore about you abandoning your post?"

"I won't be abandoning it. I'll simply convince him I am acting in his best interests by keeping an eye on his best harpooneer. You're a valuable worker, you know."

This was the same thing Buron had said when Celine bought them – that Emile was his best shot. Renn noticed *he* didn't figure into either man's estimation of value, but for once, he didn't mind. In Cimbria, he had been desperate to be thought an asset, but now, the less important he was, the better. Every person who failed to take note of him was one less person who would try to stop him from getting home. Let him be unimportant and unnoticed, and he would slip back to Cimbria without anything stopping him.

"What if he doesn't listen?" Emile asked.

"Don't worry. He'll see it my way in the end," said Fairinelle, and Renn wondered just how he was so sure of this. Did he use his reputation to intimidate Buron the same way he did Celine? And was he really so cold-blooded that he could speak of murdering his captain as calmly as if he were remarking on the weather? As if it didn't bother him at all?

At home, though the warriors were fierce, at least they let you know it. You never had to guess who would give you beating. When someone was angry at you, or like Jungbern, simply liked to torment you for fun, you knew it. But this cold disaffectedness was unsettling, and made

Renn's breakfast go down tasteless and cold, despite it being the best he'd eaten in almost three months.

"Ready to go, gentleman?" asked Fairinelle when the serving girl began to clear off the table.

"Don't forget *I'm* still their contractor. *I* decide when they leave," said Celine.

He turned his icy eyes toward her. "Are you sure that is wise?" was all he said, but he stared at her so long that she shrank back.

"Nobody asked you along, anyway," she mumbled under her breath, to which Fairinelle sighed in response.

"If it will make you stop talking, I will serve as your winger on the journey," he said. "Don't tell me you can't use one."

She looked at him for a moment, then dragged the shoulder strap of a beaten square carrying case over her head, which added another knot to her messy hair, and handed it to him.

"Don't lose my bullets. I ought to carry them myself, but I'm not going to say no to a free pack mule."

"Of course you won't," said Fairinelle.

As they left the inn, passing under the painted sign of a bowing man, with Fairinelle leading the group and Celine sulking in the back, Renn reached behind to feel for his lance, though the new weight of it strapped to his back was unmistakable. But if he was going to travel with a bounty hunter and a Butcher, it wouldn't hurt to be sure.

CHAPTER 9
Maps

It was at the next inn, in a town called Prince's Tree, that Renn learned just how far it was that he would have to travel with them.

There was a large square paper on the wall of this town's common room. While Celine went to her quarters, and Emile helped himself to a cider from the counter, Fairinelle sat at a table near the wall, pondering the paper posted there until he saw Renn looking curiously at both him and the paper.

"Forgive me, I was blocking your way," he said, moving from his spot to make room for Renn. "Would you like to take a look?"

It was a map, but not one like Renn had ever seen. There were too few green areas, and too many black dots marked with names like Isney and Sept Vœux. This was a map of Gaul.

He stared at it, trying to cement it in his mind. Did Fairinelle realize what a gift he was giving away? If Renn could remember the image, he might be able to find his way home on his own. But he had to figure out where on the map he was first. He knew they had been following a river in from the ocean, but no one had bothered to tell him its name, and he hadn't dared ask for
fear of his ignorance giving him away.

He looked for blue lines, and his heart jumped when he saw the thickest one, the one leading in from the blue ocean at the bottom, was labelled "Bronze". That was the river leading straight home! He'd had no idea it ran so far. He traced its winding way up, until at last he saw the word Cimbria, disappointingly close to the top edge of the map.

"Is something wrong?"

"I just wish Cimbria weren't so far, or that there were a faster way to get there, at least."

"There are. Coaches and boats run at least part of the way, but Celine isn't nearly careful enough with her money to afford a trip like that even for herself, much less pay for a whole party's passage."

Renn looked down at his linen shirt and trousers, and his sturdy leather shoes. If Fairinelle had the money to buy these clothes, and the money to dress himself in those tall black boots, and that fine red coat, he must have had the money to pay their way if he wanted to.

So the question was, why was he making this arduous journey on foot with a woman he obviously didn't like, if he didn't have to? Renn still didn't believe Fairinelle cared enough about the law to be doing this for his and Emile's sake.

He had mentioned Celine's money. Did she owe him something? Was he following her, dogging her until she paid him back? Maybe he was angry that she had spent five hundred livres buying slaves when she could have been paying off her debt. That must have been why she was after the bounty in the first place.

But what would happen when he finally got tired of waiting? Could Renn escape being collateral damage? For that, he realized now, was what he was. Fairinelle was guarding him and Emile not because he cared, but because they were Celine's property, and he could claim them in place of her debt.

So now, not only did he have to worry about giving his secret away, he had to hope that either Celine paid the money or Fairinelle's patience held out until they reached Cimbria, where he at least had a chance of protection. If he tried to escape before then, he would never make it. The map showed they were still hopelessly far away, and besides, how would Renn get himself food or shelter with no money? He wouldn't even be able to buy himself a copy of a map like this one, and he dreaded having to ask strange Gauls for directions every day of his life.

No, for however awful they were, it was safer to stay closer to Fairinelle and Celine. He would go on using them to get home, and then, somehow, find a way to slip away when he was in friendly country again.

In the meantime, he had better study the Gallic edge of the Cimbrian border if he was going to keep claiming that as his homeland. There were a few scattered dots in the area – not nearly so many as in the lower parts of the Gaul – but the biggest one was labelled *Misère*. In other words, Misery.

Of course the Gauls would call it that, being so close to the lands of the Wends they hated. But to Renn, it was a point of hope. If he could get that far, he was sure he could get home safely on his own from there.

It wouldn't do, though, to pretend to be from the city. Not after he had been so overwhelmed in the port town. Coming from the middle of nowhere had been his excuse for his lack of knowledge so far, so he picked out an empty spot between two small dots, as close as possible to the section of blue line marking where the Bronze ran past the Cimbrian Forest, and decided that would be his home.

The map called that area Region Martel, and the two dots were named Ligny and Vertcourt.

"Havin' a geography lesson?" Emile asked, setting two mugs of cider on the table. "Let's have a look." He pointed to a dot in the center of the map, his fingers lingering over it. "There's my hometown. Where's yours?"

"It wasn't a town. My uncle and I, we lived on our own, between Ligny and Vertcourt," He pointed to the space he'd picked.

"Aren't you going to ask where I'm from?" Celine's frigid voice joined them now.

"The world down under, probably," muttered Renn, and he was surprised to hear Fairinelle laugh, and not with the sinister sound he would have expected. It was short and clipped, but there was real mirth in it.

"No," she narrowed her eyes at both of them. "That's the place we're headed." She struck the map with her fist, just over the dot labelled Misère.

"Sounds cheerful, doesn't it?" Emile said to Renn.

"Did you not ask me to come on this mission?" Celine demanded when she heard him.

"Sure I did," he answered, shrugging. "Couldn't let Renn go alone."

"Then stop complaining."

"Who's complaining? I was just making conversation, is all."

Fairinelle spoke up. "Celine, just because you can't stop spitting poison to save your life or anyone else's doesn't mean the rest of us are the same."

All trace of laughter was now gone from his voice. For as real as it had sounded, that moment of warmth had died frighteningly quickly.

No, thought Renn. Not everyone spits poison. Some people kill you more slowly, smiling at you one minute, but driving a knife further into your back each day.

CHAPTER 10
Corrosion

He had a chance to see that knife only a few days later. They were in the woods, but still too far away from the next town to make it before nightfall, meaning there would be no evening meal unless they made themselves.

"No problem there," Emile said, cheerfully toting his gun. Within half an hour he had produced a deer for dinner, but he hesitated when it came time to dress it.

"Hmm, I'm used to cutting up sea creatures, but land animals…" he said, kneeling over it with his hands hovering uncertainly, unsure of where he was supposed to make the first cut.

"Start on the stomach," Renn said.

"That's right, you said you hunted animals back home, huh? I'd be glad if you could lend me a hand."

"Here, use this," said Fairinelle, handing him a knife Renn didn't know he carried. This weapon was almost as long as the hunting knives the Cimbria, though as with all the other Gallic weapons, it was wrought more delicately.

Renn tried not to think of what other uses it might previously have been put to as he performed his work the best he could remember. He'd never done it fully on his own before – he'd always had Linderic or someone else helping – but nobody in this group seemed to mind.

"With a skill like that, you would make a fine addition to the harpooneers," Fairinelle even commented once he'd finished and they'd gotten the meat on the fire.

Emile gave Renn a look that said "*I told you so.*"

"You can have the first watch as a reward," Celine added.

When it came to keeping guard for enemies overnight, they were to split the night into fourths, with each person taking one part. Nobody wanted the middle watches, as those would mean interrupting your sleep to take them.

Fairinelle's stood up, brushing his clothes. "No watches tonight. We may have stopped to eat, but we must keep going until we reach Latour."

"Calm down," Celine said. "We'll be fine here. You always were too straight-laced for your own good."

His head snapped toward her. "You are truly going to say that to me? Have you lost what little sense you ever had?"

"I – "

"Shall I detail for you exactly what can happen to a person as the result of such thoughtless speaking?" His voice was freezing cold, with the deadly sharpness of someone who had first-hand knowledge of the subject.

Renn had to get up to escape that terrible sound. He walked from their clearing and into the edge of the trees, looking into the gathering shadows. What would happen if he just kept walking? How long would it be until they noticed him gone?

As if in answer, the leaves rustled. It was only a slight noise, and he would have thought it was the wind, except for the fact that the woods had been still all day. Breezes struggled to blow through the trees here, compared to the winds that rolled across the water and the flat, open lands that bordered it.

He looked back at the others, but no one else seemed to have noticed the noise. Was it an animal, following the scent of the deer's blood? He strained to see through the falling dusk, but could see nothing. Remembering the Eagle's Eye, he went to Emile, to beg the use of his sharp sight.

Emile turned and scaled the nearest tree, glad to escape the tension below, but his voice soon came down with a wild edge that Renn had never heard before. "That'll be a group coming in at ten 'o clock. I'd bet a mint those are Wends."

Fairinelle's head went up like the deer's had just before Emile shot it.

"This is too far south for them," he said, his words short and quick. "Are you certain?"

Emile scrambled down the trunk and leapt to scoop up his rifle. "They're all painted like what we fought in the army," he answered breathlessly. "I'd know that sight in my sleep."

"Good," Celine's mouth curled in a hungry grin, and she pulled her pistols from their holsters. "You ready with my bullets?" she asked Fairinelle, who already had her case of shot open. It seemed he would still honor his promise to be her winger, and for the moment, their quarrel was forgotten. Better for him to hand her bullets, at least, than to use the thin sword whose swirling handle glittered at his side, thought Renn.

"Blast me for not takin' this up the tree with me," Emile said beside him as he knelt to prime his rifle. "Could've picked all three of 'em off right there." His hands were fast but sure as he worked. "You gonna be alright?" He looked up at Renn through the dark forelock of hair that had fallen in his face when he'd bent to inspect the gun. "Stick close to me. I'll tell you what to do."

Renn wondered what Emile would say if this were someone who had come to take Renn home, when the crisp crack of a pistol rang out, followed by a flurry of whooping war cries from the trees, a disgusted clicking of the tongue from Emile, and a few seconds later, the deeper, echoing bark of the rifle.

Renn still couldn't see the Wends, but Emile's aim must have been true, for he could definitely hear them, even with ears ringing from the gunshot. Their whoops turned into disembodied wails that burst into the clearing just before they did.

There were three of them. Renn searched their faces

with a thrashing heart, but saw no one he knew. They had the black sign of the Wend, but instead of the Cimbri lines, they each had one eye socket filled in with green paint.

That was the sign of the Ambrone tribe, who lived to the east of the Cimbrian Woods, beyond the Silver Marshes. They had to have travelled for weeks to get here. But why, if Wends were never seen here before? It could only be for him.

He remembered the men at home telling, as they recounted tales of battle, telling how the Ambrones preferred to fight at close quarters. Short daggers, or bare hands. Bare hands, that was the key. If he could get close enough to fight with his hands, he would be close enough to speak to them, to explain that he was the one they were looking for.

His thoughts flashed bright and hopeful, when he realized they could take him home. He dropped his lance, knowing he would not need it, but rather than seeing it for the sign of peace it was, one of the warriors took it as an easy opening and flew at him, easily knocking him over and planting her knee into his chest.

"Got you, little maggot," he heard her growl through the short, high pealing of pistols off somewhere behind them.

"You've got the wrong maggot, then," he got out in Wendish, despite the knee pressed into his sternum. "I'm a Wend – a Cimbri. I'm not your enemy."

The woman's eyes widened – they were brown behind her warpaint – and for a wild moment Renn wondered if he had succeeded. A second later, a jolt shot through him as she drove her other knee into his gut.

He groaned out a wheezing breath and tried to fight out from under her, but he was weak from lack of air and she held him fast. He wouldn't have expected any less from a Wendish warrior.

As he swatted at her sluggishly, she produced a knife from her belt, and Renn knew before he saw that it was heading for his throat. His vision blurred as her face loomed over his, too close to make out anything beyond her yellow Brawler mark. He didn't expect the rifle crack and the sudden yelp, loud in his ear.

Her weight shifted off of him, and he managed a tiny gulp of air. She wasn't dead, but she wasn't giving up either. Her knife-arm hung stiff at her side, but she was clawing for the dropped blade with her remaining hand.

Renn pushed through the burning in his lungs and forced his way over onto his stomach, digging his elbows into the dirt and scrambling for his discarded spear. He got one hand on it before he felt himself being dragged backwards by the ankles.

And then there was a second shadow over him. Emile, holding his long gun sideways like a quarterstaff, stood over him, trying to parry her still-furious blows.

Renn didn't have the time to be grateful. Why was Emile even bothering to fight this way? Why didn't he just shoot her?

He recognized Emile's movements as Badeau Number Six, one of the techniques they'd practiced on the day Renn had gotten his lance. With it, Emile landed a solid strike in the Wend's midsection, and she bent over with a gasp of pain.

"Now, Renn!" he yelled. "From beneath!"

Renn gripped his lance and thrust it upwards, through her tough hide tunic, into the soft flesh, and back out again, freezing the woman in her tracks.

He had one moment of pride in his success, one moment of happiness that he was still breathing, before the woman's innards spilled through the hole his lance had made – a grey, squishing coil that turned over and over itself as it tumbled out above him, spraying blood on his hands and face.

Renn's mouth fell open and his spear to the ground. He dragged himself to his feet and stumbled away, his head swimming, his stomach turning, and the ghost of Xavier following behind him.

He had to get away from this scene, away from this awful country. He had to get home. But home was a million miles away, and he had just killed one of the people who could take him there, so he had to settle for taking refuge on a fallen tree trunk. He tried to sit on it, but lost his balance and slid down, landing with a thump which did nothing to help the knots forming in his gut.

He stared down at the ground and his shaking, blood-speckled hands until Emile's scuffed boots appeared in his vision.

"Did you check for others? A second wave of attackers?" Renn heard himself asking. It was absurd to be thinking of fighting again after what he had just witnessed – what he had just *done* – but Linderic had always told him that was how good war parties worked.

Good war parties also killed people. Before, Renn had longed more than anything to be a part of one, but now he could have thanked Hagen a thousand times over for keeping him from such a thing.

"The other two are checking out the perimeter," Emile said. "What about you? Are you banged up too badly? Sorry I couldn't get her quicker; you were wriggling around too much for me to get a kill shot the first time. I didn't want to hit you by accident, so I aimed to at least get her off you first, but I didn't have time to reload before she was up and at you again," he explained, but it made Renn's head hurt.

"I'm telling you, it's like these people get possessed or something," Emile kept talking. "I hope she didn't warp my poor barrel." He raised up his rifle to inspect it for bends and cracks.

"Funny thing about sharpshooting – we were always able to line up our shots from far off, so we never had to worry about things like this. If we did our jobs right, people'd be dead long before they got close enough to actually fight anybody…Hey, don't forget you've got to clean your weapon, too," he said when he noticed Renn hadn't moved. "It'll need it after that hit you got in – it was a good one."

Renn looked up at him then, with a gaze the rifleman

had seen before. It was the haunted, desperate stare of men new to battle, and it was enough to stop him from speaking for a moment. When he opened his mouth again, his voice was softer.

"The first time's always the worst, remember? Pretty soon you'll stop getting that ugly sort of feeling about it."

Renn was shivering now. Did all warriors feel the way Emile had said? That the horror of killing a person was just something to be gotten over? They'd have to, in order to keep doing it. They'd have to learn to treat people the same as they treated deer – gutting them both and not caring about either. Renn had managed the gutting part. He wasn't sure if he would ever manage the second.

Something heavy and warm touched his shoulders. Somebody had placed a blanket over him, but as he pulled it closer around himself, he noticed its distinctive hue. It wasn't a blanket; Fairinelle had given him his coat, red like the blood the officer had spilled to earn the marks on his arm. Red like the shining guts of the Wendish woman lying not twenty feet away. He yanked the coat off by the cuff, and there, cold and wet, he felt blood on that too.

There was a sudden taste of salt, then he was retching at Emile's feet.

Emile sprang back frantically, and Renn discovered he could still shed tears of shame even while his turning his insides violently out. How could he be so pathetic that even a Gaul was disgusted by his display of weakness?

But when he was finally able to sit back and wipe his mouth with one hand and his eyes with the other, Emile returned, with an armful of dry, crunching leaves.

"Sorry," Renn tried, but Emile shook his head to dismiss the apology.

"Don't worry about it," he said, scattering his leaves over the mess without so much as a hint of a frown. "If I got bothered every time I saw someone get sick like that in the army, I'd have lost my ever-lovin' mind within a month. In fact, I was probably the worst offender out of anyone when I first enlisted."

Not only was he *not* frowning, he was actually almost smiling, and something about that look reminded Renn of Linderic.

"What's wrong with you, child?" Celine's voice cut into their conversation, and Emile glanced at him with a worried look.

"Just a little bad dinner," he said quickly, trying to push another clump of dirt over the evidence with the heel of his boot as he stood to face Celine, blocking Renn from her view. "Must've undercooked the deer. He'll sleep it off and be alright in the morning.

"I hope for his sake that you're right, for I've had about enough of his constantly fragile health. Don't think I won't leave him behind right here if he really does take ill."

"No, you won't," Fairinelle spoke up. "You'll make sure you squeeze every remaining ounce of usefulness out of him first, and only *then* you'll drop him, won't you?"

She turned on him. "You look down your nose, but weren't you the one who offered to wing for me? If using people for what they can give is so wrong, why are *you* doing it?"

Emile said nothing. He wasn't going to get involved in their argument, not when there was so much left to do. Blood and sweat were eating away at their weapons as they spoke, they were either going to have to either dispose of the bodies or pack up and move to a new camp, as it wasn't healthy to stick around rotting corpses, and
he, personally, wouldn't mind taking a good dunk in the river.

He moved past them to retrieve Renn's spear and was already wiping it down as he carried it back to the boy whose eyes were closed as he leaned back against the log.

"*Well, that means burying the bodies then*," he thought, as Renn didn't look like he'd be ready to move to a new camp anytime soon.

He sat down to scrub the lance clean, taking care to stay away from the leaves he'd just scattered, and saw Fairinelle's splendid red coat lying discarded where Renn had thrown it. While it had escaped getting caught in Renn's sickness – (*"Lucky he thought to remove it before losing his dinner!"*) – it   still carried marks from battle, some of them darker than others – dark enough to leave a lasting stain, if not cleaned soon enough.

"Won't you want to wash your coat out, Mr. Fairnelle. It'd be shame to let something so nice get ruined," he called hopes of getting someone to help clean up the mess.

It didn't work.

By morning, the lance was clean and the bodies were gone, but Emile had done most of that work himself. He still hadn't gotten his trip to the river, and there was a faint, blackish spot on the red coat sleeve the same color as the ones Renn had seen underneath it.

CHAPTER 11
The Night Watch

"Listen to me," Emile was saying. They had made it to the next town, and the busy noise of their inn's common room helped, at least a little, to chase the memory of the battle from Renn's mind. But it was hard to erase everything when the whole world kept talking about it. Fairinelle had informed the local authorities of the unusual presence of the Wendish band, which made it the subject of nearly every conversation in the room, including Emile's, who was trying to convince Celine that her strategy needed work.

"If you'd get rid of that left-hander, and just shoot the one with your strong hand, you'd be a lot better off. I imagine it's hard to get a good bead on two targets at a time. Didn't you notice that it took you twice as long to take out the one, when Renn and I got two?"

"I don't shoot them at the same time. What do you think a winger is for? To reload one while you use the other."

"Well, if it took you that long still using one at a time, at that close of a range, then the plain fact is you ought to practice more. It's no wonder you missed the one through the trees if you can't even hit 'em up close."

She stuck her jaw out stubbornly. "I had enough teachers when I was coming up Circle Promethio, thank you very much."

"Learning to hunt bears and bobcats isn't the same as learning to fight people, but suit yourself, if you don't mind getting someone on the wrong side killed," Emile said, shrugging.

Fairinelle made a noise that would have been a chuckle if it hadn't sounded so grim. This was nothing like the warm laugh Renn had heard from him once before.

Renn never thought he would feel sorry for Celine, but with Fairinelle staring her down like that, and laughing that strange laugh, he did. For he knew what it felt like to have that sort of danger hanging over his head, only there was no one to feel sorry for him about it.

The distance between towns was getting longer now, and staying in the woods overnight was at times their only option.

Renn looked enviously at the river they kept constantly alongside, where a passenger boat was churning its way up the water in the dark. Its passengers were probably all sleeping. He, meanwhile, was not looking forward to taking third watch that night. First and fourth watch weren't so bad, as you could either use your momentum from the previous day to stay awake, or build up your momentum for the day to come, but pulling turns in the dead of night, being shaken awake after not-enough sleep, and sitting alone while no birds sang or sunlight warmed, could be almost physically painful.

He laid down, hoping four hours was a long time in coming, but when Emile, who had second watch, shook him awake, the faintest tint of light was already visible at the edge of the sky. It was still dark, but not the complete darkness that covered the hours of third watch.

"What happened? Why didn't you wake me earlier?" he asked.

"You looked like you needed sleep, is all. You've seemed kind of low since the other night with those Wends, so I went ahead and took your watch for you."

"But that means you stayed up half the night."

"Eh, I'm used to it. We used to keep long night watches all the time in the army. Now go wake Celine up so she'll think you took your turn."

As they made ready for the march to the next town, Renn couldn't deny that he had more energy than usual, and throughout the day, Emile didn't seem to be any worse for the wear.

Several more nights passed this way. Anytime they camped between towns, and Emile had the watch before Renn, he wouldn't wake him up even when Renn made a point of telling him to, until he eventually stopped asking.

With the extra hours of rest on those nights, he felt better, at least physically, than he had since Barenhohle, and Emile seemed to like staying up nights, or at least he never complained. On the contrary, he was always telling Renn how easy it was once a fellow got trained for it.

So why not let Emile do what was enjoyable for him and helpful to Renn? That was what Renn told himself as he turned over in his pack the night before they were due to reach the city of Angel's Arrow, closing his eyes against the dark in which he knew Emile stood guard.

They flew open again, an hour later, as the report of a rifle almost burst his eardrums. He jolted up, hand already on his lance, scanning the darkness for danger. Celine shot to her feet next to him, her hair tumbling in knots around her shoulders.

"There," she said, pointing with one of her guns towards the base of the tree Emile had climbed for his nightly lookout.

She approached the form laying crumpled there, with Renn inching along behind her. As the ringing in his ears subsided, he began to hear soft moans of pain coming from the form. It was Emile's voice.

"Are you alright? Are we being attacked?" Renn hissed, throwing his back against the tree to keep it safe from enemies.

"Fine...and dandy," Emile wheezed. "Nobody's out

there. Guess I…fell asleep. Shot went off when I…hit the ground."

"It was a foolish thing to do, Mr. Badeau. Surely the army would have taught you that much," said Fairinelle, and Renn jumped as his voice seemed to materialize out of the darkness.

"Sorry," said Emile.

"He didn't mean to fall asleep," Renn tried timidly. What was worse than Fairinelle's displeasure was the knowledge that he himself was responsible for it. Emile had been too tired to stay awake because Renn had been letting him take on double duty.

"He elected to extend his watch without seeking counsel about it first, and you see the result. That shot will have been heard by any enemy within five miles. We'll have to proceed to town right now unless we want to invite any lurking Wends down on our heads."

"Right, then...No need to harp on it," said Emile, groaning and rubbing his face with his hands. Renn helped pull him upright.

"Get your things together. I expect you both to be ready to go in five minutes," said Fairinelle in his officer's voice. But Emile wobbled when he tried to walk and managed only a few steps before falling heavily onto Renn.

"Haven't taken a hit that hard since the early days on the St. Juste," he mumbled, his face pale and his chest hitching in shallow breaths against Renn's shoulder.

Instantly, Renn remembered the face of his father, and how he had labored to breathe, laying on his bed in the dim cabin which smelled of sickness, while young Renn wiped ineffectually at his sweating brow. By the time Linderic came around for his next visit to their home in the far corner of the Cimbrian Woods, Guillame LeNotre labored no more.

"Help," said Renn, though he was unsure who exactly he was talking to. He looked at Celine, who simply stood watching, as if she hadn't heard him.

The first officer came back toward them as Emile's knees buckled, and Renn staggered under the weight. They would both have fallen to the dirt had Fairinelle not stridden forward and put his own shoulder underneath Emile's free arm, lifting the weight with ease.

Renn remembered him lifting the body of the dead Wend on the St. Juste and shivered, hoping it would not be another corpse that Fairinelle had to carry.

"What's wrong with him?" Renn asked. His voice rose as he spoke more directly to the man than he ever had before, but the memory of how his father had died, combined with the knowledge that this time, it was Renn's own selfishness that had brought this on Emile, drove the usual fear from him.

"I'm no medic; it could be anything. Concussion, contusion, internal bleeding. We'd have to reach Angel's Arrow tonight with him like this, anyway, even if the gun hadn't discharged."

"Oh – the gun!" Renn remembered. "He'll need it!"

"Celine, find it," Fairinelle called over his shoulder.

"What am I, your servant?" she asked.

"You are apparently someone who wants to see what happened to Jayem repeated, for every second you stand there brings us closer to it."

Her head jerked up, and her face was as discomposed as Renn had ever seen it. She stared at Fairinelle, stricken, but he held her gaze mercilessly, until she turned mechanically, feeling through the carpet of leaves until she lay hold of the rifle. She scooped it up without a word, and followed quietly behind them.

"Make yourself useful this time," Fairinelle said to her. "Cover us in the back. Use it if you have to."

Jayem. That was the word that had given him instant control over her. But what did it mean?

"Don't let her use my gun. She's awful at it," Emile mumbled as he was jostled between the too-tall Fairinelle on one side of him, and the too-short Renn on the other.

"This won't do," said Fairinelle. "We'll never make it hobbling like this. Celine, trade with Rennesson. You're more of the right height."

She did silently as she was told, handing Renn the gun. He wanted to protest that he had only the vaguest idea of how to handle it, but there wasn't any point. He was the only one left *to* handle it, so he had no choice.

He followed after the three Gauls, gripping the gun tightly and trying to remember even one thing he'd ever seen Emile do with it. He could feel the spots on the stock where the wood was already worn smoother than the rest – the places where Emile's hands tended to rest when he shot it, cleaned it, sat watch while hugging it. He'd done too much of that last one – that was Renn's fault – and now he might never do any of it again. That was Renn's fault, too.

It was useless to try to guess how long it took to reach the town when the whole world was nothing but darkness and looming trees, but eventually the first few, dim lights of Angel's Arrow came into view. Though more lights shone behind windows than other towns they had seen, the majority of the windows, many with flowerboxes and painted gables, remained dark.

The rest of the town might have slept, but there was always one place in every town which never closed, where there was always someone to welcome travellers in the night. Inns always had their doors open. Funny to think that the first time he'd been in one, back at *The Bashful Swain*, it was he who had been sick and weak, with Emile worrying over him. Now it was the reverse, and both times they'd been carried in by Fairinelle.

"A room. On the first floor if you have one," said Fairinelle to the woman behind the counter, and even he sounded a little breathless. It had been a long walk for all of them.

The woman called towards a back room, and a sleepy-looking girl scurried out, holding a candle to lead them down the hall lined with doors. She had barely opened the one that would apparently be theirs before Fairinelle was striding in, sweeping the pillows off the bed onto the polished wood floor. "Too thick," he said.

"What's wrong with that?" Renn asked Celine as she passed.

"He needs to lay flat," she offered, speaking for the first time since the accident, as she and Fairinelle shuffled to lay Emile on the bed. But as soon as Emile was down, Celine fled the room, leaving the boy and the officer looking anxiously into the contracted brow and the unfocused eyes of the harpooneer.

Renn wondered if this was how Emile and Fairinelle had looked at him when he had collapsed at the weapons shop. Or maybe this was worse, for only seasickness, rather than selfishness, had caused *those* troubles.

"Will he be alright?" he ventured to ask of Fairinelle. Emile's look of pain, so much like the one worn by Renn's father before his death, overpowered his fear of the man.

"If I can find a medic," came the tense reply. Fairinelle straightened and turned toward the door. "Keep him talking, Rennesson. Keep him awake. Yell at him if you have to. Only do not let him go to sleep, and do not let him get up. I will come back as soon as I can."

Then he was gone and Renn was alone with Emile. Afterwards, he couldn't recall what words he had said while he waited, but he knew he spoke incessantly into the silence, trying to keep Emile awake and his own demons at bay in the room that grew more claustrophobic by the minute.

This was entirely his fault. Emile had fallen asleep and out of the tree because Renn had let him shoulder responsibilities that weren't his. He had been pulling double duty when Renn couldn't even be bothered to pull one. And now he might die because Renn had cared more about pleasing himself than about doing right by others.

Finally, mercifully, Fairinelle blew back in alongside a rumpled-looking man who carried a leather sack and squinted in the light.

The man first poked and prodded, explaining how he checked for internal injuries, then held the candle up to Emile's eyes, looking into them, asking how well he could count the fingers he held up, and altering his voice to varying volumes, asking how well Emile could hear him. When he asked Emile to recall his own name and age, and what he had been doing the day before, Renn helped to confirm the answers, or else correct them, as Emile, disturbingly wasn't always clear or accurate in his responses.

"This young man's concussed alright, but it looks to be a light one," said the doctor. "I'll come back to check up on him until he's healed but you ought to keep him in bed until then. Give him this if he's in pain," he handed a small bottle out of his case to Fairinelle. "But don't let him go traipsing around, and don't bother him with too much talk. Let him rest."

Fairinelle saw him to the door, and after a hushed conference there, the medic left and Fairinelle returned to pace the floor while Renn fidgeted in his chair by the bedside.

Renn took stock of his chances, and finally decided, or rather hoped, he could get away with not knowing much medical vocabulary, Gallic or otherwise, without raising too much suspicion. He decided to speak.

"What does 'concussed' mean?" he asked quietly.

"It means he's taken damage to his brain."

Renn's dread must have been evident on his face, for Fairinelle quickly added "Not to worry, the medic thought it was a light one, remember? It could have been much worse."

"Is there any way we can help him?"

"The best thing to do is just what the medic said. Make sure he gets his rest."

"Did I hurt him with all the talking? I kept him awake like you said to, but the medic said it would bother him."

"There is a process to an injury like this. You did what you were supposed to at the time, but now," he looked at the watch he kept on a chain in his pocket, "We can let him rest."

Renn wasn't used speaking this much to Fairinelle. It was probably the most words they had ever exchanged at one time, but Renn found that Fairinelle spoke just as gently to him as he could wish, with no hint of the hardness that marked his voice when he spoke to Celine, or even the stern tones he'd used towards Emile in the midst of the night's trouble. This was more like the courtly officer Renn had known before, the one who treated slaves like humans and earned the devotion of hardened prisoners with his kindness.

"Well, shall I procure you a room? I know you two are usually bunkmates, but there's only one bed here."

"Can't I stay here instead?" Renn nearly whispered. He didn't want to leave Emile, but neither did he know how to refuse Fairinelle.

The man stopped and looked at him. His eyes glowing eerily in the candlelight, but his words did not match them. "It does you credit that you want to stay with your friend." He said with something that sounded like admiration. "I shall arrange for a cot to be brought in."

But the cot remained unused that night, as Renn refused to leave the chair by the bed. He had slept too much already these past days. *No,* he determined. This would be *his* night watch.

Or at least that was his plan. He didn't know he hadn't kept it until he awoke with imprints from the folds of Emile's blanket pressed into his face, and the dim noises of the breakfast crowd floating down the hall from the common room.

CHAPTER 12
Child Knight

In the days that followed, Emile made up for all the sleep he'd lost before the accident. It was rare that Renn would catch him awake, and when he did, he was hesitant to speak too much, remembering the doctor's admonition not to bother the invalid.

He and Fairinelle traded shifts on watching him throughout the week, joined by the doctor at least once a day, and Renn found that he could more easily stifle his dread of Fairinelle, now that he had something else to focus on, and they had a common goal.

He saw Celine only when he would wander down to the common room during Fairinelle's shifts. She would be there, sipping a drink, and he would choose a spot as far away from her as possible. He felt bad enough already, and didn't need her attitude to make it worse.

The days went on. Emile still slept, the officer and the boy still kept watch, and every day Celine sat drinking in the common room.

Once, he saw Fairinelle approach her. They exchanged words, and she scowled when she addressed him, to which he tossed his head and said something with an angry twist of his mouth.

Renn moved closer, trying to hear, but pretending not to notice they were fighting.

"Eh, Celine! You back in these parts?" a man called from the doorway, his voice carrying laughter in it. "And you've got some friends with you?" He looked at

Fairinelle and Renn through gold-colored spectacles framed by blonde waves of hair hanging loose over his forehead.

"They're not my friends. They work for me," she said as the man approached them.

Renn didn't correct her that only one of them actually worked for her.

"Care to introduce me to 'em?"

Celine clicked her tongue. "Introduce yourself."

She stood up with her drink and brushed past him, trying to knock into his shoulder. But the man only grinned at her before dancing out of the way, and she stumbled but didn't look back.

The man turned to Fairinelle. "How d'you do? Name's Leandre Rigobert. Celine's a friend of mine."

Fairinelle looked taken aback, and Renn couldn't blame him. For one thing, nobody would've ever approached him so casually on the St. Juste. For another, the thought of Celine having friends was an entirely foreign concept.

When Fairinelle gave his own name, the other squinted at him. "I know the sound of that from somewhere." He thought for a few seconds, then snapped his fingers. "I think they called you the Child Knight or something. Wasn't it you who right sliced up a whole band of Wendish curs all on your own, when you were only fifteen years old?"

"It was," said the officer quietly.

"Imagine someone so young taking out a whole mob of mongrels like that! Some of us had to train for years before we could hunt so much as rabbits."

"I was…fortunate to have received instruction from an early age."

"Sure, sure, but there's still got to be something supernatural about a boy who can do that when plenty of grown men have died trying."

"There may be other reasons for that," Fairinelle said, but Rigobert wasn't listening.

"Bring us a drink, miss," he called to the girl behind the counter. "We've a famous Wend-killer in the house."

Unease welled up inside Renn as some a group of patrons from the next table over, having heard the request, swirled past him on their way to crowd around Fairinelle, nudged and elbowing Renn out of the way, unconcerned with his presence.

It made him sick to think just how concerned with him they would be if they knew what he was. They would likely kill him on the spot, given the adoration they were currently giving Fairinelle, who, besides being a Butcher, had apparently been one since he was only fifteen.

He tried not to let his worries show on his face as he stood up and pushed his way through the newcomers, unable to stay there and listen to the tales of the Butcher, or the Child Knight, or whoever Fairinelle was, which seemed to be someone new and more frightening every day.

He found himself at the table where Celine sat huddled with her mug.

"Some crowd over there, isn't it?" she asked darkly.

"Sure," he said, matching her tone. He hated that being here with her felt almost like a safe haven, for she would have killed him as soon as the rest. But at least she wasn't being celebrated for doing it. At least she hadn't been killing Wends since she was a child.

It didn't occur to him that when he had been at Barenhohle, the thing Fairinelle was now being cheered for was the very thing Renn had wished for himself. He wouldn't be fifteen until next year, but he, too, had already dreamed of being a great warrior. Before, he would have thought himself tremendously successful if he could accomplish what Fairinelle had at this age.

But success meant something different when you were the one being hunted.

CHAPTER 13
The Officer's Words

Celine sat alone with her mug and her memories, the former failing to drown the latter, or even to entertain her very much. If she told herself the truth, she was bored of sitting down in this common room by herself day after day, but the alternative was to go up there, to that chamber which looked so much like the one from her past, and so she stayed.

She could see Rennesson at the far side of the room this time, looking as careworn as she felt, but he didn't approach her, nor did she want him to. She was having a hard enough time answering the ghosts that had risen up from the past without having to deal with the problems of the present.

But that self-righteous Adrien Fairinelle had never cared what she wanted, and she gripped her mug harder as she saw him now striding across the room and into her business.

He stared down at her silently for a few moments. The bubbles in her amber drink frothed and burst.

"You're not going to catch many Wends that way," he said finally.

"Leave me alone."

"Believe me, if I felt I had a choice, I would."

"You're the one who invited yourself along."

"And that wasn't because I care what happens to you."

"Good, then it shouldn't bother you whether I drink or not."

"You know my reasons, Celine. I'd tell you not to act foolish, but that was never your strong suit."

"Is the rifleman healed yet?" she asked flatly, trying to change the subject.

"It will be a a few days yet. Why, are you planning to run off and leave your charges?"

"Not after what I paid for them, but people are starting to hear about the bounties, and I'm losing my lead sitting and waiting for his highness up there."

"Perhaps you ought to have paid such a sum last time, then." Fairinelle tossed his head. "In the meantime, I must remind you that men still haven't learned to heal themselves at your command, whatever else you might get them to do for you."

She took another swallow of whiskey, hoping to wash away the memory of this conversation along with the memory of everything else. He could go on accusing and threatening her as long as he liked, as long as she didn't have to remember it.

She hadn't expected that fool Rigobert to appear and start shouting the praises of her own personal specter. How was she supposed to ignore Fairinelle and his stinging accusations when Rigobert was getting the whole room to remind her of just how much power he carried?

When she was younger, she hadn't realized the extent of that power. She had made her decisions and not listened to this man, and the result had been tragedy, but she'd managed to outrun that particular memory until now, when he'd re-appeared to pick up where he'd left off. She certainly didn't want to hear now how excessively foolish she'd been – just how many reasons there were for to have paid attention when he'd warned her. Maybe no amount of alcohol could drown that knowledge, but tonight, she was going to try.

CHAPTER 14
Tiger in a Cage

Celine was forever pacing back and forth before the window.

"You should be out there," the wounded man said from behind her.

"Stop saying that. I'm not going to leave you," she answered, but she could hear how automatic it sounded. She didn't want to be automatic. She wanted very much to be sincere.

She tried to make herself remember what it felt like when she thought she had killed him, what it felt like when Adrien Fairinelle had grabbed her arm and dragged her here, and she'd been terrified that he was taking her to see a corpse.

She had determined then, that if only Jean-Marien would open his eyes, to be the most willing of nurses and never think of her own wishes again, to make up for what she had done.

But those feelings had dulled now that the worst was over, and the relief she felt when the mangled man in the bed had opened his eyes was drowning now in the vision she saw through the window now that the drapes had been drawn back for the first time in weeks.

During those days when the curtains had been kept closed so as not to disturb the patient, there had been nothing else for her to focus on but him. But now that he was awake, and she could see the world outside, she recalled that the sky was wide, the woods were deep, and the wilds were there for the taking.

"You're not cut out for nursing, you know," Jean-Marien said, though his speech was slow and halting.

Celine knew that it was as hard for him to form the words with his newly-jagged mouth as it was for her to hear them, but she couldn't help the twinge of impatience that struck her at how long it took him to say it.

"You want to be out on the hunt again," he got out. "Not stuck in here."

She didn't try to tell him that wasn't what she wanted. She was too forthright for that, and she remembered the steel in Adrien Fairinelle's voice as he had rebuked her.

"It shouldn't matter what I want," she said instead, though she couldn't make herself feel it.

"Think of it this way," said Jean-Marien, and the next words were difficult not only to form on his lips, for he would have liked very much for Celine to stay. But he could not keep a tiger in a cage simply because he enjoyed looking at it.

"I would be happy knowing you're free to do what you must...and the doctors tell me I need a positive attitude to recover."

"I'm sorry...for everything," she said, when he'd finally managed to say all he felt.

"Don't be. It was my own choice to go with you."

But Celine remembered exactly what role she had played in all this. She wanted to say so, to pour her guilt out onto him, but when she looked at his face, through all the still-swollen, half-healed breaks and jags, she could see him biting his torn lip. She realized now that she had seen him do that before, every time he had stuttered and blushed in front of her, every time he had requested something of her, full of hope that this time she would not refuse him.

"I'll come back," she said at last. She knew better than not unto promise a time for her return, because she couldn't guarantee she wouldn't break it.

"Don't. Not until you want to."

She couldn't even pray that she would be ready soon, for the relief at being freed from that room and that burden was too great to wish away, and if there was one thing she hated now more than a Wend, it was being fenced in.

CHAPTER 15
Stranger Fellows

Fairinelle didn't speak of what had happened with the man called Rigobert, and Renn didn't ask. They kept on the way they had, watching Emile by turns, until he was fully back to his smiling, talkative self.

"How are you? Have you…been sleeping alright?" Renn asked, the first time the medic had suggested that Emile would be ready for conversation. He remembered his father asking him something like that a long time ago, when he had once been ill as a child.

"Sure, after the first night, anyway. Have to say, being woken up every couple of hours doesn't feel terrific."

Renn's face fell. "I'm sorry. I've been trying to be quiet."

"It wasn't you. It was Fairinelle shakin' me awake all the time. Where is he, anyway?" He looked around the room, rubbing his neck.

"What?" Renn asked. "Why would he do that if the medic sleep was the best thing for you?"

"Don't worry, he was doing right, checking on me like that. Supposedly, for the first night, you ought to make sure folks as have hurt their heads don't go to sleep too deeply, or else it might be for keeps. That's what I used to hear from the army medics, anyway."

"For keeps?"

"Forever."

"Oh."

It dawned on Renn that not only had Fairinelle been

sharing the duties that were Renn's responsibility throughout this week, but on the first night of Emile's concussion, while Renn had slept in spite of all his good intentions, Fairinelle had stayed up until morning taking care of Emile without ever asking Renn to help him.

Renn imagined the tall figure passing through the dark silently, the serious eyes checking for signs of life in the night, and the thought filled him not with fear, but compassion. The man had to have been just as tired as Renn – and more, for he had not been skipping his night watches in the days prior – but he had sacrificed his own rest to look after someone else.

Renn knew he shouldn't be thinking of the man in anything like friendly terms. But the presence of someone who knew what to do in the face of a crisis, and who was actually willing to do it, meant he couldn't help feeling at least a little grateful. How could Renn have managed this week if Fairinelle had not been there? If he had not taken charge in the forest, had not gone for the medic, had not shared the watches with him, and even taken them all when he had to, would Emile be here talking now?

Maybe Fairinelle was a Butcher and a Child Knight, but that knight had kept safe the one friend Renn had in this whole country.

"*Yes,* he decided, "*Emile is my friend.*" Even when Renn had been secretive and closed-off (things he'd had to be) and irresponsible (something he hadn't), Emile had taken care of him. He stood ashamed before the kindness the harpooneer had shown him, and now, before the kindness of Fairinelle, of all people. Fairinelle had taken Renn's responsibility on his own shoulders, the same as Emile had. Did that make Fairinelle a friend, too?

Whatever he might do to a Wendish boy, he seemed willing to treat a Gallic one kindly enough – Renn remembered the reassuring voice that had taught him the meaning of *concussed* – so why not let him? Why not let Fairinelle be a friend, just one from whom he had to keep a secret, the same way he kept it from Emile? Wouldn't it be easier to guard one thing from a friend than to guard everything from an enemy?

After all, Celine made no effort to hide her dislike of him, or anybody else, and look where that got her. Fairinelle hounded her all the time, and if Renn didn't want to end up like her, he was going to have to get on Fairinelle's good side. Or at least that's what he told himself he was doing – merely getting on a good side. He couldn't admit to himself that some part of him actually *wanted* to be friends.

CHAPTER 16
Appointment

By the end of the next week, Emile was steadier on his feet than Celine was. She had been drinking off-and-on throughout the rest of the week, which made her crabbier than ever, and when the day finally came that the medic declared Emile fit to work again, Renn walked carefully before him down the steps, checking every few feet to make sure Emile was steady, but when they reached the common room, he saw that Celine was more likely to need it.

She had one hand on her temple and one against the wall as they gathered to leave, and as they passed back through the streets with their flowerboxed windows and painted windows, Renn looked about in wonder at how much brighter and happier they seemed in the daylight, but Celine only squinted and frowned against the sun.

On the first outdoor night since leaving Angel's Arrow, Emile drew first watch. Without complaining, he slung his rifle over his shoulder and turned to the nearest tree, humming as he checked for handholds in the trunk.

A wave of concern hit Renn as he watched. Now that he had gotten used to worrying over Emile as well as himself, it was hard to get out of the habit.

"Don't," he blurted out. "You might fall again."

Emile looked back with a faintly abashed smile. "Ah, thanks, I appreciate the concern, but I'll be alright. I won't do anything dumb this time, and it would be a lot better to have that high vantage point if trouble shows up again.

"I'm serious – don't. Please."

Emile blinked at him, surprised at his insistence. "Well, if it means that much to you."

"Just do what he asks," Celine surprised them both, speaking sharply though she looked like she was already asleep, on the ground with her eyes closed. "I'm tired of hearing you two bicker."

"We aren't bickering," said Renn.

"Whatever you're doing, you're giving me a headache with it," said Celine rubbing her forehead, and Renn didn't argue this time, for perhaps it was best not to look this particular gift horse in the mouth. She could think whatever she wanted it was going to get him what he wanted. Wasn't that what he had been doing since the first day they met? Letting her think whatever was most convenient?

She continued, addressing Emile, though her eyes stayed closed. "If you can't stay awake and end up killing yourself with another fall, then I'm out one marksman, and I'd rather not deal with the trouble of having to replace you."

"Oh, but they *are* so easily replaced," Fairinelle said to her, one corner of his mouth curling into a smile that looked nothing at all like the one he had given Renn over Emile's bedside. How could there be two so different versions of the same person?

"It was only the one time," Emile protested, looking around at the three of them. "But if it everyone's against it, I guess I'd better not." He took his hand off the trunk, and Renn breathed easier.

"Good man," said Fairinelle. "A mistake made only one time can lead to more ruin than you know."

Celine shut her eyes tighter. No one said anything more.

"Hey, I know this song!" Emile cried, sitting upright in his chair at the inn in the town called Sept Vœux, whose name meant "Seven Wishes."

A small group of musicians in the corner were playing the opening strains of a rollicking tune. It was the first time Renn had heard any kind of Gallic music beyond the tunes that the harpooneers used to sing, and which Emile still sang from time to time, even though no one else sang with him.

It was a happy melody, and Renn liked it, even though the instruments looked somewhat different from the ones he was used to at home.

"I can't tell you how we used to hop to this where I'm from."

Emile climbed to his feet. "Do you know it, Renn? What say we do it together?" He was already rocking on his heels.

But if Renn had never even seen some of the instruments the group played, he had no hope of knowing their songs or dances.

"I'll not have my slaves…er, *contractors*," Celine glanced at Fairinelle to her right, "looking like fools in public. Both of you are staying right here."

For once, Renn was glad of her bossiness.

"I believe I know this dance well enough to partner you, Mr. Badeau," said Fairinelle, standing up. Towering over the table as he did, they all knew there would be no arguing. If Fairinelle allowed them to dance, that was the end of it.

"Alright then," Emile grinned. "Never would've figured you for a reel dancer, though."

"There are many things I never thought I'd be," returned Fairinelle, and both Renn and Celine gaped as serious, steady Fairinelle hung his coat on the chair, straightened his vest, and took a position in the line of people that was forming in the open space in front of the band, while Emile jumped across from him into the second line that had formed.

All of the dancers looked so genuinely pleased to be out there moving that Renn felt bad he couldn't go join in. But it was amusing enough to watch the ex-prisoner and his jailer dance together, Fairinelle gliding and Emile bouncing, and all the more so at those times when the dance apparently called for Emile to turn Fairinelle underneath their joined right hands. Emile struggled to reach high enough for the other man to get clearance, and Fairinelle had to stoop awkwardly to make it through. Yet all the time, he still carried himself like as elegantly as a prince, and the juxtaposition of his graceful carriage and the undignified movement made Renn smile.

"What are *you* grinning at?" Celine asked from beside Renn, her voice a discordant note against the cheerful tune.

"Buron would die of the fits if he saw this," he said.

"Who? Oh, your old master on the ship. Yes, I believe he would, that walrus," she said, and even she cracked smiled then.

Maybe it was because the music was rising, wild and heady, the pounding rhythm of feet on the floor was vibrating in his chest, Emile was belting out the words like someone who had never had a concussion, and Fairinelle's rare, warm laugh that Renn had heard only once before now floated above it all, but it struck Renn that Celine had been quite wrong.

Anything that could make each of these strange companions of his look so happy – that could give a kind, faithful friend a few minutes' joy, that could make a grave man laugh, and make a harsh, hard woman smile – such a thing was not foolish at all.

Celine really ought to smile more, he thought. She had a lovely smile.

At morning training, Emile stopped halfway through Badeau Number Five, confiding to Renn that he thought he'd overstretched something in his rifle-arm. "Suppose I got a little too excited in the dance last night," he said. "It's better than a knock to the head like before, but I guess I'd better sit out this time, just in case," he winked, and Renn knew he recalled his plea from days before, when he'd asked Emile not to climb the tree during his watch, just in case he got hurt again.

"A sharpshooter won't be any good if he wears his arm out and can't even hold his own weapon. You keep going, though. I'll watch you," he nodded at Renn. "Turn your foot in. No, the other way."

Renn saw Fairinelle approaching from behind. It seemed he was always appearing out of thin air, just at the moment he was needed. He could almost be a Cimbri with how silently he materialized sometimes. At least on the St. Juste, you could always hear his boots coming, but here on the soft dirt paths of the towns, and the leaf-covered grounds of the woods, there was nothing to give him away.

"If you are indisposed, allow me to help," he said to Emile. "The Wends are coming this far south these days, and who knows what we may find the further we go." He lifted his eyes to the treetops visible beyond the city roofs, then turned to Renn. "You can't afford not to practice, so if I may, I'll offer myself as your sparring partner today."

Fairinelle had never offered to participate in their trainings before, but then, he had never offered to dance with anyone before either, and a hint of last night's smile still lingered on his face.

"It's alright with me. What do you say, Renn?" Emile asked, curling his arm in and out, and Renn nodded.

He would have expected himself to be too afraid to say yes, but now that Fairinelle was his friend, now that Renn had seen him acting...well, like a normal human who could laugh and enjoy himself, he found, somehow, that he didn't mind.

"Ready?" Fairinelle asked, and pulled his rapier from its sheath. It was the first time Renn had ever seen the bare blade. It was slender, like its owner, and sparkled in the morning sun, looking as clean as if it had never seen battle. But of course it had. One didn't get to be a Butcher without using one's weapon. Renn wondered why he never used it, why he chose instead to be Celine's winger. Perhaps someone like him wouldn't deign to fight unless it was a battle worthy of his skill.

"Let's begin."

Sparring with him was different than doing it with Emile. Fairinelle was straighter, smoother, cleaner in his movements, gliding the same way he had in his dancing, and Renn, having first been trained to fight boars at Barenhohle, then to fight men with only a makeshift training regimen, wasn't used to such liquid movements. Every time he tried to strike a point, Fairinelle evaporated from the spot, spinning away as effortlessly as water.

Fairinelle would pass and feint with his small, shining blade, giving Renn something to follow with his staff, but the session was unsatisfactory for them both, as Renn grew increasingly frustrated with his inability to keep up, and Fairinelle, seemingly unhappy with his progress, called for an early stop after a quarter of an hour. He stood, gazing past Renn, his mind apparently far away, then closed his eyes and shook his head.

"Take it easy on him," Emile called to him. "He's still learning."

"I don't need to be gone easy on," Renn protested. He'd thought he'd been progressing, and perhaps he had learned enough to kill a Wend too dumb to know her own kind, but how was he supposed to protect himself from the enemies that lay ahead if he was still this bad at it?

He wanted to grumble, and braced himself for how much worse things were going to get if Celine showed up in her usual bad mood, but when she did arrive, she did not complain of her usual headache, and Renn didn't want to spoil this rarity of a day.

So he bit his tongue and was rewarded with one of the most pleasant legs of the trip they'd had yet. The next town was only a day's hike, Fairinelle showed no other signs of disappointment in Renn, Emile was still humming the bouncing tune from the night before, and when they reached the inn of *The Cracked Chestnut*, Celine did not go immediately to the bar.

She actually sat willingly and quietly with Renn at the table he had chosen near the wall, where another map like the one at Murat hung on the wall. Renn had rushed to begin studying it, for it had been weeks since they'd left Murat, and he hadn't any idea of just how far down the river they'd gone. He looked for the town of Angel's Arrow, which he definitely knew after Emile's concussion, and tried to follow the line of the river upwards.

"Are we making satisfactory progress?" Fairinelle asked, indicating the map.

"I'm – not sure. I'm...bad at reading these things," Renn stalled.

Celine spoke up. "If your skills at tracking through the woods are anything like your skills at tracking on a map, I may have made a terrible mistake...one of many, really. We're only following the river, child. Surely you've realized that much."

"Surely you know not *only* following that way," Fairinelle answered her. "We're passing by here first." He pointed a long finger towards a spot on the map that was further removed from the river than any of the other dots they'd been in so far.

"You have an appointment on that road that's long since overdue. Do you even remember what it is?" His eyes glittered like his rapier, and he wasn't smiling any longer. His face had gone hard again, as it so often did whenever Celine started talking.

Celine turned pale. "Are you really going to...? Why can't you mind your own business?" she asked, her voice weak.

"Because you never learned to mind yours." He spoke as quietly as ever, but Celine flinched as if he had shouted. Her lip trembled, and Renn noticed for the first time that the line of it was not completely even. One side was slightly swollen, as if someone had once struck her on the mouth and the welt had never fully disappeared.

She said nothing else but turned and almost ran to the bar. Renn could see the yellow liquid splashing over the rim of the mug she ordered.

He looked at Fairinelle. Why had he had to act that way? Why couldn't he have afforded her the warmth and kindness he was clearly capable of showing to others? Celine had been doing so well all day, and now he had driven right back to where she'd started. Just what had she done to deserve this from him?

But he couldn't ask Fairinelle any of this. Not after he'd seen for himself that morning how easily Fairinelle could outmaneuver him. Instead, he turned and looked at the mark on the map that had left Celine white and shaking.

It was called Faubourg.

CHAPTER 17
Circle Promethio

"No prior experience?"

"No."

"But you studied at the Lillianic School?"

"Yes."

The man at the desk leaned forward on his elbows, looking up at the young man standing before him. "What is he, then? A duke? An earl?"

"A baron...and a magistrate."

"So tell me, what is a baron's son is doing here? Why aren't you off in Circle Ambrosia or somewhere with the other nobles? You'd probably get your hands a lot less dirty."

"Here is where I wanted," answered the young man simply.

"You've made a smart choice, then" the man at the desk said, straightening the name plate in front of him that read 'Georges'.

"We don't mind taking applicants without practical experience, but unlike some circles, we don't expect them to stay that way. So if you don't mind working hard, it surely wouldn't hurt us to have a future baron on the roster."

"I don't mind."

"Good," said Georges. "Then I'll get to work on your papers." He tapped the folio in his hand against the desk, before setting it side-by-side with a ledger he had spread

open before him. "Welcome to Circle Promethio, my lord."

"No need for that. You can call me Adrien."

"Alright then, Lord Adrien."

Lord Adrien sighed.

"You'll have to work with a mentor before being let out on the real hunts," Georges said, not looking up while he copied the information from the folio into his ledger.

"How long will such a process take?"

"That depends on you. The mentor decides when you've learned enough to hunt on your own, so the harder you work, the quicker you get out there. Though we've had some who just couldn't cut it no matter what they did. Just a complete lack of natural talent. That's not you, is it?"

Adrien was silent.

"I'd say not," Georges answered his own question. "Not after having gone to the Lillianic School. Anyway, let's see who can take you."

He pulled open another ledger and scanned its columns. "Hmm…looks like Jayem's last one just graduated to Deucalion rank , so I'll put you down as his for now…or at least I will after these blockheads settle down!" he raised his voice on the last words, half-shouting them at the crowd of chattering young men spilling into the wood-panelled room from a corridor on the right.

Adrien stepped back to avoid being jostled, the new arrivals being too absorbed in conversation to notice they were about to collide with him.

"Fine lot of hunters those are," grumbled Georges. "Can't even pay attention to what's in front of their noses…Hey, watch it!"

The group had nearly knocked over a man coming from the room's left door, who had been keeping his head down as he skimmed the wall with his shoulder.

"You lot want to wash out?" Georges hollered, the business-like manner he'd used on the new arrival having evaporated. "If you act like that in the field, and you won't live to make it out of Pandora rank."

The noisy group ambled off grumbling, leaving the other man still standing and blinking at Georges, reminding Adrien of the way the boys at school would look when Mistress Lillia caught them misbehaving.

"You alright, Jayem? Sorry if I scared you there."

"Oh – I'm not – I'm, I'm fine."

"Good. Because I've got a new trainee for you, just arrived."

"So soon?" he asked with dismay in his voice, but seemed to realize how it sounded, and darted a concerned look at Adrien. "I'm mean, it's not that I mind, it's just –"

"Your last protegé only recently graduated," Adrien supplied for him. "I apologize; I seem to have come at an inopportune time."

"Don't, it's alright,"

"Your name is Jayem? Is that correct?" Adrien asked, extending his hand as he noticed the man absently wringing his own.

"Oh, no, no," the man looked startled at the question. "Some people call me that because those are my initials, but my real name is Jean-Marien." When he reached out his own hand, Adrien could feel it shaking.

"I'll call you Jean-Marien, then," Adrien said.

"No, I don't mind 'Jayem', really. Sometimes it's nice to have your own name to yourself, if that makes sense?"

It made all the sense in the world to Adrien Fairinelle.

CHAPTER 18
The Bashful Swain

At the end of their first training session, Jean-Marien shrugged with an embarrassed look at his student. The session had been meant for the mentor to evaluate the strengths and potential of his protegé, but Adrien, with his fine rapier, had matched him almost step-for-step.

"I'm not sure there's much I can teach you, at least in this respect," Jean-Marien said. "You've already got excellent form."

Adrien couldn't make himself thank Jean-Marien for the compliment.

"Your record says you haven't had much experience in tracking, though, so I think that's where we'll focus," his mentor went on, and Adrien noticed that without so many other people around, Jean-Marien seemed to stutter less.

"Once you've got your target where you want it, it seems like you know what to do already. But it takes a lot of work to get to that spot in the first place, you know what I mean? When you see an animal, you can't just jump out and expect to take it down right then."

"Sometimes you can," *thought Adrien.* "At least with humans."

"The key to being a Promethean is to make friends with the solitude. You have to learn stealth and patience. You have to learn to tough it out when it feels like you've been on the lookout for ages. When your back is stiff from waiting and your legs are asleep, and all you want to do is go home, that's when the best opportunities show up.

You've got to be alright being alone out there. Some people can't stand the silence after so long, but that what I like best about it."

"I can imagine," said Adrien. "No one around to bother you, or make you talk when you don't want to."

"Exactly," Jean-Marien said. "It's being with so many others that's the hardest work for me...I can never think of anything clever to say," he turned slightly red as he admitted it.

"But out here," he looked up, "it's only myself I have to talk to."

"Then I'm certain I chose the right profession," said Adrien.

"I'm glad," was all Jean-Marien replied. Adrien noted he didn't ask him to share any reason for being averse to talking. People at home didn't hesitate to ask him all manner of questions, but how nice it would be here, not having to share information he would rather not. How nice to know someone else in the world saw the merits of silence.

"Yes," Adrien decided. It would certainly be helpful having someone like this for a friend.

CHAPTER 19
White Night

It was past midnight when Renn and Fairinelle herded a stumbling Celine in front of them down the hall. Emile had already gone to bed, but he poked his head out the door when he heard the noise of their approach.

"What's going on, Renn?" he asked.

Celine fell on her way past, and he reached out to grab her.

"Hey, I guess this old arm is better, if I can carry this weight." He handed Celine off to Fairinelle, so that he could roll his shoulder and curl his arm, testing out his newly-returned form.

"I'm glad," said Renn, pleased to see his friend back to normal.

But in the morning, Emile paid for it with the broad side of Celine's pistol smacking across his head as she emerged – an hour later than everyone else – into the common room.

"What was that for?" Renn cried. Emile had already suffered one head injury; did she not care if he got another? He marched up to her, his face growing hot with indignation, and reached to take the gun from her, but she swatted him away.

"He deserves worse," she said. "It's mighty bold of him to even show his face to me at all, after that embarrassing scene in the hallway last night, grabbing at me as he did."

"Bold of me...?" Emile repeated, blinking as he

rubbed his head. "I didn't do a thing last night except keep you from falling down drunk, if that's what you mean."

"You're a fine one to speak of boldness," Fairinelle told her. "I was also there last night, though it seems you were unaware, and I can confirm he's telling the truth. He handed you over to Renn and me as soon as he dragged you to your feet.

"Why should I trust *you*?"

"I suppose I have a talent for remembering when wrongs committed." He stepped forward, wresting the gun from her grip where Renn hadn't managed to do so. "If you are so concerned about laying hands on others, then remember this: You are never to hurt either of these boys like that again. Do you understand?"

For the first time, Renn was actually glad to hear him threaten her. If, just this once, he could stop her from putting Emile in danger again, then Renn had to admit he was alright with it.

Yes, he decided. It could definitely be an advantage having a Butcher for a friend.

If Celine had been about worried being embarrassed that night, her worry came too early. As the days went on, she slowly ceased to care what she looked like in front of others, just so long as she had a drop of drink on her tongue.

When they hiked along the river, she trailed behind the other three, staggering over tree roots, complaining constantly of the pain in her head. She looked like Renn had felt that first day off of the St. Juste. How he had felt on the way out Cimbria, when must have passed through these very same trees.

No wonder Willow and Badger had always been so cross. It was irritating to have to wait for someone to constantly find their feet, or worse, wait for them to stop vomiting long enough to make any dent in the distance they had to go. Renn tried to be patient with her, remembering how kind Emile and Fairinelle had been during the times when he'd been sick himself. But that was different, for Renn couldn't help his sickness, while Celine could stop it anytime she wanted. She just didn't want to.

They had more nights in the woods thanks to her slow progress, and the others eventually decided to take her off the night watches. Half of the time, she couldn't be roused when it was her turn, and when she was able to wake up, they were afraid she wouldn't be any use as a watchman anyway.

"We'll have to split her turn between us," said Fairinelle over the fire near which Celine had already dozed off.

"But that's how Emile got hurt last time," Renn reminded him. "You said we weren't to do that anymore, didn't you?"

"Unfortunately, she always finds a way to make others pay for her selfishness."

A flash of heat shot through Renn's face. That was exactly what he had done to Emile the first time. Just like Celine, he'd been far too interested in getting his own rest, and not nearly interested enough in anyone else's. He was embarrassed to think of how he had acted now.

"It isn't right," he insisted, his hands curling into fists. "She's taking advantage of us!"

Fairinelle looked faintly surprised at his outburst, but it was soon followed by a look of – was that pride?

"Quite so," he said. "I'm proud of you for having sense enough to see it."

It *was* pride. Pride in him. Renn hadn't expected that, and he certainly hadn't expected to be pleased by it. For this strange, kind, frightening man to praise him, the boy who had never been good enough for his uncle Hagen or his cousin Jungbern back home, who hadn't been smart enough to escape the slavers, or responsible enough not to hurt his friend, it felt like he had finally, for once in his life, done something right.

For Fairinelle was a warrior, wasn't he, and a good one?

A warrior's approval meant something, after all.

When they reached the town of *Vent-sur-Rivière*, or "Wind on the River", Renn was only too glad to step inside the inn called The White Night, knowing that sturdy walls protected him and the others from the night, and that they would not have to sit up and watch out for themselves this time.

He wondered if anyone like them was out there tonight, any travellers sitting watch for unfriendly faces in the dark, while Renn took his turn safe in the city.

"*It's only the work we do out there which keeps them safe within their precious little walls,*" Celine had once said. She had been right, but for some time now, she hadn't been doing any work out there either.

Now, as ever, she sat idly by, indulging her taste for alcohol. Nobody seemed to notice her sitting there alone or how she slumped further and further back in her chair, her eyes drooping more and more, until they closed completely.

"You want to try learning this one, Renn?" Emile gestured to the lines of people that whirled before the small group that played here, like the group that had played in Seven Wishes when he had danced with Fairinelle.

Renn decided that he would do it this time. The other option was sitting and watching Celine, and if she didn't care about taking care of herself, then Renn decided that, at least for this night, he wouldn't care about taking care of her either.

He went with Emile, and soon learned the pattern, crossing and passing and turning between other pairs of dancers in the line. It wasn't so hard, once he got used to it, and really, it was a lot of fun.

"Hey, don't I know you?" a man as Renn passed through the line opposite him.

It was Leandre Rigobert, Celine's friend, who had been at Angel's Arrow while Emile was on bed rest from his concussion. Renn had never actually spoken to him, only heard him shouting on about the Child Knight, and he wondered how this man would have recognized him.

"Um, I – ?" was all Renn got out before he had to move down the line to another pair. He looked back at Celine, but her chair was empty.

She had fallen down to the floor and hadn't even woken up. Somebody stepped over her on their way to the bar.

"*Serves her right*," thought Renn. She had stepped over a good many people herself.

He smiled at the thought of leaving her there all night, and of what her reaction would be when she woke up to find herself in so undignified a state.

But still, when they finished the dance, and he saw Celine still on the ground, he wondered what if something really did happen to her overnight? For as much as she deserved to be left there, how would he get home if she were gone? Would either Emile or Fairinelle have reason to keep going towards Cimbria if not for her and her bounty? No, it was better to have her around, to keep them together, to keep them moving towards home.

He knelt down and grabbed her arms, thinking to drag her back into the chair, but he couldn't quite manage it alone, as she was like dead weight. Maybe he could do it if he had some shark-hauling rope.

"So that's where I know you from." Leandre Rigobert was approaching, looking between Renn and the unconscious body on the floor. "I saw you with her back in Angel's Arrow, didn't I? And she was drinking then, too." He slid easily into a chair of his own, looking at Renn over the rim of his glasses.

"Seems you're still with her. So tell me, how does a kid like you come to travel with Celine the dragon lady?"

"Uh, it was…" Renn couldn't tell this stranger that he'd been bought off a prison barge. If he explained that, he would have to explain why he was on it in the first place.

"Through a mutual friend," Emile cut in, sitting across

the table and resting his hand casually on his chin, though he cut a sideways look at Renn. It seemed neither of them were anxious to share that bit of their history.

"There's another of you?" asked Rigobert, swivelling his head to look at Emile. "And she said she wasn't running around with a bunch of boys. I knew she was lying. Are you two Circlars like her?"

"What?" asked Renn, stalling again.

"How is it you're travelling in the same direction as us?" Emile asked, deflecting the attention off of their story and onto his.

"I heard about the bounty same as Celine. Speaking of which, where's the other one that was with her? The Child Knight?"

"He was around...don't know where he went," said Emile, looking to the corners of the room. "I was about to go looking for him."

"I'll go with you. I wouldn't mind the chance to meet him again." Rigobert got up in tandem with Emile.

"Um, I still need some help?" Renn called after them.

Rigobert turned back, slung Celine's arm unceremoniously over his shoulder, and began dragging her towards the hall of guest rooms.

"Anybody know her room number?" he asked the other two, who were following behind.

"Beats me," said Emile, while Renn shook his head.

Rigobert gingerly reached into her skirt pocket and pulled out her key with the number engraved into the metal. "Here we are," he said, lugged her to the door matching it, unlocked it, and dropped her on the bed.

He looked down at her, putting his hands on his hips. "Isn't this a laugh? The ice queen lolling about like common street trash? Can't wait to see what she does tomorrow when we tell her."

*   *   *

It seemed Rigobert meant what he said, for in the morning, he approached them wearing a travelling cloak.

"What are you doing here?" Celine asked.

"I heard about the bounty, same as you, but I realized that if this man's working on your side, I don't stand a chance" he gestured at Fairinelle.

"I'm not on her side," said Fairinelle flatly.

"So I thought I'd join up with you," Rigobert continued talking to Celine, seeming not to hear. "Get myself at least a share of the money."

Celine tried to forbid him, saying she would not share her money with one more person, but but Rigobert only laughed and said "What are you going to do? Shoot me and take my share off my corpse? It'll be hard to spend a bounty in prison."

"Maybe I could have you put on the St. Juste. Wouldn't you like to me oversee you?" teased Fairinelle, and that was the end of the matter.

Rigobert was coming with them.

"I'm glad you're coming," Renn said to him as they walked. "Celine's no good when she's drunk all the time, and we could use someone else to split the watches with."

"Heh, thanks, friend," Rigobert said. "She would've liked to keep me out, but I knew I was joining one way or the other."

"How did you make friends with her?"

"Bounty hunters have to know a lot of people and hear a lot of things, otherwise we'd never get the good prizes. Half the worthwhile marks aren't ever advertised in public; you've got to be a Circlar to hear about some of them, and for someone like me, who isn't a part of one, well, we've got to be doubly alert. I thought you would've known that, already travelling on a bounty as you are."

"It's our first time doing one," Emile interjected from behind.

"What a monster of a first time, seeing as it's for *people*," Rigobert said. "Usually, it's just for rogue bears or nuisance wolves or something."

Renn remembered what Emile had said about Xavier's giant shark. "*You picked a devil of a one to get started on.*" But the truth was, he hadn't really picked any of this at all.

"Well, we didn't get scouted for nothing," said Emile.

"Fair enough," Rigobert conceded, and looked forward.

Celine walked ahead of them, with Fairinelle behind her, their boots crunching through the leaves. He made her walk in front, as he refused to keep checking behind him to see if she had fallen down on the side of the path somewhere.

Renn watched them, Fairinelle straight-backed and Celine trying to be. A leaf fell into her hair, making the her head look more like a bird's nest than usual.

Another leaf brushed Renn's face. He watched it float down and become lost in the blanket of hundreds of others, and he wondered if some impression of him, who it had touched, would remain there with it. After he was gone, safe back at home, would some memory of him still be here?

CHAPTER 20
That Type of Thinking

"You, what's this list for?"

"Excuse me?" Adrien blinked at the strange person addressing him as if he were one of his father's servants back home.

"Who are all these people on this paper?" The girl pointed to the row of names tacked to the corkboard in the hallway of Circle Promethio's lodge.

"Those are people who have completed marks or gotten rank promotions this month. Do you know what a mark is? Or a rank?"

The girl rolled her eyes. "Not only do I know, I'll be on this list by the next time it's printed."

"Are you a member here?" Adrien asked. He didn't the brashness of this person who obviously didn't even know how Circles worked.

"Not yet, but that's no obstacle."

"Well, joining would be a start, not to mention the months of training you'll have to go through to even get a foot in the field."

"That's fine for people who are too scared or too lacking in talent to do any better, but you can't bag the big game by sitting around waiting for it. I fully intend to go for what I want, and see if I don't see my name on these lists soon enough." She turned from him and ran her finger down the rows of names on the list, stopping between Pascal Laurent and Jean Lavalle.

"Now I know why you're not a member. If you were,

you would know that type of thinking is foolish." It was exactly the type of thinking Jean-Marien had always advised against. It was exactly that type of thinking which had once forced a young baron to become a Child Knight.

"Alright, if you're such the master hunter, why don't I see your name on any of these lists?"

"You don't even know what it is."

She was undeterred. "That's proof enough in itself. If you were so good, you'd be famous already, and I wouldn't have to ask it."

"You must not be from Misère," *thought Adrien, feeling his right arm burn just above the elbow.*

"What good is a Circlar who won't go out and fight for glory?"

"We hunt down marks because people need protection from them, not because it's something glamorous."

"Hey, Adrien, you ready? I –" Jean-Marien stopped halfway through the doorway when he saw his protégé conversing with the girl. Instantly, his eyes lowered to the ground.

"Sorry, I, um, didn't mean to interrupt. I didn't know you had a friend with you."

"We're not friends," the girl rolled her eyes, but Jean-Marien didn't see it. "I don't even know this person."

"He's Adrien, and I'm – " he said, looking up for a moment before dropping his gaze again. "I'm Jean-Marien."

"Hmm. Is that so?" She had gone back to scanning the list.

"Hadn't we better go?" Adrien asked, turning his back on the irritating new applicant. Jayem had never been good with introductions, and Adrien was glad for the excuse to leave her presence.

"Was it alright that I told her your name?" Jean-Marien asked as they left. "You seemed sort of hesitant about it, so I wondered..."

"It's fine," said Adrien, though he wasn't sure he would have told her if he'd had the choice. She hadn't even had

the decency to meet Jayem halfway when he'd made the effort to introduce himself. Aside from the fact that it was only proper etiquette, he had obviously been nervous, and she hadn't even looked at him.

"We still don't know who **she** was, though," said Jean-Marien.

"All I know is she had some terribly uninformed ideas about what makes for a good Circlar."

"If she's new, maybe she hasn't had time to learn any better."

"I wouldn't say so to her. I'm sure she'd give you an earful in return."

"Oh, I don't think she'd have much to say to me."

Adrien thought about that conversation afterwards, after everything had ended in blood and brokenness.

In the end, she had said enough.

CHAPTER 21
A-Rovin'

There were some days when nothing happened besides their coming a few miles closer to Cimbria. Nobody fell out of trees, or got into blazing arguments, or had to fight for their lives against a rogue band of Wends.

But before Cimbria, they had to reach Faubourg, the town Fairinelle had pointed out on the map, and as the days drew on, Celine alternated between becoming more irritable and more withdrawn. When she spoke, she snapped more than ever, and when she was silent, her eyes were glassy and her mind was clearly far away.

The rest of the group did not much miss her barbs in conversation, but to see her sitting alone, outside the cheerful circle of the others reminded Renn of himself from a few years prior, newly arrived and afraid in Barenhohle, knowing almost no one. Of course it was Celine's own fault that nobody wanted to talk to her, but that didn't change the resemblance.

"How long have you known Celine?" Renn asked Rigobert one day. He couldn't ask her or Fairinelle truth about Faubourg and "Jayem", but maybe he could get some shred of an idea from Rigobert.

"Eh, since about three years back, I guess."

How long ago had "Jayem" happened? Renn wondered.

"Where was that? Did you ever meet her in Faubourg?"

"Not at all. Why would I have gone there when the Wends were practically trying to take it as their own, and there weren't even any bounties out back then? Never understood that one – there were attacks all over the place, but nobody did anything about it.

It's getting to be like that again now, but at least they the sense post bounties for the brutes this time."

He looked at Renn and squinted. "But how do *you* know about Faubourg? You had to have been awfully young then."

"We didn't put up a bounty 'cause we were trying to get the treaty to go through," Emile cut in from where he was striking a flint for the fire. "Wouldn't have looked good to be putting hits on people we were claiming to want peace with."

"They didn't sign the treaty anyway," Rigobert said. "If there had been a bounty, at least there would have been fewer of them to fight when they backed out. On the whole, I can't say I much care for how your army handled things."

"I'm not sure I care too much for that anymore, either," said Emile, his eyes back on his flint.

After a minute, he began humming one of the many snatches of songs that he had carried with him from the St. Juste. It was one Renn recognized, as Emile sang it often, and he'd even begun to learn some of the lyrics himself, though, according to Emile, only the chorus was in its original form. He'd made up his own lines on the verses, explaining that the original ones he'd heard from the men on the ship were not exactly "polite."

Renn joined his voice to Emile's, and they grinned at each other over the fire as they sang out loud on the chorus.

"A-rovin', a-rovin', for roving's been my ru-i-n."

"Sing something else" demanded Celine from her isolated spot. "I hate that song."

"How can you hate it? Most of it isn't even the same lines," Renn argued.

"That part you're singing is, and it's that part which is the most offensive."

But they went on singing just the same, and Celine gave

a sigh that was half a groan. Renn faltered only when he saw her pull a silver container from her coat pocket, unscrew the lid, and tip its contents into her mouth.

It wasn't hard to guess what was inside it, and, strangely enough, in between gulps, he could hear her finishing the verse, muttering darkly to herself.

"I'll go no more a-rovin' with you, fair maid."

CHAPTER 22
Proper Introductions

"Her name is Celine Lauvin," said Jean-Marien. "That girl you were talking to before"

"Who? Oh…" Adrien's brow creased when he remembered the rude girl by the notice board. "How did you find that out?" It wasn't like Jayem to actively seek out acquaintance with anybody.

"I asked Georges," Jean-Marien tried to shrug casually. "I figured he would know, as he's got everyone's files."

"Thank you. You've, err, saved me the trouble of finding out myself," said Adrien. To tell the truth, he hadn't had any intention of getting know that impolite girl, but how could he say that to his friend, who seemed so pleased that he'd gotten the information? "Though I suppose Georges will have to give us an official introduction now."

As little as he wanted to, it was the only thing to do. The proper rules of society must be followed. Perhaps it might show that Celine a little of how civilized people behaved.

"You can try," said Jean-Marien, "but Georges said she's trying to get her training done as fast as possible, so she's out with Marina all day almost every day. I haven't seen her myself more than twice."

Good. The more she was out in the field, the less they'd have to see her. And maybe out there she would actually learn something that would teach her to stop spouting those ridiculous, self-important notions.

"How long do you think it'll be before we see her name on the lists?" Jean-Marien asked.

"Longer than she thinks, I'd wager," replied Adrien.

He had been right. For though Celine put in more hours than most other protegés in Circle Promethio, she was impatient to a fault, and struggled with the waiting, or the "sticking it out" as Jayem had called it. If she couldn't get her target within two hours, she was ready to call the hunt off for the day, and when she did see her target, she would not take the time to line up her shots, and usually ended up scaring the animal away.

All this Jean-Marien had gotten from Marina, who was Celine's mentor, and he related everything he heard to Adrien, whose only pleasure in hearing about Celine came from the secret, grim satisfaction of knowing that she was quickly finding out wrong she'd been.

But even that pleasure had evaporated on the day Jean-Marien had told him he'd put in to be Celine's second mentor.

"Why?" Adrien asked flatly, nearly stopping in his tracks as the two of them walked. Second mentors were for people who were trying their hardest, and still just needed some extra help to hone their skills. It was hard work and lots of effort for everyone involved. So why would Jayem, who trembled to speak to more than two people at a time, and blushed even when speaking to his friends, choose to insert himself into this mess of a situation, with a student who was clearly on the way to washing out, not because of her skill but because of her bad attitude? It was strangely out-of-character for him.

"Why would you want to mentor a washout like her?" Adrien demanded again. "She'll only bring you down."

"Because she needs help," Jean-Marien said. "She's struggling."

"And it is entirely her own fault. I told her from the beginning she was rushing into this, but she would do it anyway. Don't throw yourself on the sword of someone who is committing suicide."

"But, well…" Jean-Marien tried again. His began to turn red and wring his hands. "I want to."

Adrien's heart sank as he watched Jean-Marien fidget and stutter. His friend was much too shy to want something like that, unless…

"Are you – ?" he started, taking a step back. No. He couldn't bear to ask. It would make things awkward and terrible.

But things were already awkward and terrible, for his friend was in love with Celine Lauvin. That must have been why he always pestered Adrien with news of her progress, why he assumed Adrien cared about her all. Because he cared himself.

The only thing Adrien couldn't tell was why. She was reckless and brash, where Jean-Marien never put himself forward if he could help it. She was loudmouthed and callow, and never seemed to care about anyone else's existence, least of all this timid, sensitive person who, though he was Deucalion rank, seemed at times to be more in need of guidance and care than any of his students.

It wasn't that Adrien minded sharing his mentor. Jean-Marien had other students, and Adrien got along with them just fine. He wouldn't even have minded if his friend had gone off and fallen in love with someone else, anyone else. What bothered him was that Jean-Marien was devoting himself to someone as unsuited to him as that Lauvin girl. She who didn't see him blushing as she swept past all his gentle attempts at conversation, didn't hear him making excuses for her, blaming himself for her rudeness.

"I shouldn't have bothered her," he would say. "Not when she's trying to so hard to catch up. She must be so busy."

She who was so cold to him that he had to resort to this, an official assignment, just to make her look at him as a person rather than some sort of irksome object in her way. She, who treated Jean-Marien's silence, which had been *such a balm to Adrien, as something to be scorned. That was what made all of this so wrong.*

If Jean-Marien went through with this, the man who had trouble even meeting people's eyes was only going to be hurt by Celine's sharp, uncaring glances. The man who could barely stutter a word to anyone was going to be cut to pieces by her harsh tongue. He would break himself on the rocks of her indifference, and there would be nothing Adrien could do about it.

CHAPTER 23
Faubourg

"Here we are. Come on, Celine, don't dawdle," Rigobert called, looking over his shoulder to where Celine trailed far behind the rest, and extending his other arm towards the cobbled street leading into Faubourg, lined by peaceful-looking buildings. "Did you hear what he said?" Fairinelle asked, falling back alongside her. "You don't want to be late."

"I heard," Celine answered, her head down as she slunk through the neatly-painted city gates.

For all that Faubourg had seemed to Renn like a part of a mysterious, dangerous game amongst the shadows of the forest, today it seemed nothing but a pleasant and welcoming rest. It was strange that all this existed so close to the border, but Renn could almost forget to be puzzled by it once Emile whisked him away to squares where the sun shone, water splashed in fountains, and shops sold unfamiliar foods that melted creamy cold and sweet in his mouth.

"Where did you get the money for this?" Renn asked from one side of the table in front of the shop whose sign read *"Joyful Ices"*.

"Fairinelle gave it to me. Said for us to go enjoy ourselves," explained Emile, pulling a stick of peppermint out of his cup of pink ice. "Here, try this."

"Why didn't he come with us?"

"I wondered that myself, especially as he looked serious as an ox at an auction all the while he's telling us to have fun, and he must have said five times for us 'stick together and not go beyond the city gates,' but who am I to question what he does?"

Renn chewed the peppermint and wondered. Fairinelle had spoken so grimly about this place and Celine's appointment here, so what reason would he have to send them out to have fun on the town...unless it was to get them out of the way? What if Celine's appointment was to finally pay him her due? What if he told them to stay inside the gates, because outside of them was where he was going to leave her body?

"You don't think..." he started to say, but how could he explain his concerns to Emile? Emile never worried about anything, and he would likely only tell Renn not to worry either, while Celine might be dying somewhere.

It was ridiculous to care so much about Celine, but if she really was the first to fall by Fairinelle's hand, if he had started collecting his dues, who among them would be the next target? By keeping Fairinelle away from Celine, he was also keeping the man away from himself.

"You all right?" Emile asked. "You're looking sort of grey all of a sudden."

"I'll be back," Renn said, rising suddenly as the peppermint fell to the table and bounced off onto the dusty ground. "I...forgot something at the inn."

He jogged off without giving Emile time to question him, and though he heard metal scraping the pavement, and the muffled clinking of coins behind him as Emile rose and struggled to find payment to leave on the table, Renn couldn't stop to give an explanation.

He was short of breath by the time he burst back into the common room of *The Fair Boatman*, hoping she was there. At least if she were drinking, it would be better than the alternative.

But only Rigobert was inside, tipping his chair back with a newspaper in front of his face and his feet pushing on the table legs.

"Rigobert!" Renn called. "Where's Celine?"

Rigobert blinked at him, but didn't sit up. "My, aren't you in a rush this morning?"

Renn sighed in frustration. He didn't have time for this.

"Have you seen her?"

"Sure, I saw her – heading into the potions shop this morning when I was coming out of it. I was surprised to see her up so early. She looked a wreck, though."

"Was Fairinelle with her?"

"Hmm? No, I didn't see him."

Well, that was a start. As long as she were alone, she might still be safe.

Renn turned around the way he had come, calling back thanks to Rigobert, whose glasses rims were just visible over the top of the paper.

He ran back past the same sparkling fountains, the same cafés, through the same sunshine, but they did not hold the charm of before, not while the Butcher was on the loose, and the woman he hated was unaccounted for.

But where was the potions shop? What did Rigobert mean by "potions" anyway?

"*Weapons, balms, such things as we use are relegated to the outskirts of town,*" he remembered Celine saying on the first day he had known her, and he ran towards the gates where Fairinelle had forbidden them to go, hoping his guess was right.

He ran until he saw a sign hanging over doorway showing sparrow holding a vial, with a painted name on the fading wood: "Jean-Marien Hironde, Apothecary". He had no hope of deciphering the last word, but the picture told him he must be in the right place.

He pushed the door open timidly, half-expecting to see the floor inside soaked in blood, a strangled body, and Fairinelle standing triumphant in the midst of it all. But what he saw nothing more than a quiet, vacant shop with that looked like any other, save perhaps for more cobwebs than usual behind the unlit torch lamps, and the fact that while the lower shelves were neatly lined with glass containers filled with varying colors of liquid, all of the upper shelves were empty.

Gray dust motes floated through the beams of sun streaming through the windows, as Renn looked around. To the far left was a narrow stairway which seemed as if no one had used it for years. The boards, separating from each other, were blanched by a layer of dust. Celine could not have gone that way, or he would have seen the print of her boots. But between the stairs and counter was hall, not nearly as narrow as the stairs, and the floor there was clean.

Renn crept into it, trying to control his breathing, and watching for rough spots in the planks which might creak and give him away, but the floor here was not only clean but smooth, almost as if someone had purposely worn down the wood for the convenience of a half-Wendish boy stealing through the halls.

He passed by two closed doors with only shade and silence spilling out from under them, before he reached one under which light and unhappy murmurs floated. Not daring to push it open, he sidled up to it, fixing one eye on the crack between the door and the frame.

He had been right. Celine was inside, and it was she that was making those painful sounds. But it was nothing else like what he had expected.

She was not alone. There with her was – not Fairinelle, but a man in a chair that was unlike anything Renn had seen before. It had wheels on either side, and a plank attached to its front, upon which the man rested his feet.

But this chair was not nearly as surprising as the man himself. His legs were thin and twisted, and Renn could only describe his face as broken. It looked as if someone had held it to a grindstone until the skin was a mess of ragged lines stretched over the jagged edges of his bones.

A flashing memory of Jungbern's face with its ring of scars passed through Renn's mind. This was how his cousin might have looked if Linderic hadn't dragged

Siegher away on the day that the huge dog had attacked him.

Celine sat next to the man's wheeled chair, her head bent over onto the armrest of her own, her bird's nest of curls falling over it, hiding her face as she mumbled something that sounded like "I'm sorry", though it did not sound like her at all. For one thing, she never apologized to anyone. For another, she never spoke in tones so soft and quavering. Where was the sharp, hard-edged person Renn was used to?

He looked on in silence, wanting, and at the same time dreading to interrupt this strange scene. Had she been hurt? Did she need help? And what about this man? His wounds were not new, but perhaps he might need...something, though Renn didn't know what. He looked at the scarred face, trying to think of what to do, and realized the man was looking back at him.

"Hello there," said the man, his mouth struggling slightly to form the words. "Are you looking to buy something?"

"I, um…" Renn stuttered. The man's words were soft and gentle, but they gripped him as tightly as Badger's hand when he'd been pulled out of the Cimbrian tree.

"I was looking for...um, my boss. She was missing and I worried that….I mean, I wondered if...I heard she had come here."

"Looks like a lot of people care about you, Celine. You had better go on." the man smiled down at the messy head next to him.

She sat up then, and Renn saw her face was swollen and streaked with tears. He stepped back in shock and dread, certain she would not take kindly to his seeing her like this. He expected her to fly at him in a fury, to yell at him to mind his own business and leave her alone. But she did none of these things.

She took hold of the man's hands, staring at him as if she were praying to some saint, and said "I'll come back this time."

"Don't. Not until you want to."

She stood and bent over him, hovering for a moment, then turned and brushed past Renn as if he were not there.

Only Renn and the man in the wheeled chair were left, staring at each other. Renn felt he ought to say something, but what could he say to a stranger of whose life he had just seen something far too personal?

The man wrung his crooked hands for a moment, before setting them back in his lap and sighing gently. Even through the scars, Renn could see the wistfulness in his face.

"You had better go after her," he said. "Before she gets into trouble."

Renn turned. Though grateful for the excuse to leave, he tried not to flee outright. It might hurt the man's feelings, though the truth was Renn ran not from revulsion at him, but from discomfort at himself. Though he had done it with the best of intentions, he knew not that he shouldn't have gone poking about here.

He reached Celine as she strode through the door, under the sign of the sparrow. Already she looked more like herself, here in the bright sunlight.

She walked on, not looking at him or acknowledging him except to speak these words as Emile appeared at the end of the cobbled road, waving his arms and rushing towards them:

"If I find that you don't know how to keep your mouth shut, I will kill you, make no mistake."

There was no danger of that. Renn had long since learned to keep secrets.

"Law!" Emile huffed as he reached them. "Why don't you just run the rest of the way to Cimbria? You'll be there and back in no time," he said between breaths, with one hand on his side. "What in the blazes got into you? You disappeared before I could even get money on the table, and when I get to the inn, you're gone again! Where'd you find him, Boss? Goodness knows I couldn't do it."

Celine said nothing.

"Sorry, I thought I'd lost something," Renn lied.

"I could've helped you look," Emile sounded slightly wounded. "But you had me thinking I'd lost *you*, what with the all the talk of Wends prowling about. How could I have looked Fairinelle in the eye if you'd been killed? How could I have looked *myself* in the eye?"

"Sorry," Renn repeated.

"Anyway, did you find it?" Emile asked.

"Um, yeah..." said Renn. He'd found something, he just wasn't sure *what.*

He turned over and over in his mind all that he had seen, and all he thought he knew, until the name under the painted sparrow came together into a meaning.

Jean-Marien. JM. Taken together, those initials were a word. Jayem.

Jayem was not a thing. It was person. The man in the chair.

He meant something to Celine, enough that she would cry over him when she cried over nothing else. He was the threat Fairinelle had been using on her all this time.

Had he known this man was important to her, and hurt him as a way to force her to act? Every time he had hung the name Jayem over her head, was he threatening to do something worse to this already damaged man? But why would he treat Celine and Jean-Marien like this when he was perfectly kind to everyone else? When he was so generous as to buy Renn and Emile new clothes, to pay for the things they needed, and never once complain about it? There had to be more than simple money to this story.

Fairinelle came back to the inn late that night, and when he got there, he was not his usual self. By turns he paced the common room, sitting and drumming his long fingers on the table, or staring out the window. When he had dropped into his chair for the fifth time in an hour, Emile's mug went down on the table with a soft thud.

"Listen, Mr. Fairinelle, I'm not usually one for prying, but it strikes me something's bothering you."

"Does it?"

"You're restless as a new pony on plow day. It's not like you."

"I'm not sure what *is* like me these days."

"Would it help to talk about it?"

"I wonder..."

"Lots of times when I think I just can't take something, it helps to talk it over with someone, if there's someone to be had. Half the time, when I say it out loud, I realize it's wasn't much to worry about after all."

"*I guess my problem is part of the other half,*" thought Renn.

Fairinelle's eyes, which had been roving uneasily all evening, fixed on Emile then, steady and intense.

"You know of Circles, yes?" he asked.

"Sure, professional animal hunters and the like. Thought about joining one before I settled on the army, but chasing after applause wasn't quite up my alley."

"It's true they can attract attention-seekers, who only want glory, but they attract other types of people, too."

CHAPTER 24
Truths

"*I don't* want *a second mentor. Is there nothing I can do about it?" Celine wailed to her mentor Marina, pulling on the end of her long braid as she paced across the study.*

"You don't have to accept the help, but I would if I were you. Let's be honest, Celine, you're struggling."

"Is that really what you think of me?" said Celine, her eyes wide as she turned to face her mentor.

"It's not what I think, it's the truth. We're going in the field every day, and you still haven't even gotten out of Pandora rank. There are students who came after you that already outrank you."

"That's because – because – " Celine tried, her face burning with indignation, but she couldn't find a good excuse. "Come out with me tonight, and by tomorrow I know I'll have made it." She set her chin stubbornly, not giving up.

"You can't tonight. There's a hold on hunts. The army sent a message that the Cimbri Wends are on the move. Nobody's allowed out until it's lifted."

"What do I care about Cimbri? If I killed one, wouldn't that earn me a promotion?"

"That's your trouble," Marina said. "You're so impatient that you'd rush off and get yourself killed for half a chance of glory. I think you need a steadier hand to help you get control of yourself, and Jean-Marien is – "

"So steady I'll be an old lady before he gets around to

saying a full sentence in front of me. How am I supposed to learn anything that way?"

"He's volunteering his own time," Marina said. "Just give it a try. Honestly, you can't end up much worse than you are now."

"Maybe I'm so bad at it because I have a mentor who doesn't believe in me!" Celine shot back, feeling the heat of embarrassment rise to her face again, and refusing to believe she might deserve it. She turned and ran from the room so that Marina wouldn't see her lip trembling, only to run into her new mentor, who was trembling himself.

"Oh! I was just coming to see – if you …" he started.

"If I wanted to go out and train tonight?" she rolled her eyes. "Can't. Didn't you hear about the hold on hunts? Aren't we all supposed to be hiding in fear until it's over?" She made a face over her shoulder towards the room she had just left.

*Jean-Marien managed a small laugh. "I can see **you're** not. Good for you." But he dropped his eyes again as soon as he'd said it.*

If only Marina had found this so amusing, thought Celine. But no, she had to sit there, looking sorry and pretending like she cared, telling Celine to improve, but all the while insulting her and keeping her from the things that would actually get her there.

"You don't think I'm stupid to want to fight them?"

"I think it shows…" he stopped, then took a breath and looked straight in her eyes again. "It shows you've got spirit."

He seemed almost as proud of himself for saying so as he was of her for being so.

She cocked her head at him. This was something new. He was perhaps the first person since she had come here to act as if her ideas were worth anything.

"Don't let Marina hear you say that."

"She just doesn't want you to get hurt."

Jean-Marien, having once astounded himself by speaking his mind in front of her, somehow found the courage to keep going. Perhaps some of her fire was rubbing off on him. "Even the bravest people can't do everything alone."

"What if I had someone helping me if I went out tonight?" Celine's eyes lit up, for what he'd said had given her an idea. Who knew this quiet, stammering man would have such good ideas hidden his head?

"You're supposed to be pretty good, aren't you?" she continued. "Marina said you were. I know if you were with me,

between us we could bring back a trophy that would put Promethio on the map, couldn't we?"

Or what was it the other boy called him?

"Jayem?"

Had it been anyone else who asked him, Jean-Marien's "steady hand" would have prevailed, as Marina predicted. But he stood in awe of this girl who knew what she wanted and didn't hesitate to reach for it with both hands. And this girl who never before had reason to notice him – sad, shy, pathetic Jean-Marien – was now asking him for help. How could refuse her when she looked at him with that hurt, desperate expression? When she called him by that name used only by those close to him?

When he led her through the gates and into the forest as the night winds began to blow through the branches above, Celine smiled as sweetly as she could at him.

Marina had been right after all, she thought. Jean-Marien would get her where she wanted to go. Yes, it could be useful to have someone like this for a mentor.

"What happened then?" asked Emile.

"He came to grief." The words came strangled in Fairinelle's throat.

"The Wends got him?" Emile leaned forward incredulously.

Fairinelle nodded. "Here, just outside Faubourg, the

very area in which we now find ourselves. If I am uneasy, this is the reason for it."

"Ah, don't worry. Last time, you didn't have the rest of us there to help." Emile tapped the barrel of his gun lightly, where it stood propped against the table.

Renn wondered how much of this story had actually happened. The last part, at least, was questionable. Fairinelle was making it sound like the man had died, but Renn knew better.

He had seen Jean-Marien himself. But if the first part was true, if this "Jayem" had really been Fairinelle's friend first, and Celine had taken advantage of him and turned him to her side, maybe Fairinelle had chosen to take revenge on both of them – on Jayem by hurting him, and on Celine by haunting her with it. Maybe there had been no Wends at all but only an angry Butcher.

He looked at Fairinelle's pensive face, the gloved hands crossed in front of his mouth, and the firelight from the great hearth that flickered across them. What was he hiding behind that look, those hands?

But then, if he really was hiding the truth, Renn supposed that was another thing he could learn from him. Not just battle and swordplay, but how to hide awful secrets about yourself, and make others love you in spite of them.

Yes, it really could be useful to have such a friend.

CHAPTER 25
The Least They Could Do

As Fairinelle had feared, when they next spent a night in the woods, the Wends did not fail to appear.

Renn still hoped wildly that he could save at least one of them this time, but neither would he make the mistake of leaving himself vulnerable again.

"Get out of here now," Renn hissed to the painted man whose dagger had nicked him on the forehead as they fought. He swung his own staff forward, blood from his cut slinging down in front of his eyes. "Go home and save yourself from getting killed."

But just like that woman from Renn's first battle, whose gutted body rotted somewhere in the distance and the past, the Wendish man didn't listen.

"Get those words out of your dirty mouth," he growled back, darting aside so that Renn's blade only grazed his ribs.

"I'm trying to help you."

"By trying to invade us? By taking – "

He didn't get to finish. Badeau Number Eight hit home, and the man crumpled to the ground.

It was Renn's second kill, but this time, he didn't run, and he didn't get sick. This time, it was his own blood running down his face. Trying to catch his breath, he brushed at the slippery skin below where the Wend had cut him. He thought he'd be ready this time, but while he didn't get sick, he still couldn't be indifferent to what he'd done. It still bothered him that again, he had tried to help this one, but again, the result had been the same. The man had still refused to listen, still attacked him, and still died. Renn had been forced once again to kill his own kind. But he'd kept himself safe – that was the important part. He looked at his hand, now as bloody as his face.

"The least they could do is die cleanly," Celine tutted, picking her way through the splashes of red on the ground. "Look at this, leaving filth everywhere. Wendish blood..." she hiked up her skirt to keep it from touching the wetness. "Ugh."

Renn wiped his hand on his sleeve.

CHAPTER 26
Left Standing

It had taken everything in him for Adrien not to turn and run from the sight. But what disturbed him more than the sight – red and horrific as it was – was the fact that it hadn't really been the Wends who had done this.

All of this had been caused by nothing more the selfishness of a girl who loved nothing so much as herself, a girl who had confidence enough to entice a lovestruck man into danger, but not enough to help him when he threw himself between her and the jaws of the giant Wendish dogs she had been certain would never come. A girl who had pride enough to enter the path of those dogs, but not enough pride to do anything but scream so loud and helplessly as Jean-Marien fought for his life and hers, that old Yves Decourt and his daughter had rushed into the woods wielding their farming tools as weapons, sure that someone was being murdered out there in the tangle of trees.

And someone was. Adrien had been afraid Celine would break Jayem's heart. She had broken much more than that.

When the other Prometheans finally found them, old man Decourt was still hacking at the corpse of an enormous dog heaped over the figure of man whose breathing was the too-shallow breathing of a baby bird, fallen and dying far from its nest. They couldn't tell who it was underneath the animal, for when they finally pried its stiff jaws from his face, he was so covered with blood, so torn and twisted, that he was unrecognizable. They searched his pockets for membership papers, but both the pockets and the papers were shredded to bits, and had Celine not finally regained her power of speech and identified him through the blood dripping down her own lips – where the dog had caught her before Jean-Marien leapt between them – they would only have realized it was him by the fact that he ceased to show up for his daily appointments in the many weeks that followed, for the bleeding figure they carried back to the medical wing of Promethio Lodge remained there, unconscious, for a month.

As soon as they had allowed him in, Adrien came to Jean-Marien's room, desperate for the fate of his gentle friend. That had been weeks ago, and still here he stood, still waiting for Jean-Marien to wake up.

His friend had been cleaned of the gore that had covered him. Adrien had winced to hear how when they first lifted him from the ground, he was so slick with it that they lost their grip and dropped him, but he was unsure that his being clean was much better, for it only served to expose the cracked and misshapen nose, the line of grinning teeth now visible through the holes in his cheeks. They said the skin that used to cover them had been found in the dead dog's jaws, while the splinters of what had once been Jean-Marien's leg bones had been scattered around the second dog. That dog had ensured that if he ever woke up at all, Jean-Marien would never again enjoy being alone on a hunt, looking out in solitude until "his back was stiff from waiting and his legs were asleep." He might never again speak words of cheer and comfort to a melancholy Pandora while the trees whispered softly overhead and the wind blew away the gloom of reminiscence.

For a person whose only other option was to go home and be the Butcher of Misère, to be looked up to and lauded for having committed bloody murder, it had been nice to have someone to take care of him instead. Someone who was quiet and gentle, and didn't ask questions, who made him feel as if he could still be a normal person, and not one fated to live as a marked killer for the rest of his life.

But all of that was gone now, and for what? So that some stupid novice could play at fame and grandeur? Fame and grandeur were only ever bought with blood and suffering, Adrien knew. He could have told her so, nut no, she had been determined to learn for herself. Determined to bring death and misery to this place, this Circle which was supposed to have been Adrien's refuge from all of that.

She was no better than the Wends had been on that day back when he was fifteen years old. Not caring who they hurt or killed so long as they could get something out of it.

And both times, thought Adrien bitterly, he had been the one left standing to absorb the shock. Then and now, he had stood over broken, dying bodies; for Jean-Marien was surely dying. Adrien couldn't even rally himself to hope for anything more. He had already hoped against this ever happening in the first place, and this had been the result. What was the use of hoping further?

And where was Celine, who had caused it all? Who ought to be here, facing up to what she had done? Who ought to be crying the way he was trying not to? Adrien had yet to see her anywhere near this room. The others said she was in shock, but who could afford shock when people were fighting for their lives?

Adrien began to stalk her door almost as much as he did Jean-Marien's, and the first time it cracked open and her pale face peered out, he had grabbed her by the arm and pulled her to Jean-Marien's room, muttering grimly all the while about choices and consequences.

"I can't do this right now," Celine whimpered as he pulled her along.

"That's exactly your problem," Adrien growled through his teeth. "You care a great deal about what you want, but you refuse to think about the consequences. You wanted to go out on your fool's errand, even if you had to get

someone else to pay the price for it. You wanted nothing to do with Jayem until you saw how you could use him to your advantage.

If you had gambled with your own life, it would have been one thing. But betting with someone else's – taking advantage of him because you knew you could – that's…" his voice wavered as he tossed a trembling hand in the direction of Jean-Marien's door, "— that's something I can't forgive. Now you get in there and take a good look at what you've done."

Head down, she crept past him into the room and softly closed the door behind her. Adrien almost wanted to follow her, to make sure she was suitably horrified by what she saw, but the only thing more revolting than the idea of her not repenting of what she had done was the thought of how disgustingly pathetic she would look actually doing it, because she would not be mourning Jean-Marien, but rather the fact that his tragedy had inconvenienced her, that it exposed her own sad lack of skill in spite of all her boasting.

Adrien waited there outside the door, determined to let her see when she emerged that he would always be watching to make sure she did not shirk her duty. It worked for a time, as Celine did make a few efforts own her own to go see him. But one day, she left and did not come back. After all her determination to earn the highest rank as fast as possible, she had disappeared without finishing.

Adrien later learned that she transferred somewhere else learned she had transferred to another Circle to complete her training. Somewhere we she could keep on with her foolish hunts without the reminders of the past to bother her.

He was angry that she would even be allowed to remain a Circlar at all. Why wasn't she dismissed from the program entirely? How could he stay and be part of a group that allowed such things to happen without punishment? He'd thought he'd found a place he could belong, but it seemed he been mistaken. And so, as soon as he had graduated to Pyrrha rank, he put on the splendid, richly red coat Georges, Marina, and poor Jayem had given him as a gift for the occasion, and walked with a bowed head and aching heart through the doors of Promethio Lodge, out through the gates of Faubourg. And while he did return from time to time, to visit the friends he had left behind in sorrow, it was fourteen years before he managed to bring Celine back with him.

CHAPTER 27
What He Did For You

On the way down to the ocean with Willow and Badger, Renn had been too sick to keep track of the days. On the way back, the days blurred together simply because there were so many of them, each of them filled with walking for miles and miles, getting closer to the black dot called Misère, and the borders of Cimbria beyond it.

There were still days when nothing happened, but there were more and more days when everything did, and Celine grew more drunk and less useful with each one. During the slow days, she was a bother, but during the hard ones, she was liability to them all. She, who was supposed to be the leader of this hunting party, barely even registered when the next Wends were sighted in the distance. She had been sitting between two gnarled tree roots when the alarm was raised, and while the others jumped to their feet, Celine didn't move.

As Renn gripped his lance, side-by-side with Emile priming his gun, Renn heard Fairinelle, who was supposed to be her winger, barking down at her.

"Is this how it was back then, too? Were you too stupid to stand up take care of yourself, and that's why he –"

"Don't you say that name to me!"

"You are completely right. I wouldn't want to throw it before swine."

"Can you hurry this up?" Rigobert called, cracking his knuckles anxiously. "We're going to need at least one of you."

Fairinelle knelt down, wrested a pistol out of its holster, and stuffed it into her hands, wrapping her limp fingers around the grip for her, though none too gently was it done . "Of all the times for you to discover timidity! If you'd learnt this five years ago we would've all been better off, but no, if it was all or nothing then, it's got to be all or nothing now. Tell me, did you ever even make it out of Pandora?"

Renn had no idea what Pandora meant, but he only hoped whatever charm Fairinelle had always had over her would hold, and she would stir herself to action.

She didn't.

Instead of getting angry, Celine only let the guns slide out of her grip, covered her face with her hands, and sank further down between the roots with moan.

The Wends were nearing the edge of the trees.

"Don't expect me to go down with you," Fairinelle spat at Celine, "You did that to Jayem, but you won't do it to me."

He yanked the pistol from her, then swung around with a look so dark and savage that Renn hardly recognized him as the gun blazed fire in his hand. He shot at the feet of the Wends as they burst through the clearing, scattering their formation long enough that Emile and Rigobert picked them off easily, before they even got within range of Renn's staff.

It was what Celine had tried to do on the day Renn had killed his first Wend. Break them up, make them easy targets, finish them off before they reached you. It was the same strategy, and Emile congratulated Fairinelle on the timing when everything was over, saying how it was just what the gunmen used to do in the army.

Fairinelle had obviously mastered the technique that Celine hadn't. She wasn't mastering much of anything, as she still sat, moaning on the ground. Renn wondered why Fairinelle, who was obviously better at it than she was, chose to serve as her winger, instead of the other way around.

But in the midst of all the praise, Fairinelle flung the pistol down in disgust, then turned and hauled Celine up by the arm.

"Celine Lauvin, stand up this instant. There will be more of them coming, mark my word, and I refuse to be caught out here with you again when they do. Get moving. We are going to reach Misère tonight, whether any of us likes it or not."

CHAPTER 28
Port Misery

For a city named Misery, it was the most pleasant place in Gaul that Renn had seen so far. It was Faubourg amplified, with cobbled streets that were wider and smoother, and flames in the streetlamps that were were brighter and cleaner. Dainty boats bobbed at the river docks, and stately houses sat behind rows of neat hedges. Every shop, every pristinely painted building boasted quiet courtyards fenced in by prim ivy-covered railings.

Past these many elegant yards trooped Renn and Emile, searching for a place to spar. They no longer trained on the outskirts of the towns, for neither of them dared after hearing the story of Jean-Marien, and anyway, with the cities in this part of the country being walled and guarded, it was a hassle to go in and out past the watchmen every time.

At last they came upon a wide space before a long building that bore in golden letters, the name: *LILLIANIC SCHOOL OF SWORDSMANSHIP*. There were a few boys and girls in its front courtyard, swinging blades around in wild arcs that left Renn questioning whether the Lillianic School of Swordsmanship was any better than a makeshift training regimen thought up by a self-taught harpooneer in the back yard of a weapons shop.

"Put them away," sighed a tall woman who emerged from the doorway under the golden letters. "Let me remind you that we do not slow down our practices to accommodate anyone who breaks their weapons or themselves."

"Yes, yes, we don't want you to hurt yourselves," repeated a shorter, plumper woman who followed after her.

While a few of the children dropped their blades and made
cursory moves to sheathe them, many seemed to pay little attention at all.

The tall woman sighed again, with the air of someone who knew she ought not to have expected any differently, while the shorter woman merely shook her head, though she seemed far less troubled by the children's lack of response.

"Maybe we'd better not practice in there," Renn said.

Emile nodded in agreement. "Let's get back and find Fairinelle, at least until this place clears out," he said just as the two women approached the gate where the newcomers still stood.

"Good luck, boys," the shorter woman said to them as she passed. "For all that we used to teach his son, it still takes us three weeks when we need to get an audience with the baron."

"I, um...I'm sorry. Who?" asked Renn.

"Baron Fairinelle, of course. The person you were just speaking of."

"Sorry, we don't know any Baron Fairinelle,"
explained Emile. "We're new to town, actually. Our Fairinelle is just a Mister. An officer."

"Mister Fairinelle..." the taller woman mused. "The only other was...Can you mean...Adrien Fairinelle?"

"A serious, quiet young man?" the short one supplied. "Though I suppose he's a full-grown man by now."

"Always stepping softly?" the other added. "But cold and fierce when something bothers him?"

Yes. That was the perfect description, Renn thought, and nodded.

"Then is he back home again?" The shorter woman was

quickly growing excited. She bounced on the balls of her feet. "How did you know he was back?"

"We came here with him. We've been travelling together up the river," said Emile.

"Are you…his sons? Oh, let me look at you," she took Emile's chin in her hand, turning his face to one side. "Yes, I think you look like him."

"Calm down, Charlotte," the other woman laughed gently. It was a nice laugh, and Renn liked the sound of it. "I think that one's a little old. This one *might* be the right age, but only barely." She looked down at Renn. "You're not his son, are you?"

"No," said Emile with a laugh of his own. "We work for him. We used to...ah, sail under him, and now we're helping him go after the bounty on Wends."

"So he's become a bounty hunter now!" said Charlotte. "Leave it to him to try to work for his money when he could've asked his father for it from the start."

"You know his father would have told him to do the same thing," said the tall woman. "He would never encourage his children to laziness."

"I suppose you're right," Charlotte agreed, almost automatically. "That must be why he's the baron and I'm not."

"Are you serious? Is Fairinelle really from a noble family?" asked Emile.

"You knew him when he was young?" asked Renn at the same time.

"We trained him since he was boy." said Charlotte proudly beaming. "Right here at this school. See, my sister's name is there on the front; Lillia" she pointed at the large gold letters that said LILLIANIC SCHOOL.

"His father is the baron and magistrate of Misère," said Lillia.

"What was he like before?" asked Renn. If these women had known him since his early days, they might know how he became the Child Knight, or the even the Butcher.

"Bless you, lads. You've come up all the way from the

sea with him and you didn't even know he was a baron's child?" Charlotte asked.

"He doesn't talk about himself too much."

"That's true, he never was one to brag. Not even when…"

"Even when?" Renn leaned forward, gripping the leafy railing between them. It leaves were smooth and cool under the heat of his hand.

Lillia looked up at a bird sailing through the clouds overhead.

"He killed two Wends, all by himself, when he was just about your age, with nothing more than a fencing rapier. He'd always been so quiet, but he just walked out from practice one day, and the next thing we knew, he was standing there in the middle of a bunch corpses, blood all over the place. They had come down from the border; they often did in those days."

"These days, too," Charlotte added. "I don't know why, but they seem to come in cycles. I don't know what we'd do if we didn't have a family like that protecting us, being so close to the border as we are. I always said something serious was going to happen with that boy, do you remember Lillia? I could see it."

"What did you see?" Renn asked, heart thumping, skin tingling with the breeze that blew in and rustled the ivy leaves. "Please, tell me."

CHAPTER 29
History of the Officer

"That will be all for today, young lord. You can go on and join the others outside."

"Yes, Mistress," said the tall boy, and if his hair had not been matted against his forehead, it would have fallen in his eyes as he made a stiff bow.

"Ten years my student," said Lillia, looking at lanky form as he walked away. "A young man now, and he's never yet failed to call me by my title."

"Oh, I wouldn't worry about it," said Charlotte. "You know how those types are. Their society breeds it into them."

"I'm not worried about it. It does him credit, for I don't know that society does breed it into them. Some of the other children have quite grown into their pride, with less claim to it than he has. I believe it's bred into that one, but that's the baron's doing, not society's."

"You don't think he's too strict? I wish he would allow his boy to have a little fun."

"I'm not sure you can afford fun when you're training to be a lord and a magistrate."

"I worry about him, though. It can't be healthy for his spirit never to enjoy himself, to balance out all the responsibility he'll have to carry. People can break under that kind of pressure.

"I would rather a boy be too serious, than treat everything like his own personal playground like some of these others do." Lillia clucked her tongue as she leaned

to pick up a glove someone had discarded on the ground. In the corner of the room was a face mask that had clearly been thrown and rolled, its user not having

bothered to stow it properly. "Look at this. They must think I'm their maidservant, just here to clean up after their revels."

"But at least they have fun," Charlotte held up the mate to Lillia's glove, having found it on the other side of the room.

"How much fun will they have coming to class with no rapiers because they broke them horsing around after-hours? Or if they don't come at all because they stabbed each other with them?" Lillia asked, glancing through the window to the square outside, where many of the young Fairinelle's classmates lingered, parrying and thrusting at each other with the instruments they had been told to use only in training.

Charlotte didn't answer, for a noise was coming from outside, the sound racing up from the forest path at the edge of town in peal upon ever-shriller peal. The shrieks and cries, like the sound of a hunted animal, filled the air as the women ran outside, Lillia easily reaching the flock of students outside, Charlotte trailing behind, still holding the glove.

The boys and girls were not playing now. They had stopped and pricked their ears up to the sound, staring as a boy in tatters came flying up the road and out of the trees that led to the Fairinelle estate, barely seeming to draw breath for the endless screams that flew from his mouth.

Charlotte grabbed the child as he sped forward. "What's wrong, child?"

"They're trying to kill us!" he panted.

"Who?"

The child fought against Charlotte's hold. "They -- the tall boy's got a sword!"

Charlotte looked at her sister. People can break under that kind of pressure, *she had said. "Would he really...?"*

"Elisabeth, give me your rapier," Lillia demanded of the student nearest her, snatched it from his offered hand, and took off running down the path through the trees that led to the estate of the Fairinelles.

"Everyone called him a hero. It was more than even I knew he was capable of. He got his tattoos but he never said a word about it afterwards, and he left home not long after that," Lillia said. "All he would say was that couldn't stand to stay here anymore. I suppose the adventurer's life was more exciting for someone with a skill like his."

"But now he's back to protect us again! Always dependable, Adrien was," said Charlotte. Then she laughed. "How funny, that we need our own student to protect us, when we were the ones who taught him how to do it in the first place."

"We didn't teach him everything. Much of that came on his own. I've always said so."

"It's true, you have."

They were like some comical alternate version of Willow and Badger. One always played off the other, only this time it was to agree with everything, rather than argue about it.

Renn would never get the story out of them at this rate.

"What sort of things came on his own?" he prodded. "Can you tell me more about how he fought the Wends?"

"Aiming to be like him, are you?" Charlotte smiled.

"I can't tell you much more," Lillia answered, more to the point. "That's all we knew about it. He just went out one day and saved the town – the Wends were all dead by the time we got there – and then he went out and left us. Beyond that, you probably know more about him at this point than we do."

Renn looked down. What was it that he really knew? He knew that Adrien Fairinelle was the type of man to work on a slaver ship, to kill warriors single-handed, to turn imperious bounty hunters into cowardly drunkards.

But he also knew that Adrien Fairinelle was kind and generous, a reassuring presence in times of trouble, a steady hand trying to hold their little group together.

What he didn't know how he could be both at the same time, or whether only one side was the *real* Adrien Fairinelle.

But then, nobody knew the *real* Rennesson LeNotre either.

CHAPTER 30
Smile

"Here's something to help us on our way," Emile stooped to pick up a coin in the doorway of the inn, and handed it to Renn with a pleased expression. If he had been at all disturbed by the two sisters' story, he didn't show it.

"Smile, Renn! It's good luck to find one of these."

"Was I not?" Renn asked, rousing himself. He'd been too busy mulling over the tale of the young killer Fairinelle to notice what he'd looked like.

Emile laughed and tapped Renn's arm with the back of his hand. "Are you ever?"

This didn't make Renn feel much more like smiling.

"Alright, what's eating you this time?" Emile asked as they found an empty table.

"I was just thinking, do you suppose I'll ever be as good as Fairinelle, at fighting, I mean?" This sounded a passable enough cxcuse.

"Don't worry, you're doing just fine," said Emile. "I wouldn't get fussed about all that fancy stuff they teach them in places like that school. You and I, we're surviving, aren't we? We've made it this far, and that's what matters."

"But you were trained in the army. Of course *you're* going to make it."

"Eh, that's true. Didn't do me much good when they took my gun and shipped me off to prison, though. Had to learn to survive on my own there, just like you." He picked up the coin Renn had set on the table and began spinning it on its side.

Renn tried to imagine Emile fighting his way through the harsh conditions on the St. Juste, learning how to handle people like Xavier, who would kill someone over the slightest complaint. And yet, even after all that, Emile hadn't hesitated to befriend Renn at the first opportunity.

"Weren't you afraid I'd be unfriendly as the rest of them, when you met me?"

"Huh," Emile rubbed his cheek absently. "Now that you mention it, I guess it didn't occur to me. You just sort of struck me as the trustworthy type."

"It didn't occur to you?" Renn repeated incredulously. What sort of person just forgot to be consumed by their secrets? What went on in the head of someone who wasn't always worrying about the consequences of the truth?

"Anyway, I'd figured out my way around a harpoon by that time, so I suppose I could've killed you if you'd really tried anything."

Yes, it definitely looked like Renn would have to keep doing all the worrying for the both of them.

"That's a joke, Renn. Smile, remember?" Emile tapped him again.

"I don't wonder he doesn't care for your jokes. They're irritating."

That was Celine. For what reason she had slunk from her isolated corner of the room to them, Renn could not guess, other than that her brain was too addled to remember that she disliked them both.

"Go away, Celine," he said. The scent of alcohol hung about her, and the longer she stood near him, the more it singed Renn's lungs and frayed his patience.

"Listen to the boy, telling *me* what to do. Who do you think bought you off that boat, child?"

"If you don't stop this, I'll – "

"You'll what?"

Renn clenched his fist. Unless he was planning on attacking her with his lance the way Emile had joked, what could he really do to stop her? But there *was* one who could force her to behave.

"I'll – I'll have Fairinelle send you home!" he burst out at last. It was the best he could think of. He certainly wasn't going to say he would have Fairinelle kill her.

"Ha, what home? Faubourg?"

"At least you have a home to go to. What happened is never going to be less awful than it is, and no amount of staying away is going to change that. But it's there for you when you want it, which is more than some people can say."

"And why shouldn't you have a home to go to? Isn't that just where we're headed? Your home on the borderlands?"

"I…" Renn cast around for some answer. He hadn't intended for her to discern so clearly that he'd been talking about himself. His eyes fell on Emile, and he remembered how they'd talked of the St. Juste.

"They wouldn't want to see me at home, not after I got packed off to prison," he finished.

"And just what was *your* crime?"

"Unless you're willing to share whatever's causing your troubles, maybe you shouldn't ask too much about his," Emile cut in, thumping his palm down on the coin he'd been spinning so carelessly.

"Trouble!" Celine barked out a too-shrill laugh. "Is that what you call it when you've ruined someone's life and they refuse to hate you for it? At least this boy has the relief of not having to go back and face whatever it was he did."

"If it's hate you want, there's no lack of that. Trust me." Fairinelle materialized next to them, his cold voice preceding him.

"If you hate me so much, why don't you leave? Go wherever it is perfect people go. I'm sure you'll never run into me there," Celine said, but she backed away from him all the same.

"I wish I could," he sounded almost wistful, and he sent

one glance to the ceiling before his face and expression hardened again. "But I have other obligations, too — one of them being to look after your pathetic self, because I refuse to have to bring Jayem your death certificate. Now leave these two alone." He pulled her away from them, and she stumbled behind in his iron grip.

Renn watched them go, and just as suddenly as he had wished Celine away, he now found he wanted to follow them. Not because he wanted to be near Celine any more than before, but because, in the span of a few sentences, what he thought he knew about Jayem had been turned on its head. If Fairinelle didn't mind maiming the man who had once been his friend, why would he care if Celine died, or if Jayem knew of it? And how could he ask either of them any of this?

Emile had suggested that Celine not go poking into others' business unless she were willing to share her own. It was a good suggestion, and maybe someday Renn would learn to heed it, but today would not be that day, so he put his arms up on the table and flopped his head down on top of them.

"You alright?" Emile asked. "I remembered how you didn't like to talk about what happened before you came to the St. Juste."

Here, at least, was one friend he didn't have to worry about – who had never hidden anything at all from him.

"Sure, I'm fine," said Renn, as Rigobert slid up to the table next to them, on Emile's left.

"So, I've been trying to figure out what the issue with her is," Rigobert said matter-of-factly, sliding a mug towards each of them, though neither touched them.

"There's something more here than simple addiction to the bottle. I've known her for three years, and while she wouldn't say no to a drink, she was never this bad."

Rigobert leaned forward, lowering his voice a fraction. "Have either of you gotten anything? I think Fairinelle knows, but he's not telling, and I don't dare press a Butcher about his business."

It was eerie to hear him speak so plainly the words that had been spiralling silently in Renn's mind for months. But Emile only went back to spinning the coin.

"Nope, haven't heard a thing. If people don't want their business known, maybe it's for a reason."

"And what if that reason were dangerous to yourself? Wouldn't you want to know then?"

"I can take care of myself when things get tough."

"Well then, what about you, Renn?"

"He can take care of himself, too, and if he can't, then I'll take care of the both of us," Emile said stubbornly.

His eyes didn't leave the coin but his jaw stuck out. What a difference from the Emile who hadn't even thought to worry about the safety of his own secrets just minutes before.

"If you say so," Rigobert responded.

"Listen, I'm a sharpshooter. That means I know how to take danger out of other people's paths before they can even see it themselves. We'll be fine."

"Maybe so, but I don't think I'll be sticking around. We've been moving so slowly, somebody else will snatch up all the bounties before we ever get to the border."

"Go on, then, and leave us alone," said Emile under his breath. Then, more brightly, to Rigobert he said "You might be on to a plan there."

"I always am," said Rigobert, standing up. "See you on the other side."

When the noise had finally died in the tavern had died down, and Renn and Emile had retreated to their room, Renn called across to the other cot in the dimness, hoping Emile wasn't asleep.

"Thanks for taking care of things back there. For getting Celine to leave me alone."

"Anytime," Emile's voice came through the dark. "Everybody gets on edge when they get close to border; it was the same way in the army. You just have to ignore half of what people say, and tell 'em to get lost for the rest."

A thought occurred to Renn then. If all it took was the confidence to tell Celine to get lost, why couldn't they use that same confidence to get lost themselves? Now could be the perfect time to slip out on her, like Renn had imagined he'd do way back at the start of this journey. With Celine out of her head half the time, she wouldn't notice until it was too late.

"With Celine like this," he spoke again, hesitantly, though his heartbeat quickened at the mere mention of it. "Do you think we could…"

"Run off, you mean?" Emile anticipated him.

"Right. Couldn't we just, you know, disappear one of these nights? We could be long gone before she realized anything."

"Hmm, " Emile pondered for a moment. "No good. Celine might not notice, but Fairinelle would, and I've no doubt he'd come to get us. You know he's a stickler for doing things by the book, and, well, we've seen what happens to people who get on his bad side."

Of course. Fairinelle.

Witnessing his anger secondhand, during those terrible clashes with Celine, was frightening enough. How awful would it to be the actual target of that anger? It was enough to drive a person to tears and drunkenness every night to forget it. That was how Celine had gotten to where she was in the first place.

Emile was right. They might have been friends with Fairinelle now, but the man was still an officer and Butcher, and they couldn't afford to take the chance.

"Besides, even if he did let us go," Emile went on, "who's to say someone else wouldn't find out where we came from and throw us right back onto the St. Juste? There'd be no getting off a second time after trying something like that. At least this way we get some freedom, and it's all in the clear because it's sanctioned under Fairinelle. He's the one who gave us special permission to be off the boat, remember? He said that Celine buying us wasn't legal, but he'd let us do it as a work program. So I think it's better to stick with him and try to ride it out, at least for now."

"But what happens when the bounty is done and he tries to take us back to the St. Juste afterwards?"

"We'll have to think on that one a bit. I don't want to go back any more than you do, but right now I can't figure how to get around it. Fairinelle's the one who could take us back, but he's also the one helping us the most at the moment."

"By the way," Emile added, "assuming we figure out some way for him to let us off, where *do* you want to go after this? Can you really not go back home?"

"I don't know."

"Alright, then. If you can't go home, do you want to come with me?"

"Sounds…" Renn tried to make himself say something, but he found a tightness had gripped in his throat and silenced his voice. And even if it hadn't, what could he say? He wanted so much to say yes, to say it as easily as it had been asked, but he could never go with Emile, and he could never tell him why.

If they stayed together, Emile was bound to find out the truth, and Renn couldn't bear to think what the reaction of the former soldier would be to that. He would rather remember their friendship as it was, even if that meant leaving it behind, than risk breaking it for certain. They were going to have to part ways in either case, and Renn would prefer it not be because Emile hated him.

"Sounds great," he managed at last. What could it hurt to pretend they could go on together as they'd always been? The end would come soon enough, so why not let Emile – and himself – have this comfortable deception now?

"It's a deal, then." Emile's voice was bright in the darkness.

"Deal," said Renn, smiling through the salt in his eyes as he spoke this false promise to his real friend.

CHAPTER 31
Eagle's Eye

"If I remember rightly, there's a little wayhouse hereabouts," Emile squinted through the trees, raising his hand to block the sunlight glinting off the river water to their left. "Shouldn't be too far ahead."

Renn wondered how or why any Gaul would choose to build a business so close to the border. Misère, already considered by most to be closer to the border than they cared to go, was three days behind them.

Aren't the people here afraid of roving bands of Wends attacking? Renn asked himself. But perhaps the people of the border were braver, less fearful than those further inland. After all, his father had come from the borderlands and he'd had no fear of crossing the river to meet Renn's mother. And Renn, as far as any of the others knew, had come from this land as well. He had pretended to be tough and uncaring when he'd lied to Celine on the St. Juste, hadn't he? Maybe that attitude came from his father, too.

He wondered if his father had ever visited this waystation Emile spoke of, or how he'd felt about the ongoing battles. Had the battles even been going on back then? It wasn't something he'd ever talked about with his father, and he couldn't ask anyone now, for fear of his giving himself away. How could a native not know the history of their own country?

Emile certainly knew his, though, for as they made their way up the river, he stopped and surveyed the remnants of burned bridges that clung to the banks at intervals, charred and broken.

"I remember these," said Emile. "Remember building them, and burning them, too. Back when we thought the treaty was going through, these were supposed to make it easier to cross between the two sides, but when it fell apart, we had to burn down everything we'd just built."

"Didn't it make you feel bad, to have to tear down what you worked so hard for?" Renn asked.

"Sure, but what else could we have done? We couldn't leave an open path for the enemy to come charging through to us."

Perhaps there really was nothing to be done. Perhaps bridges really did have to be burned. Renn was going to have to burn his own soon.

"The administration ought to have thought of that before they had you build them," said Fairinelle. "It would have saved time, money, and effort."

"Can't fault 'em for being optimistic, though" shrugged Emile. "It's a hard life thinking the worst all the time."

"It's better than not thinking at all," said Fairinelle with a look at Celine, which she either did not see or chose not to acknowledge. "Refusing to think of what would happen should plans fall apart is worse."

"I'm not arguing that, but what I mean is, even if things might go bad, you've got to keep your hope up until they do. We all wanted the treaty to go back then, and things would've been better for us all if it had. For one thing, I wouldn't have been packed off the St. Juste," he went quiet for moment.

"But I suppose if I hadn't gone there, I wouldn't have met any of you fine folks, either." He brightened again, ruffling Renn's hair. "We hoped until the moment it fell apart, and then, when the worst came true, there was still something good to be found in it afterwards, see?"

"Not exactly," said Fairinelle.

"Ugh," said Celine.

"Yes, something good even came from meeting you,

Celine," said Emile in response. "Us hired hands wouldn't have gotten out here in this fine open air, and seen these fine burned-up bridges without your generous patronage," he said, putting an arm around Renn's shoulder.

Renn smiled, for they all knew Fairinelle, not Celine, paid for most of their expenses.

"Come along on the 'Celine Lauvin Hiking Program for Health and Good Spirits!'" Emile went on, projecting his voice like he were selling goods at a market. "Hiking is good for your health, so why not do it until your legs fall off? Want to see the stars? Double watches every night gives you double the time to appreciate them!"

Celine rolled her eyes. "Stop," she said, but Emile ignored her.

"If you want to become a fighter, she'll let you do your part *and* hers in battle, the faster to improve."

"Good spirits of both the tangible *and* intangible variety, of course," Fairinelle offered, his mouth pulling upwards at one corner, though he kept his arms crossed.

Renn couldn't quite follow that one. He didn't know what half of the words meant, but Emile's face lit up to hear Fairinelle join in the joke.

"Ha, of course. That's how she keeps you coming back – the first kind of spirit makes you sick and low, so you need the other kind to shake off its effects. That's what you call a supply chain."

Celine's jaw clenched.

"Perhaps she's cleverer than we gave her credit for, if only a little," said Fairinelle.

"Nah, if she were, she'd know the person running the scheme isn't supposed to fall for it herself."

Celine had had enough. She sprang towards Emile, her hands out like claws, but he stepped back from her, and she fell into the river mud with a splashing thud, going face down with her tangled hair thrown out in front of her. There was a moment of silence, as the others peered down at her, before all three burst out laughing.

Fairinelle held his hand before his mouth, but it did

nothing to stem the waves of great, warm laughter such as hadn't been heard since that day when they'd looked at great map on the wall at Murat, while Emile fought for breath against the chiming giggles that rang out constant succession.

Renn's stomach ached by the time Celine sat up, fiercely and quickly, but the twigs and dead leaves dangling from her hair, now stiff with mud, undermined the anger of her expression, and only made her look the more ridiculous. Her hair looked more like a bird's nest than ever.

"You're filthy," Emile managed through bursts of laughter.

Celine rolled her eyes again, two white spots in the midst of the dirt on her face. "If you want to see filth, look at your beloved bridge back there; it's covered with it." She climbed to her feet, a viscous squishing following her all the way, and tried to stalk off, but her skirts, like everything else, were soaked in mud, and clung to her knees, making it hard for her to stalk very fiercely.

"You'd better go after her," Emile said to Fairinelle. "Make sure she doesn't try and drown herself from shame."

"If that's her goal, I might stay here," Fairinelle answered, breathless and grinning. But he loped after her just the same.

"Never seen him smile so much before," Renn said, wiping his eyes, as he knelt by the remains of the bridge.

"What do you see there, Renn? Any idea what Celine was on about? It can't look any worse off than *she* did, can it?" asked Emile, coming alongside to inspect it. After a bit of inspection, he pointed to a set of carved markings in the soft, rotting wood. "Maybe she meant this."

"What's wrong with it?" asked Renn, still giddy with laughter. "All it says is 'keep out.'"

"Does it?" Emile scratched his head. "Guess I couldn't make it out with the wood all warped like that."

"Maybe you need glasses, Mr. Eagle Eye," teased

Renn, still smiling as he climbed to his feet again. "Didn't all this outdoors stuff improve your eyesight along with your health?"

"Maybe," Emile repeated, staring back at the post as he climbed up after Renn. "But this is…"

"Come on, don't dwell on the past, right? You said it yourself," Renn tried to remind him. "You didn't want to burn down your hard work, but don't worry about what you had to do back then. It wasn't your fault."

"Yeah," said Emile slowly.

It was only a few more minutes' walk to the tiny settlement of Plainte, and the lone, lonely tavern Emile had remembered, but he remained pensive through all of them, and the mood inside the tavern didn't help him.

No loud voices rang, no glasses clinked, and no music played here on the border, where few dared or wished to come even for a bounty. The only sound was the quiet treading of the owner in the back, so quiet, as if he were apologizing for daring to run a business this close to the tainted lands of the Wends.

Emile sat next to Renn, not speaking, elbows on the table and fingers steepled in front of his mouth, staring over his fingertips off into the distance. Renn had never seen him this silent in all the time he'd known him. Annoyed, yes, and even angry, but this stillness was something new.

There had to have been some memory, perhaps some battle, some comrade lost, that had been dredged up by the site of the bridge.

"Hey, whatever happened at the bridge, it does no good carrying it around with you, right? What's important is moving forward. Isn't that what you always say?" Renn tried encouraging him.

It was a first – that Renn was the one smiling where Emile was not – but it felt good, here at last, to be able to return the favor his friend had so often given him, at least once before he had to go away.

"Sure," said Emile, but his smile was only half-formed.

"Hey, Renn, can I ask you something?"

For the first time since Renn had known him, Emile seemed to have trouble choosing his words. Something that looked like puzzlement – or rather, more like concern – was settling into his face. He reached out to run his hands up and down the length of the rifle leaning against the table, as if trying to draw strength from it, then took a breath, raised unhappy eyes, and asked:

"How do you know how to read Wendish?"

The words froze Renn's blood as no battle had yet done.

"What?" was all he managed, though he'd heard the question perfectly.

"That writing on the bridge – that wasn't any Gallic word I know."

Had Renn really come all this way, fighting through bands of Wends who should have been his friends, while hiding himself in the midst of Gauls who should have been his enemies, just to give himself away within miles of home? He'd been too distracted by laughing at Celine to realize what he was really seeing on that bridge. He hadn't even noticed it was Wendish writing, and not Gallic. This was the cost of letting himself get too close. Sharing in all that laughter, letting himself become friends, it had led to this.

Emile was running his hands along the gun again. Renn had to say something, and quickly.

"I come from around here, by, um, Ligny..." attempted after a few hard swallows, but that old excuse now sounded hopelessly tired even to him. "I've been into Cimbria lots of times. That's the whole reason Celine brought me along—to serve as her guide once we got here. When you go into their lands, you can't help seeing how they mark things up with their ugly words all the time." He tried to emulate Celine's disgust at seeing the carving, though he didn't feel at all successful.

Emile didn't look convinced. "That's not like you, to say such a thing," he said softly.

Renn fought down the rising panic. What had happened

to that boy who "might have killed a man", who'd swaggered and lied and fooled Celine into thinking he hated those dirty Cimbrian animals who were only fit to lick a man's boots?

"You know some of their words yourself, don't you?" he said. "You saw the warpaint on those Wends way back at our first battle. You said you'd recognize them anywhere." He heard a note of pleading come into his own voice, but forced it back. It would give him away more than anything else had so far. He hadn't survived this long by begging.

"Of course I learned 'em when I saw them up close – I was in the army," Emile said, sounding half-desperate himself. "But unless there's something else you're not telling me, you never were."

"That doesn't mean I never saw them up close, either," Renn shot back, trying his hardest to inject a defiance he didn't feel into the words. At least this part was true. He had seen Wends up close. Plenty of them.

"If you had, I don't know how you would've survived, because whatever it was that got you on the St. Juste, it couldn't have been for fighting. You were shyer than a baby mouse when you got there."

"Who wouldn't be?" countered Renn. "That place was awful. We've talked about that lots of times together, haven't we?"

Emile threw his hands up. "But you didn't even know how to use any weapons, Renn! Nobody who goes into Cimbria does it without knowing how to survive there."

"I told you, I used spears for boar hunting before. I knew how to use those."

"The Wends themselves use spears for boar hunting! That doesn't mean anything. I had to teach you how to use one to fight people."

"You want to know how I got onto the St. Juste? I've already told you I was kidnapped and sold to Buron. I didn't have to earn my way on, unlike you."

Emile's eyes snapped up, hurt swimming in them.

Renn wanted to say that he hadn't meant to be so harsh, but the problem was, he had. He needed to be imperious and cruel. The only other choice was being found out. If he let Emile ask everything he wanted, the truth would come to the surface, and everything would be over.

This was the start of it, then. The separation.

This was the where he began to leave behind his companions. It was the moment he'd been waiting for all these months, the one he'd envisioned over and over. Only he never used to envision it being so painful.

"Renn…" Emile said, and his was tone distant. "You're not really...you're not a Gaul, are you?"

"I am!" Renn cried, but the vehemence was wasted. Emile didn't seem to hear him.

"Your accent…" he said.

"I know it's a little different, but I can't help that. You never minded it before now."

"You're always asking Fairinelle to explain himself, 'cause he uses those kind of fancy words sometimes."

"How should I know how to speak like a nobleman?"

Emile looked at his hands. "I even had to teach you how to do the Cotton Reel. I thought everybody knew that dance."

His face was working into a new expression. A rueful smile touched his mouth now, and he shook his head, closing his eyes.

"Blast me if I don't have a soft spot for Wendish kids or something." He leaned back in his chair, scrubbing his hands over his face and groaning.

"I don't know what you're talking about," Renn tried wildly, his heart beating faster than ever.

Emile didn't sit up. "There's a lot you don't know," he said, muffled through his hands.

Renn wanted to yell that he didn't care. Anything to get Emile to stop talking, stop thinking of him as Wend.

"Being a Wend was really why you were sold off to Buron, wasn't it?"

"I am not a Wend!" Renn's had to fight to keep his voice down. It was bad enough having one person know the truth. He didn't need the whole room knowing. "Listen, if you can't get it through your thick head that it isn't true, then you're stupider than I thought, but don't you dare go taking those stupid ideas to the others."

"Why would I do that?" Emile asked. He did sit up then, his hands dropping away from his face. "It's my job to look out for you."

"I don't know what –" Renn started again, but Emile's fist banging on the knotted wood between them shocked him into silence.

"If you would listen to me for one blessed minute!" Emile cried with a look that many a Wend must have seen at the long end of a rifle.

Renn shrank into his chair. Had the moment finally come? Was now when he would have to start running?

"Didn't you ever wonder why my captain got so riled up that he took away my medal and shipped me off to Buron just for disobeying orders one time? When the most he ought to have done was flogged me, maybe? The thing I went against him on was when he told me to shoot a little Wendish girl. They said it was treason – that I betrayed my country."

"Treason…" Renn echoed, stunned. It was the first time he'd heard that Gallic word. He didn't have to ask what it meant. He remembered a sunny day on thc deck of the St. Juste, when Xavier had spat salt and blood and declared that he'd throw Renn overboard, and Emile along with him.

"*Like I care what that Wend-lover says. I'll throw him overboard, too.*"

All this time, Renn had been in company with a Wend-lover, and not known it. Xavier had known the truth back then, but it hadn't been the truth about Renn.

"A kid that young couldn't have known there was a war on, much less the difference between the two sides," Emile explained. "Punishing her, letting her die just because of what happened to be in her blood was taking it a bit too far, if you ask me."

"*Had to learn how to defend myself pretty quick on the St. Juste ...well, you remember what it was like. The boys got sort of riled up sometimes,*" Renn remembered him saying in the weapon shop by the sea.

It wasn't just the everyday violence of criminals and slaves that Emile had faced. He'd fought his way through the same prejudice and hate surrounding than Wends than Renn himself had always been afraid of, though at least Renn had been lucky enough that Buron hadn't believed Willow's story about Cimbria. But Emile couldn't have hidden the truth of why he'd been sent to the boat. He'd been an official transfer, not one of Buron's secrets, and it was just like Buron to tell everyone the reason, whether Emile wanted it shared or not.

"What do I care?" Emile was ranting on. "What do I care where someone's from? It's only when a person's trying to hurt someone else that I've got a problem with them," he looked down with defiant, shining eyes, and slapped his hand on the table again. "And if someone tries to hurt you because of this, I'll kill them myself, even if they send me back to the St. Juste for it."

All power of speech, Gallic or otherwise, had left Renn's tongue. His mouth opened and closed, but the tears sliding down his face took his voice with them. The quaking dread that he had felt every second since crossing the border – Emile had actually lived through all of it. But where that fear and worry had hollowed Renn out, carving away at his spirit like water on stone, Emile had felt it all, too.

But instead of filling those carved spaces with fear and loneliness, Emile had filled them with love. He could have kept to himself back on the St. Juste, kept his head down and let Renn struggle alone, and he had every right to let Renn find his own way now. But he, who had known what it was to be hated, had offered himself as friend and protector from the very beginning. Renn had been silent and secretive for fear of being found out. Emile had been caring and tender in spite of the same. He hadn't been worn away by his sorrows. He'd been refined by them.

Renn threw himself forward, wrapping his arms around this strange friend who worried for himself not at all yet feared for others to the point of murder. This lonely friend who had done everything to make Renn feel wanted, but had been alone himself as he'd done it. This brave friend who smiled though everything though nobody smiled back, and more than anything, this true friend who knew what Renn was, and did all of this anyway.

"There now," Emile said, and his voice, so strong and bold just moments before, was soft and kind again as he patted Renn's back.

"Do you really not mind what I am?" Renn managed to ask, his voice muffled in Emile's shirt, when his voice finally returned through his tears.

"Well, you've got arms and legs the same as other people, don't you? Never mind the stuff they're made of. A house is a house whether it's built of wood or brick, and you've just been built of bricks instead of wood, is all. What matters is the person living inside the house, is how I see it."

"Half-brick, maybe. My mother was a Wend, but my father really was a Gaul."

"There you go, then," Emile smiled down at him. "I was wondering how a Wend comes to speak Gallic as well as you do. Why don't you tell me all about it?"

"Yes, please. Enlighten us."

Emile's hand tightened into a fist on Renn's back. With sinking heart and a growing dread, Renn looked over his shoulder to see the blazing, betrayed eyes of Celine.

"If a Wend is even *capable* of telling the truth," she finished with a snarl, her lip curled and her chin lowered.

"Ah, you're out of your head again." Emile tried to bluff. He picked up his rifle and pushed Renn towards the door, carefully keeping himself between him and Celine. "Come on, Renn, we've got to practice."

But Celine wouldn't be dismissed so easily. "I'm always out of my head," she said, close on their heels. "But somehow my body's still here, and I'm still able to hear things. You've let this mutt convince you to keep him!"

"And why shouldn't we keep him?" Renn could hear the tension in Emile's voice.

"He's a Wend, isn't he?" Her words shot like an arrow. "That means he's as guilty as the rest of them – a liar and traitor at the very least." She laid a hand on Emile's elbow, as if to pull him away from Renn, but he wheeled on her, throwing her back.

"If you call that lying, then we've each of us been lying since the first moment we met!" he burst out, all hope of deception gone. "*You* didn't tell us you were planning on letting us do all the work while you drank your life away. And as for 'traitor,' when did Renn ever betray us? He's fought alongside us every step 'til now, unlike some who sat around crying on a tree stump in the thick of it all."

"He's been using us as a free ticket home," Celine countered. "He'll turn right back around on us as soon as it's convenient. You know he might."

"Any of us *might* do anything! *I* was known for sniping Wends at hundreds of yards, and then I turned around and saved an innocent Wendish kid from being murdered. Are you going to call me a traitor, too? Me, who got distinguished service in the army, which is a good sight more than you've ever done? Are you going to be like the rest of them who forgot it all the minute *that* was convenient and sent me to prison to fit their own prejudices, and didn't bother to count all the good I'd done for them in the rest of my life?"

Renn was struck by how freely Emile had told his secret for the second time. He'd been guarding it even longer than Renn had been guarding his own, but he had willingly offered it up to protect him. The truth was out now, and the consequences were in motion. Renn's worst fears had come true...and he couldn't have been happier.

The river of fear and worry that had been wearing away

at his heart had suddenly ceased, leaving only a great, wide, airy space within him. He looked up at Emile's back, and how the light from the lamps shone on the shoulders that stood between him and Celine.

"If you had any nerve," Emile went on, his brow knitted and his voice impassioned. "You'd look at what Renn's done in *his* life. But I guess Fairinelle's right –you always take the easy way out. You'd rather drink away your guilt over that person you hurt instead of facing it, and you'd rather convict Renn for *what* he is than face up to *who* he is, and that's a blasted decent fellow who's done more to keep you alive than you've done for yourself."

"Oh yes, I suppose you'll be thanking him when he runs across the river and brings his Wendish beasts down on us?"

"I wouldn't!" cried Renn. "I was going to tell them to stop crossing into Gaul. I was planning on helping you, if you wanted to know!" he leaned out from behind Emile to frown at her. He had moved so quickly from relief to anger that he was surprised to hear the tone coming from his own mouth. Who was she to doubt him, after all this time? He never *had* meant to hurt them, only escape from them, even at the beginning.

"Now's not the time, Renn," Emile said under his breath, but it was too late.

Celine's cheeks flushed red to match the angry heat in Renn's own, then her hand flashed, and she was aiming both her pistols at him. "I believe you'd tell them *something* in that devil tongue, but it would be nothing to help me."

Emile's rifle was in his hands the same instant.

Gunfire flashed between them, and scattered shouts came from within the tavern, followed by Fairinelle's roaring voice, commanding whoever was inside to stay there, before he burst through the door, taking in the scene with his wide blue eyes, then storming to where Celine reeled, but still stood, glaring.

"Run," Emile urged, shoving Renn before him towards

the trees beyond the clearing. They dodged through trees and over gnarled roots, Renn's legs and lungs burning, but Emile kept pushing him onward. Behind them, they heard two pairs of boots, and Celine's wild shrieking, crashing through the underbrush behind them.

When the constant pressure of Emile's hand dropped from Renn's back, he turned, and caught his already-short breath at how pale and ragged Emile looked. His hair was matted to his forehead, and a stain of blood ran from his shoulder to the hemline of his
shirt. Finger-streaks of it covered the muzzle of his gun, his face, and neck, stark against the pale, glistening skin.

"You're a better shot than her!" Renn cried in dismay. "Why didn't you shoot her first?"

"She's always been all talk. Didn't think she'd actually do it," Emile panted as slowed to stop, squeezed his eyes shut and leaned back on a tree.

"Go on, I'll catch up," he huffed. "You know the way from here, don't you?"

Yes, Renn did know the way now. But how could Emile find it on his own? On one side was Celine and Fairinelle, on the other was the wild and the Wends, and Emile looked too weak to face either of them.

Renn told him so, but he only opened his eyes and said, much more slowly than before. "Come here. You've got dirt on your face."

Did he not notice the blood on his own?

He reached out and wiped Renn's cheek with a bloody thumb. "Make a clean break of it, yeah? Don't take any of this old dirt with you when you go home. Can't imagine you'd want to, anyway," he said, and for the first time since Renn had known him, he failed at trying to smile.

"Of course I want to!" insisted Renn, and he hoped Emile understood. He hoped Emile knew he would carry the memories of this gentle soldier for the rest of his life. He would have died a long time ago, if not from danger, than certainly from loneliness and heartache without this kind sharpshooter guarding him from both, never once leaving him alone no matter how ungrateful Renn had been for it.

How, then, could he leave Emile to die alone now?

No, Renn realized. Here at the last, he wouldn't run. He would face Celine and Fairinelle alongside this dying Gaul, his friend, even if meant dying within sight of the home he'd fought so hard to reach.

Emile was kneeling now, no longer able to stand. Renn cast a last, desperate look north towards his home, and knelt too. Soft, cool mud covered his knees and the leaves crackled beneath him. He'd once wondered if these leaves would keep the memory of him when he was gone. Perhaps they would keep his body now, too.

He gripped the stock of his lance, listening for the sounds of approach. He was grateful to Emile for drilling technique into him since day one, as it meant he wouldn't have to lean on his friend for directions now. He might never have the chance to lean on Emile again.

"Can't say I don't appreciate this," Emile said, his eyes bright in his ashen face. "But you've got to go on. Don't know if you knew this, but it always broke my heart when you didn't smile, and there won't be much smiling here soon. I don't want you around to see..."

Those bright, tearful eyes flicked to a place behind Renn's head, but before Renn could turn around, Emile nodded, Renn was lifted out of the mud and off the ground. The trees blurred past him, and somewhere in what was now the distance, high, angry shots cut off low, barking, desperate ones, and the echoes chased after Renn as the strong arms of Fairinelle carried him away toward the shadows on the border.

CHAPTER 32
Devil's Work

"Put me down!" Renn tore at Fairinelle's red coat. "I have to go back!"

"Has all the world gone mad?" Fairinelle wondered aloud, but didn't stop. "I assume you know Celine has finally left all her senses – was this not why you were running?"

"I don't care! Let me go!" Renn shouted, writhing so violently that Fairinelle was forced to stop. He set Renn on his feet, looking at him in amazement.

"Rennesson…"

But Renn was already running. He tripped and dodged around the trees back toward the direction where Emile lay. He moved quickly at first, for he was not winded like the officer trailing after him. But he didn't have such long legs as Fairinelle, either, and the familiar vice grip soon closed on his arm, halting him.

"Rennesson, you must understand, you'll be killed if you keep on this way," Fairinelle breathed hard. "Celine is coming for you."

"What does that matter to me?" Renn protested, imagining Emile's bloodless face somewhere behind them.

But a look of anger clouded over Fairinelle, and his eyes seemed to look straight through Renn now. "Is this woman a witch?" he demanded, stamping his boot heel. "What is it that makes men want to die by her hand?"

Renn's answer was prevented by Fairinelle lunging for him, knocking him into the ground. The stock of the lance still strapped to Renn's back slammed into his spine as pine needles and mud sprayed up around him.

Fairinelle was on top of him, and above his red coat hovered Celine, swaying like a rabid dog.

Fairinelle pushed himself up on muddy gloves. "Why would you not listen?" he hissed at Renn, his hair in his face, before flipping over and flinging out his arm to ward off Celine's attack.

Renn gasped, trying to regain any air in his lungs, trying to get out from under the others, but they fought and slipped and thrashed, climbed halfway to their feet, and fell on top of him again. Fairinelle was trying to get hold of her arms, but his grip, so sure before, was unable to catch hold of Celine now, as she slipped on the mud and insanity the drove her. In her madness, it seemed she had forgotten her guns, for she dove at him heedless of the pistols she had used to shoot Emile.

It wasn't until she was lifted in the air by her collar and flung sideways that Renn managed to squirm free and draw a full breath. But it wasn't Fairinelle who had thrown her, for he had rolled aside when Celine was lifted off him.

There were not three, but four people in this fight.

Celine scrambled up again, this time remembering exactly where her guns were, and aimed them at Renn.

"Hold off there, sister!" said the figure who had thrown her, and this time, the newcomer tackled her with all the force of someone used to wrestling wild boars, knocking her to the ground, sending one pistol flying into the brush, and pulling the other from her hand.

"Good thing I know how to use this, right?" The eyes sparkled at Renn and the voice spoke in perfect Wendish as the figure leapt up and swung around to point the pistol at Celine, who did not get up again.

Henny, the Barenhohle archer who had once been banned from hunts for endangering Renn with a Gallic gun – a weapon the warrior Cressido had called "the devil's work" – pointed one now at Celine to save Renn. After all this time, someone had finally come for him.

She laid her head back and closed her eyes, her dirty hair splayed out around her, and she smiled, waiting for the shot. She did have such a lovely smile.

But the shot never came, for Henny stiffened, the pistol fell from his grasp, and he collapsed across Celine's knees. In the place where he had been, now stood Fairinelle, rapier in shaking hand. The hand of the Butcher of Misère.

Celine's eyes opened to see the dead Wend on top of her, and her beautiful smile gave way to awful shrieking. They clawed their way out of her throat, not frightened shrieks, but accusing and angry, as she kicked and flailed with a wild desperation to get out from under the corpse.

Renn couldn't blame her. He felt like screaming himself.

Fairinelle reached, not to help Celine, but to grab the gun from Henny's still-warm fingers. He emptied the cartridge, then threw the remaining bullets and the pistol in opposite directions.

"How could you do this?!" Celine cried, crawling to her knees and clutching at Fairinelle's arm. There was no laughter now, as there had been a few hours before, the last time she had pulled herself from the dirt.

"I was ready to...I wanted to...! You, who have wanted me dead all this time – you choose *now* to let me live and suffer longer?!"

"I don't want you dead, Celine!" he shook her, his voice rising to match hers. "Why would I have stabbcd this poor boy if I did? Instead of letting him do me such a favor as to kill you?"

"Liar. It's all you think about."

"What do you think would happen to Jayem if you died?" he snapped.

Jayem. Jean-Marien. The man with the kind eyes and the broken body.

"He gave himself up to save you, and if you died now, it would all be in vain. You had your chance to let yourself be killed the first time, and I wish that you had taken it!"

She staggered back from the face of his rebuke.

"Oh yes, I do wish that," he leaned towards her. "But that chance is long gone. Jayem took it for you, and though you pretend to suffer over him, you will kill him a second time if you do this, if you value your life as cheaply as you did his. Though all the world would be better off if you did end your miserable existence, Jean-Marien would not, and I will not let you hurt him again, not even for all the world. No, not even if I have to kill every Wend in the world to do it."

Celine bent and vomited, covering Henny's body in desecration.

Renn's face burned and his fingernails cut into his palms as his hands clenched into shaking fists. Between the two of them, would they ever be done dishonoring the dead warrior? Celine had sullied his corpse, but Fairinelle's words were every bit as wicked. How could he speak like this, so self-righteous, as if he disdained taking Henny's life?

Celine had killed Emile, and had tried her best to kill Renn. She *deserved* to lose her own life for what she'd done. That much, even Fairinelle admitted. How could Jean-Marien be worth Emile's life, and Henny's, and Renn's himself? Renn had imagined that Fairinelle was his friend, but after all, he was still a Butcher.

"Was it all a lie?" he asked Fairinelle, his voice shaking as much as his hands.

"Was it...excuse me?" Fairinelle's eyes, bright with fire, struggled to focus on Renn, as if he had forgotten the boy was there.

"How can you pretend to care whether people die or not? You're so bothered by losing your friend, but you have no issue killing mine." Renn advanced toward him, growing angrier with each step.

"What I've done to…?" Fairinelle trailed off. The fire in his eyes flickered.

"He was going to take me home. Why couldn't you just let him? Why did you bother taking me away from Emile if this is what you were going to do?"

"You knew this warrior..." breathed Fairinelle, and his voice sounded like the wind dying away on a cold night. "You really *are* a Wend.

"His name was Henny," Renn went on, and it pleased him to see the Butcher's proud face fall further with each word. "You might at least mark *that* on your arm, instead of just a dagger like the others."

"The others." The rapier dropped from Fairinelle's hand as he reached to pull his dirty coat cuff back to the elbow, revealing   the dreaded tattoos for the first time since that day on the St. Juste.

"You mean this?" he pushed his arm into Renn's face. "So you know about it after all. Would you like to know how I got it?"

"I know how you got it," Renn spat. "Two Wends, killed on the road when you were only fifteen."

"That's how I *earned* it. Everyone knows that part, it seems." Fairinelle shook his head, smiling ruefully. "Let me tell you how they marked me with it."

CHAPTER 33
The Butcher

Adrien's shoulders heaved. He could barely believe it was over.

When he had stepped onto the road running between the town center and his father's manor, still wearing his practice clothes from Mistress Lillia's lesson, he hadn't known any of this was coming, but when the dark figures dressed in furs had slid from the shadows of the trees and rushed after the cart driven by the white-haired man with the child beside him, Adrien knew he could not just hide and watch it happen.

When first he saw them, he had darted off the road and skidded into a crouch behind the a thick tree trunk, peering around it to see the horse rearing in its traces and rocking the cart dangerously as the first man from the woods tried to catch it – his huge arm easily reached around its neck – and the other man, only slightly smaller than the first, clambered aboard the wagon.

But first one lost his grip as the horse reared and reared again, its shrill whinnies matched by the panicked cries of the child, and with the weight of the man climbing up the sideboard, the cart tipped to the side and crashed to the ground. The driver, child, and attacker fell into a heap together.

The man with the horse yelled something to the other, who threw the old man off of him with a snarl. Their words were gruff and terse, and Adrien hadn't understood them. It was then that he knew what these people were. Why they dressed like that, and carried such large, crude weapons. They were more than just common thieves; they were Wends.

How could this be happening? Barely a mile out of town, and there were Wends here? Adrien's heart pounded in indignation. This was his father's land. How dare these wicked people come here bringing violence upon the innocent? If they wanted to fight a Gaul, let them fight one who could defend himself!

And so with a shout he hadn't realized he was making, he stepped out from his hiding place, rapier in his outstretched hand.

The old man, crumpled on the side of the road, made a muffled moan and lay still. The child, his face smudged with dirt and his clothes torn from the crash, managed to find his feet, but when he saw the shining point of Fairinelle's blade, he opened his mouth wide, started screaming, and did not stop. He turned and ran down towards the town, and his high, wailing voice carried back to them even after he had disappeared down the road.

Adrien looked at the Wends. They were both bigger than him, and they looked none too pleased with the interference of this Gaul frowning at them in the road, stopping them from taking what they wanted.

It would never work if he tried to take them on directly. Such a thin little sword would easily break under a direct blow from such large axes, and a young, willowy student would break just as easily under a blow from a huge, hulking warrior. Logic told him what experience didn't. There had to be another way.

What had Mistress Lillia always taught him? She said there was a balance in everything. To pack a hit with power, you had to give up speed, and hope your blows landed accurately, for you wouldn't quickly get another chance. It took time to gather up the energy for a stronger hit. But if your blows were weaker, you could make up for it with their quantity. A thousand rapid pinpricks were easier to make, and could take out an opponent just as effectively as a few heavy, slow strikes. He only had to keep his focus, never let himself stop moving, looking, thinking, analyzing.

He gripped his sword, took a breath, and stepped forward.

At the end of it, he stood, breathing hard, wiping his brow. He was alive. All of his attention in Mistress Lillia's lessons had paid off. She would be proud of him. He was proud of himself.

But when he looked down at the bodies, bleeding from a thousand places, he could no longer feel proud. He felt sick and empty, as if the life were draining out of him the same as he had drained it from these Wends.

There was the noise of someone coming up the road, but it sounded slow, distorted, and far away. He turned towards it, with barely time to tense for another attack before Mistress Lillia appeared, her normally tidy hair streaming behind her, closely trailed by Mistress Charlotte and several of the other students, many still in their fencing gear.

Lillia ground to a halt when she saw the scene, her eyes scarcely wider than those of Adrien himself, who still clutched his bloody sword in his hand.

"Young lord," she breathed as looked from his shaken face to the bodies at his feet. "We thought...there was a boy who said there was trouble...but these are Wends! Did you do all this by yourself?"

He nodded slowly.

"Then you've done extremely well. Better than I would've hoped, even for a Fairinelle," she said, her chin lifting. "I'm proud of you."

"You always did pay such good attention in your lessons," Mistress Charlotte added with her quick smile, which seemed horribly out of place to Adrien, when faced with such murder as he had committed.

"What about him?" called one of the boys, catching sight of the old man huddled on the side of the road. "Is that one of them?"

"No!" cried Adrien. He had almost forgotten the man was even there. "He's innocent. He was attacked by these…" He gestured toward the bodies, trying not to look at them.

"You saved him, then!" cried one of the younger students.

"As if it weren't enough to take out a bunch of Wends singlehanded, you've gone and become a hero in the bargain," said a young, sandy-haired man named Jehan, and shook his head.

"Don't be sore over it," said another. "That's what his family does. They can't help it. They didn't get to be the barons of this town for nothing, you know."

"Your father will be so pleased," Mistress Charlotte agreed, speaking to Adrien. "You're in a very fine way to succeed him," she smiled.

"Here's to the next baron of Misère!" someone cried.

"The protector of the border!" shouted another.

"The Wend-killer!" called a third.

The shouts grew louder and the praise more extravagant as the students surged around him, pushing him back toward the town.

As horrifying as it was to look on the slumped bodies killed by his own hand, it was even more so to be dragged away from them, to see them kicked aside aside and left to bleed in the dust, to be unable to pay any sort of respect to the lives he had just extinguished.

"Tell everyone!" his schoolmates cried as they ran along. "Let's show them was the Lillianics can do!" Several people at once volunteered to take the news to the estate of Baron Fairinelle while others pounded on every door they could find along the way to the town center, sharing the news.

"Come see what Adrien Fairinelle has done. See what

happens to Wends who cross a Lillianic – a Misèrien – a Gaul!

Curious townsfolk opened their doors. Those who hadn't come out when the child from cart ran screaming now poked their heads out at this second disturbance. Shopkeepers stepped from their storefronts, joining the growing crowd. Everyone cheered and congratulated Adrien Fairinelle, but if any had paid close attention, they would have seen an uneasy young man searching hard for a way out.

Adrien's eyes fell upon his father, standing tall above the crowd.

The throng parted before the baron. The people grew quiet, watching in awe as he approached his son and looked seriously into his face.

"Is this true, son, that you have killed two Wends on the Pauline Road, unassisted?" he asked, though Adrien had the bloodstains to prove it.

"Yes, sir." The words were bitter in his mouth, but more bitter still was the look of pride in his father's eyes.

Baron Fairinelle turned to his secretary, who stood beside him, "Find Mr. Villiers. Tell him to bring his inks and needles."

The crowd broke out in cheers again. Adrien blanched, but no one saw it.

"Am I not too young, sir?" he asked, fighting to keep his feet as the crush of people swirled around him again. His voice rose in panic, but it seemed to those around him that he was only trying to be heard above the din as as they clapped him on the back, shook his hand, and tried to be near their new young hero who would soon be named a Butcher.

"Your modesty does you credit," said the baron. "But your skill is a greater credit still, and your age makes it all the more merited. If you are skilled enough to have done this, even being young as you are, then you've earned the right to tell the world."

His father put a hand on his shoulder, steering him towards the pavilion in the town square from which he made all of his public speeches, where all the ceremonies and festivals were initiated, and townsfolk gathered for events of any importance.

It felt more like his father was driving him, prodding him up the steps of the pavilion like a calf pushed towards the altar. Mr. Villiers appeared, nearly leaping up the stairs to open his bag of inks and needles.

Somebody lifted Adrien's arm and laid it bare on the wood.

Stop, *he wanted to say.* I don't want this. *But he saw the look in the people's eyes. It was the same way they had always looked at his father, their lord and protector. It was a look of admiration, of hope.*

And now, most painful of all, was the fact that his father was looking at him in the same way.

What would the crowd do if he raised the objections he wanted to? They had been so quick to celebrate him; would they turn on him just as quickly? If he had killed any other kind of person, they might have praised his distaste for it. They would have said he was too genteel to take pleasure in bloodshed, too well-bred to glory in gore, and the whole affair would have worked to raise their opinion of the family Fairinelle.

But to show regret over killing a Wend was a different thing entirely. Adrien would be labelled a sympathizer, a traitor, and his father would be marred by the association. The people would say he had no control over his son and would doubt his ability to govern the town if he could not even govern his own family. They might accuse him of harboring the same traitorous sentiment himself and call for his removal, or worse.

Adrien glanced again from the baron to the people, and all the while the needle came nearer. The faces of the two Wends loomed before him, their eyes empty as their lives left them. That image would be inside his mind forever. He did not want it written on the outside too, carried on the very arm which had committed the act. But how could he refuse a mark he had earned when it meant marking his father with a reputation he had not?

If he accepted the tattoo, Adrien would be the only one inconvenienced. If he did not, both himself and others would suffer for it, and Adrien never could bear the suffering of innocents, never could accept those who made others suffer for their own misdeeds. So he made himself think of the honor of the house of Fairinelle, of the old man and the child who had been saved, of the good he had done for his country.

He forced himself to watch the red well up on his own arm as the needle bit into his skin. He hoped it might ease some of the guilt, hoped that repaying the blood he took with blood of his own would somehow settle the score.

It didn't.

The needle scraped and scratched, hurting more than it should have but less than he wanted it to, until several raised lines of pale, shocked skin could be seen near his elbow, and he felt even worse than before when he saw the shape that he'd only seen in his father's books, telling of the land across the border. It was the mark of the Wendish nation, and crossing it were two daggers, one for each Wend he had killed.

The lines on his skin were now quickly brimming red. Mr. Villiers dabbed the blood away while cheers rose behind him. Adrien looked at his father's proud and grateful face, and he forced himself to stay where he was, to not bolt down the steps and away from this nightmarish celebration. But he could not force himself to smile back.

On the Pauline Road, an old man brushed himself off, gathered what he could from the overturned cart, and limped off down the road, leaving the remaining goods, the horse, and the Wends where they lay in the dust. He would have liked to set everything in order himself, but his two weak hands could only do so much…

*　　　*　　　*

"All he would say was that couldn't stand to stay here anymore." Lillia said.

*   *   *

"What's a baron's son doing here? Why aren't you in Circle Ambrosia with the other nobles?"
   "Here is where I wanted."

*   *   *

"It's nice to have your own name to yourself, if you know what I mean," Jean-Marien said.
   "I think I do," said Adrien.

*   *   *

"I would have gone mad if I'd stayed there and been worshipped every day for what I'd done, so I left home and joined a Circle in a place where no one would know me, in the middle of the wilds – that was Faubourg. I was happy there, in Faubourg. But Celine…"

He looked over at her whimpering quietly. She seemed not to hear them.

"As you know, Celine so kindly destroyed any happiness I had there. She took my best friend, the only one who saw me not as *what* I was but *who* I was, and threw him to Wendish hounds. After that, there was nothing left for me there. I could have gone to another Circle, but the same thing would have happened. Grief would have followed me, and how could I not deserve it, after what I'd done? So I kept on drifting until I reached the lowest of the low places. The only place someone like me belonged."

"The St. Juste," said Renn. It was a prison ship and a slaver's barge. For criminals and murderers. For boys who were lost and far from home.

"Exactly, and do you not agree that it suits me? At least

Celine only hurts the friends of those she doesn't care about. I'm the one who kills friends of people I do care for." Fairinelle gestured towards Henny. He almost laughed as he spoke, but his eyes were shards of blue, broken glass.

"Yes, perhaps I *should* get a new tattoo," he said, then abruptly sank down hard, and covered his face with his hand while shuddering sobs broke under it.

Renn stood paralyzed. How could he have been so very right about this man, and so very wrong at the same time?

It was true that violence was in Fairinelle's nature. Renn had seen that correctly from the start. But the protective side of his nature had not been a mask for that violence at all. Rather, it was the reason *for* it. This was a man who had been raised to watch over those weaker than him, and though he was scared and sick to death of bloodshed, he would always do his duty. He would punish those who hurt others, whether it was roving Wends, careless girls, or his own self. He could never let any of them forget what they had done, and Renn saw now that it was rotting his heart out.

Fairinelle still sobbed, and the plaintive note in his cries was picked up by a mighty, wailing howl just behind Renn's ear, before a rush of wind and weight barrelled past him, and a blur of claws, teeth, and black-and-tan fur slammed into the weeping officer.

The huge jaws of Siegher, Renn's favorite warhound from Barenhohle, snapped shut around Fairinelle's forearm, and he fell backwards, knocked flat by the animal's weight. The hand he had put to his face to cover his tears had kept him from seeing the oncoming attack, but it was only because his hand had been there at all that the dog's teeth hadn't yet reached his throat. The poor, breaking barrier of his arm had stood in the way.

With one arm thus pinned in the dog's great mouth, Fairinelle kicked at the animal, but with as much effect as kicking at a rolling boulder, doing nothing to stop the onslaught.

Renn jumped forward to help, but was thrown back by the dog's huge, swinging haunches. He scrambled to jump in again, but this time collided with black, muddy jackboots as Fairinelle tried vainly to twist his way out.

There was a crack and a groan, in that same ragged voice that been sobbing before, and the boots stopped kicking. Tears ran down Fairinelle's color-drained face. It was how Emile had looked before he'd...

It took Renn a moment to hear the screaming. It took another moment to realize it was himself. Last of all he realized that he was screaming the houndsmen's commands that Linderic had taught him not so long and forever ago in the halls of Barenhohle.

CHAPTER 34
Die Cleanly

The dog wheeled around, Fairinelle's blood staining his iron teeth.

"It's me," said Renn, panting for breath. He held out his hand, remembering the nights when an orphan boy and a warhound would sleep curled up together in the hay, and trusting – hoping – that Siegher remembered the same.

But Renn had been wrong about so many things today.

"Don't tempt a dog on the hunt," Linderic used to tell him.

Siegher lunged, fast as thunder, but Renn was faster. He was too much in practice with the Badeau Numbers to miss now, and Siegher fell on top of him, red foam dripping onto Renn's cheek the way so many others' blood had touched him before.

He looked to his left. Celine had disappeared sometime during the fight. On his right, Fairinelle lay moaning.

Renn thought to move toward him, but he had forgotten that war dogs never went to battle on their own. Without Emile's sharp eyes, he hadn't seen the young man on whose tanned face tricolor paint was broken by a circle of jagged scars, watching him from the trees.

"How many times do I have to tell you, Ranizone? Leave my dog alone."

Jungbern, prince of Barenhohle, stepped out from the shadows, his face still wearing the same, mocking expression as when Renn had last seen him on the morning of the war party all those months ago.

"So you ran off to join your people after all," Jungbern said. "Just like I knew you would."

"I didn't run off anywhere. I was taken," Renn said defiantly, though he was still prone beneath the body of Siegher. There was a time when he might have been deterred by his cousin's anger, but he'd dealt with so many other threats, with so much loneliness and danger and fear since leaving home, that Jungbern's silly barbs didn't frighten him anymore.

"Do you know how many war parties we've sent out looking for you?" Jungbern asked. "And not just us Cimbri. Our neighbors came out, too. The Ambrones and the Teutons even crossed the border for you. A waste of time, really, for half of them never came back. My father finally had to ask me to do what they couldn't, as you see." He waved his hand, indicating himself. "But look at you, running to this Gaul. All of our people, killed for a traitor who would repay him like this."

Renn went cold, for Jungbern was right in more ways than he knew. The first person Renn had ever killed was the Ambrone woman who hadn't believed he was Gaul, and he'd gutted her for it. All the others after her, who he had learned to stop feeling bad over just as Emile predicted, they'd all been searching for *him*.

It was why everyone had said that the Wends were too far south, why they were attacking more frequently than anyone had seen in years, why the bounty on Wends was put out by the army again. He was why they had come, and he was also why they never made it home.

"That dog was trained to kill Gauls," Jungbern said. "He knew what you are. Shame he couldn't kill you, but least he got your friend over there." He gestured toward Fairinelle, grinning.

"That's not my friend," said Renn. He knew that Fairinelle, if he did not die from his wounds, would certainly be doomed by Renn admitting any friendship with him, for Jungbern would surely finish what Siegher couldn't.

"You came to look for *me,* and here I am, so help me up, and let's go," Renn said, fighting against every instinct to look at Fairinelle. It was all so horribly wrong to leave him there without a single word of goodbye, to never know if he had lived, or died with his heartbreak still glistening in the tears on his face. Renn had spent so long trying *not* to look at, *not* to speak to Fairinelle, and now he only wished he could do so one more time.

Jungbern didn't move. "You think I'll take you back so you can spy for *them* when you get there?"

"Will you just help me up?" Renn bit out. "Isn't that what you came for, to take me home? I'm telling you there is nothing and nobody here I will ever see or speak to again." Did Jungbern even know how hard it was to say these things?

"Why should I trust a Gaul like you?"

"Because you're not as smart as you think you are!" Renn finally snapped. What did Jungbern know about Gauls except how to kill them? Did he know about the Gaul who befriended young boys with terrible secrets, who was lying dead out there somewhere because he had protected that secret? Did he know about the one who carried the guilt of the world on his shoulders and in the skin of his arm?

Jungbern's face contorted and he dropped down, his face inches from Renn's.

"Say that again," he threatened. This was something Jungbern had done before, pinning him to ground and threatening him, and Renn had learned how to fight his way free, only this time he was stuck under Siegher's huge carcass, and couldn't go anywhere.

He heard the creak of the leather sheath as Jungbern pulled his hunting knife from his waist.

But he didn't see the man who had again heard the sound of angry Wendish words in the woods, and had risen from the ground, pushing himself up on his unbroken arm, stumbling again toward the crisis, pushing through the pain in his body and the trembling in his heart.

Fairinelle, limping, looked at the boy sprawled on the ground, and he saw again an old man by an overturned cart. He saw Jean-Marien lying unmoving, covered in blood, and he saw Emile now dead somewhere in the forest. Lastly, he saw himself, standing before the slain, standing over the all the people he had ever fought to protect, and he *understood.*

Unfolding before him was the answer to why Jean-Marien never complained about his fate, while Adrien couldn't bear to think of it. It was why Emile, who had known war and prison and slavery, could still sing in deepest night, while a few drops of inkwere enough to darken the years of Adrien's life.

It was because there was a reason for the suffering they endured. To protect meant to be satisfied knowing someone else's life would go on even if your own would not. It was worth taking horror and death onto yourself when it meant that someone else would not have to.

Jean-Marien had known this when he had gone with Celine on the hunt. Emile had known it when he chose to confront her over Renn, and Fairinelle himself had known in when he fought the Wends in Misère, and killed the one named Henny just now.

The only difference was that Fairinelle had not realized he'd known it. He'd always feared that the feelings which forced him to kill meant he was a monster, but he knew now that it was love, only love, like that of Jean-Marien and Emile, which had driven him every time. Love for his people in Misère, love for Jean-Marien who would be hurt by Celine's death, and now, love for this unhappy boy who had come from across the border and turned everything upside down made Fairinelle stand once more when all his body wanted was to rest.

He had fallen into an abyss by killing a Wend to protect a child. He would get out the same way.

Jungbern's knee cut into Renn's ribs as his knife began to draw blood from the skin, but it went slack, and sharp gasp rattled through the air, which Renn knew by now was the sound of a life leaving a body on the point of a blade. Jungbern slumped over him, limp and heavy, and at the other end of the sword in his back, Fairinelle fell after him, smiling.

The woods were hushed, and even the river seemed to stop moving as Renn clambered out from under the pile of bodies. He never knew how he was able to lift the weight of the dog, the prince, and the officer, but he did it, even as his hands and knees sank in the puddles of blood now flowing freely from the Fairinelle's body.

Fairinelle's effort had cost him dearly. That he had been able to rise at all had been surprising, but then, Fairinelle had always been stronger than he looked.

"I'm sorry, I'm sorry," Renn repeated, frantically running his hands over Fairinelle's many wounds, as if he could close them by his touch. "You didn't have to do this. I lied to you and used you…I'm sorry."

"Don't be," Fairinelle's voice was weak and his eyes were closed. "It's because of you that I'm not afraid anymore."

"Are you hurt badly?" Renn asked, though he could see the answer for himself.

"It's an honor," Fairinelle sucked in a sharp breath. "To suffer like he did."

"Like Jayem did? You won't end up like him. I won't let you."

In all the months that Renn had tried to puzzle out the secret of Jayem, he had never thought it would end like this. He hung his head until his hair brushed Fairinelle's shirt, which was red now to match his coat, and wondered how he was going to get this tall man to safety by himself.

With his head hung over, the world was upside down in more ways than one. The trees shot down towards the sky, and – he could have laughed at the absurdity of it – a huge pair of bear-hide stockings stood as high as any of them.

Surely three Wends surprising him in one day was too much to be believed. But these were no ordinary Wendish warriors. The whole reason Celine had come here, the whole reason there was a bounty in the first place, was because the Cimbri were the best, most fearsome woodsmen in Wendland, who could slip silently through the woods, tracking their prey for miles without tiring, and without ever letting them know it. Because they could take whole platoons unawares, much less one dying man and one distraught boy.

"For shame, Ranizone, to do such a thing. Crying won't help him now." The voice came booming down, and when Renn looked up, Hagen, his uncle and chief of the Cimbri, stood in battle dress, towering above and frowning down at the bleeding Gaul and the boy who cried over him.

"Hurry up and kill the Gaul. That's the only way to avenge your cousin."

"Avenge him? But Fair – I mean – this Gaul saved me!"

Hagen's frown deepened. "Saved you from your own kin?"

"Siegher attacked me. He wouldn't listen. I had to kill him, but Jungbern got angry over it. He said I was a Gallic spy...he tried to slit my throat. But this man," he motioned to Fairinelle, "he only meant to help. He didn't know who Jungbern was."

Hagen studied him. "You poor child," he said finally, his black eyebrows knitting together. "What chance could you have against such cunning? To be tricked into thinking they mean you no harm? After months of being steeped in their witchcraft, it's no wonder your mind is addled. Your fool of a mother was the same way. But don't fear, little Rani, I shall free you from this spell, even if I couldn't free her."

He stepped towards them, and Renn could feel the ground shaking until Hagen stood directly over them, his head as tall as a ship's mast, his bear hide boots as tall as Renn's shoulders, and his mace lowered like a storm cloud over the sea, above the body of Fairinelle.

Renn's eyes glowed white as he stared up into the dark mass of Hagen's shadow. He knew what would happen to Fairinelle, and it was worse than anything a Butcher could do. All the Gauls he had faced before, Willow and Badger, Buron, Xavier, Celine – none could match the terror of the Cimbrian war chief, this great lord of wild Wendish wood.

"There are more than mere men in Cimbria, my boy," Celine had once warned him, and she had been right.

Renn had not known he'd reached for Fairinelle's hand until the officer's slick grasp touched his own. Fairinelle pressed weakly with his shredded fingers, smiling reassurance at him.

It was the same smile he had given Renn while Xavier lay dead on the deck of the St. Juste, and while Emile lay unconscious in a dark room in Angel's Arrow. It was the smile that had first made Renn depend on him in spite of himself, one that said "Don't be afraid. I'm here with you."

It was too much to hope that he would rise a second time. If anyone could have stood a chance against Hagen, it would have been Fairinelle the Butcher, the Child Knight of the North. But there was a reason Jean-Marien had not walked in fourteen years. The dogs of Cimbria knew their work too well; tear down the enemy and make an easy kill for the warriors who came after.

But one thing was not too much to hope: That for whatever other madness raged in her mind, Celine would remember how much she hated Wends. From wherever she had run to, she had still heard the voices of the Wends, and a pistol shot now whistled through the trees, nicking hairs off the beaver-fur mantle on Hagen's shoulder.

Hagen turned his bear-like head toward the shot, no longer interested in the fallen prey beneath him.

Celine, balancing against a tree with one hand, her gun smoking in the other, had caught her breath enough to growl at him.

"Stand away from my kill."

Hagen hadn't understood any of her words, but he recognized the cut of the bullet and the challenge in her voice. "Another of your *friends*, Ranizone?" he rumbled, but even as he asked, he was already loping toward her.

Celine stood fast as the giant man bore down on her, grabbed her by the neck, one hand fitting all the way around, and lifted her completely off the ground. Her skirts swayed in the air beautifully, sickeningly, while Hagen glowered into the face of this new brash, stupid enemy.

Nausea clawed at Renn as he waited for the sound of snapping bones to begin. He had seen this happen once before, to a boy not much older than himself, who had been caught stealing. He remembered the uselessly flailing hands, the garbled choking moans, and worst of all, the moment they had ceased, when his windpipe was crushed and his neck bones cracked.

But Celine did not flinch. Even with the Hagen's hot, angry breath in her face, and his deadly hands clenched around her neck, she held her head aloft.

It was what she wanted, after all. This was why she had chosen the Cimbrian bounty. It was why she drank herself senseless every night. Because she was stumbling, staggering, under the weight of her guilt and sorrow. She was looking for a way to end it.

It was why, now, with her matted, muddy hair hanging down between Hagen's bulging knuckles, and her face turning violet, she closed her eyes and smiled. She sought to absolve the tragedy of Jean-Marien not by taking a Wendish life, as she had always said, but by ending her own. She would rather die, removing herself and her crimes from the world, than try to forgive what she had done.

She did have such a beautiful smile.

It was all that was left now of the band of Gauls with whom he had laughed and fought with every step between here and the sea. Of Emile who had known his secret and loved him anyway. Of Fairinelle who had learned it and had been saved by it. Of Dumoulin the harpooneer who had protected him when he was only a slave, of Rigobert, Charlotte, and Lillia, and all the others who had shown him so much of kindness, and so much of heartache.

They were strange and wild, these Gauls, but they were

kind and brave, too. They were killers, kidnappers, slavers and soldiers. But they were also men who threw themselves before wild animals to save someone they loved, marksmen who cheerfully went to prison to protect an innocent, barons' sons who abandoned all the luxury they knew in an effort at repentance...and a woman who hated Wends only less than she hated herself, who was harsh and imperious, and for all of that, held a despair that was no less worth absolving than Fairinelle's, or of Renn's himself.

Fairinelle had smiled as he fell because, by giving his life, he had come out of the darkness. Celine smiled now because, by dying, she was going into it.

How could Renn let her go there alone? How could he let her die without even trying to stop it? He would save her, and bring her out of her darkness, as all the others had done for him. That was what it meant to be a warrior. Not to kill and destroy, but to protect, and it had not been this Wendish chief, but the Gauls who had shown him that.

Renn climbed to his feet, the mud sliding off him, and stood where Fairinelle had stood before, planting his feet as he faced his uncle and shouted out to let her go, as he had shouted to Siegher only minutes before.

Hagen released his grip, if only a little, and growled. "I begin to think you *want* to be one of them, Ranizone, and this is no witchcraft at all."

"You're right, it isn't!" cried Renn, anger welling up in him the same as it had that day of the war party back in Barenhohle. He had thought Hagen was wrong back then. He knew Hagen was right now.

"After I took you in, sheltered you in spite of your half-blood, treated you as one of us...you choose to betray me?"

"If I'm betraying you, then it's no more than I'd be betraying them if I let you do this."

"Your wicked father's people –"

"They're not my father's people," said Renn. When he had lived at Barenhohle, he had never wanted to think of them so, but now, he *knew* they were not so.

"They're not his people," he repeated. "They're mine. Whatever loyalty I owe to you, I owe as much to them."

Hagen's eyes blazed at him.

How could Renn have ever wanted to be like this man?

"So you are your mother's child, after all. You carry a chieftan's blood, and you choose the Gallic pigs instead. If you love them that much, are you prepared to die with them?"

Renn bit his lip, but only for a moment. He had already decided to die once today; it couldn't be that hard a second time.

"It will be an honor to suffer as they did."

Celine dropped to ground with a crunch, and even as Hagen came toward him, it was a relief to hear her weak gasp for air. Renn reached for his lance in its harness, and realized too late it was left stuck in Siegher's chest. He ran to it, slipping, and scrambled to plant a foot on the dead dog's side, yanking to get the weapon loose. After several pulls, the dog's ribs finally shifted beneath his shoe, and the blade slid free past fur and flesh. Renn turned, and Hagen was upon him.

There was barely room to maneuver, save for Badeau Number Nine, a low-swinging move meant to buy space, rather than attack. He swung out, and swung again, but still his uncle's hulking form bore down on him. Renn was barely able to dodge the wide arcs of the axe, and he could not kick his way free as he had with Jungbern, and the Wendish enemies in the forest so many times before. Hagen was too huge, with too many decades of experience, to fall before a boy who'd only trained for a few months.

"And you wondered why I never let you join the warriors," Hagen laughed, the sound like thunder as the breeze of his axe fluttered the hem of Renn's shirt.

"What hope has a pathetic Gaul in any kind of fight? You'd have been nothing but a liability, assuming you would have stayed on our side at all. Jungbern was right about you all along."

"*You would've made a fine addition to the harpooners,*" Renn remembered Fairinelle telling him.

"*That was some fancy work you did,*" Emile's voice echoed next in his ears.

Even haughty Celine had once deigned to say "*You've got the right spirit, at least.*"

No, Jungbern had not been right about him. Jungbern did not know anything about him. He did not know how Renn had fought his way through slavery and war parties, alongside decorated soldiers and legendary swordsman, and none of them had ever told him he was less than worthy. For all that he had feared and hated them, they had respected and encouraged him. And more than that, they had shown him how to fight.

He'd thought it tremendous bad luck to travel with the elite killers of the Gallic world, who could have ended him at any moment, but now it was that very thing which would save him.

To his mind came that weapons yard on the edge of Concertine, on the very first day Renn had held a lance in his hands. Leave it to Emile to teach the most important things first.

"*Slice him once going forward.*"

Renn thrust the pole out in front of him. After all the dodging, Hagen had not expected it.

"*Then catch him again the other way.*"

He yanked the blade back towards himself.

"*See? That's all there is to it.*"

There would be no overpowering Hagen, but he could outmaneuver him. He could outsmart him.

"*A thousand rapid pricks were easier to make, and could take out an opponent just as effectively as a few heavy, slow strikes.*"

That one was a lesson from Fairinelle.

Renn had outwitted his way through an entire country. He could outwit one man. He tried to remember how Fairinelle had always looked, flitting back and forth as Celine's winger, and how Emile had moved, swinging his gun like a staff against the Ambrone woman. He even remembered Dumoulin again, parrying and thrusting his harpoon as he fought to keep the peace on the St. Juste.

Renn swung around, not cowering, but driving, spearing forward. He refused to recoil when Hagen swung at him, and the shaft shook in his hands with the impact, but it was Hagen who came away bleeding.

Hagen never had seen what a warrior he could be. That simple fact was what had started him on this journey, and the same fact would finish it.

If Mistress Lillia could have seen him at the end of it, she would have sworn it was the Child Knight reborn, standing and shaking, victorious over a dead Wend twice his size, and all alone.

Yes, Renn was all alone now. Everything he'd learned to love in Gaul was gone, and everything ahead in Wendland was lost to him now, too. How could he ever go home after this? He was a Butcher now himself. He had killed not just any warrior, but Hagen, the chief of the Cimbri. What would they say to him if he showed his face at Barenhohle?

And even if he could hide what he'd done, even if everyone at Barenhohle welcomed him back, he came to the sinking realization that he was next in line to be chief. If he went home, he would be expected to order war parties to raid and attack the Gauls. To cause more suffering like Jean-Marien and Celine's, and send someone else to traumatize another young Fairinelle, or send another Emile to prison.

He could not go forward that way, and he could not go back the way he came. He looked at Celine. She was not moving. Behind him, Fairinelle was still, and somewhere far away, Emile's body lay alone

He closed his eyes, his head throbbing and spinning as it hadn't done since the first day off the boat in Concertine.

His legs trembled under him, and the lance grew heavy in his grasp. His strength was draining out of him, and not just in spirit, for Butchers didn't earn that title without gaining a few wounds of their own. He touched the weeping gashes on his arms with cold fingertips as his vision darkened, and when his knees buckled, he didn't try to catch himself, for he knew he was going to join the others who were waiting for him.

It wasn't such a bad thing to die in Gaul, in the end.

CHAPTER 35
Ghosts

Renn was forever waking up in strange places without knowing how he'd gotten there. But this time, the place wasn't strange at all. It was his own bed in the Houndsmen's barracks at Barenhohle. Sunlight flooded his eyes, and he wondered whether he had gone to Heaven, or if he had ever really left home at all, until he moved, and the aching stiffness in every part of his body reassured him that he had really lived all that he remembered.

The houndsman named Keno sat on a stool at the end of the cot, with his feet kicked up on the rough blanket, a block of wood in one hand and a short knife in the other.

Beyond him lay houndsmen in the other cots across the room, but only one thing was wrong. One of them, Renn couldn't tell who, was using a tattered red coat as a blanket. How could they dare to do such a thing? How could they plunder the precious body of the son of the baron of Misère? Renn gathered what small strength he could and sat up to see what else had been stolen off the dead.

He saw the long, battered, Gallic-made rifle leaning against one of the other cots, and pushed the blanket off in what passed for a rage in his tired body, stiffly sliding his legs over the edge.

"Easy there," said Keno, setting down his whittling to ease Renn back into bed, but Renn batted at him feebly.

"How could you? Isn't it enough that they died? Why

do you have to bring those in here?" he pointed to the relics of the fallen.

If he were chief, he would certainly keep the ban on bringing trophies back from the dead, but for an entirely different reason than Hagen had.

Keno shifted uneasily. "Err...are they not your friends? We'll have a lot explaining to do if they aren't. People get curious if you bring a bunch of Gauls home, you know. But that one over there keeps insisting, and we couldn't wake you up to ask you."

This conversation was making no sense. What could Keno mean by 'bringing a bunch of Gauls'? Did they dare bring the bodies of his friends themselves back as trophies, too? And which of the houndsmen would think of doing such a thing.

"What *friend*? Who suggested this?" Renn demanded, his heart on fire but his voice weak.

"That one over there keeps telling Linderic he knows you. I can't understand most of what he says, but according to Linde, his name's...Em...Em something." Henny struggled to remember. "You know any Gauls like that?"

Someone who could speak only to Linderic, who slept with a rifle by his side, whose name was...

"Emile? Was he called Emile?!" Renn pressed.

"That's it. He – "

But Keno was interrupted by the houndsman who kept the rifle by his cot. Only it was no houndsman at all, for when the figure stirred and sat up, trying to shake himself out his blankets, Renn saw his right side wrapped round with bandages, and the friendly, if wan, face looked around until he found Renn, equally bandaged, and equally piqued.

"You alright?" Emile peered at him dazedly. "Thought I heard you calling."

That was definitely Emile. Who else would have been shot, left for dead, and still risen from the grave to ask if *Renn* needed anything?

"How are you alive?" Renn wondered. "I saw Celine shoot you."

"Tch, yeah," Emile said, "But it's like I've said before; she shoots too early. If she'd taken the time to line up her shot, with her strong hand, she might've got me. Lucky for me, she never listens to advice."

"But how are you *here*?" Renn asked, then looked to Keno. "What stopped you from killing him? How did you know they were my friends?"

"This one," Keno gestured to Emile. "I was supposed to be
with Jungbern and the chief, but I fell a bit behind and ended up on a different track than the rest."

"Late as usual?" Renn asked.

"Maybe…" Keno admitted, ducking his head. "Linde had to come back and get me, and that's when we ran across him."

Renn smiled. It had been Keno's paints and mirror, left laying out due to his chronic tardiness, which had made Renn look so much like a warrior that he'd been mistaken for one and taken away from home. How that tendency to lateness had angered him the day he'd left!   And how grateful he was for it now!

"It seemed like somebody else had gotten to him first," Keno said. "He couldn't even get off the ground, but he was snarling at me like any of our dogs, and holding that gun straight at my face, though he looked hurt as anything. Lucky for me, Linde was there to talk him down."

Renn remembered the fierce look on Emile's face in the last Gallic tavern, and could well believe what Keno said. He turned to Emile, but was interrupted by the rough-hewn wooden door banging inward, and Linderic hurriedly half-dragging someone in with him. Renn saw the brown paw of a dog outside the doorway before Linderic kicked the door closed behind him.

"I don't need you to baby me. Sickness isn't worst thing I've ever gotten for my troubles," complained the person he was dragging, and Renn had never been so happy to hear anyone be so irritated. For unless Linderic could touch ghosts, it was no phantom that he so stoically deposited back to her cot.

"Will you tell him that, Rennesson?" asked Celine, but she nearly jumped out of her skin when Linderic answered her himself, in her own language.

"You're not making it any easier, you know. What in the world were you doing to yourself, anyway? I've never seen someone get so sick. Now, I'm sorry, but I've got to go clean it before the dogs get to it. Please just use that pail we've left you and don't run outside unless one of us goes with you." He made a face, but straightened it out, resolutely dusted his hands, and left back the way he had come.

Celine was still staring agog at the door after this Wend who spoke in her own words, but Renn could only laugh with relief.

The effort hurt his ribs, but he couldn't stop, not even when Celine, hunched over on her cot, commanded him to be quiet. He was too pleased to see her breathing, even as out of humor as she was, to be bothered by her bad moods now. But he would leave her alone, at any rate. When he caught his breath, he turned back to Emile, grinning, not caring how it hurt his chapped lips.

"Keno said you were threatening him like anything, even when you couldn't get up. That you were fierce as any war dog when they found you.

"Ah, he told you that?" Emile flushed, and gave an sheepish smile that turned into a grimace as he shifted and leaned on his bad side.

"Sure," Celine put in. "I've no doubt you would have torn my throat out with your teeth to keep me from him, if I hadn't shot you first."

"Right, thanks for that," said Emile, wincing as he touched his wound.

"Don't look at me like that," Celine looked up then, sounding suddenly earnest. "Perhaps it was wrong, but didn't I make up for it when I – ?" She cut herself off abruptly, looked at Renn, then looked down at her fingernails.

"When you challenged the chief to protect Renn yourself," Fairinelle's hoarse voice finished for her.

Renn's head snapped back to his right. He had forgotten the cot with the tattered red coat.

It had been no ghost Linderic helped in from outside, and it had been no houndsman bearing a rifle as a war trophy. If being surprised by three Wends in one day was too much to believe, but had still happened, perhaps three Gauls could do the same.

The figure under the coat did not sit up as Emile had done, but he shifted slowly, and when he turned, a poorly-suppressed smile was edging over that familiar noble, though bruised, face.

"Don't tell me you were only trying to claim your rightful kill," Fairinelle said to Celine. "If you were really set on killing him, you would've done it already. You've had plenty of time." His smile broke out fully now. "I think you do have a heart somewhere in there, after all."

A huff came from Celine. "Oh, *all right*, then. Don't think I'm not still furious at you for lying to me – all of you," she swept her eyes over each of them.

"That, we can handle. But can we trust that Renn's safe from you, finally and for all?" Emile asked.

"He was true to his word," said Celine, "and I can't fault a man for that. He didn't hand us over, even when it went worse for him not to."

She turned to Renn.

"I saw how you threw yourself over Adrien. I've seen someone do that in the face of those dogs before, and I did nothing to stop it then. I couldn't let it happen a second time." She shook her head. "No, death's not for you, Rennesson. Not by that chief's hand, and not by mine."

That was it. The last great obstacle done away. The last of the three Gauls, this awful person who had tried to

destroy both him and herself, no longer wished to kill him.

He could only hope she had changed her mind about herself, too.

"And is death still for you?" he asked cautiously.

She shook her head softly.

"Seeing you standing up to him, trying your best when you didn't have a chance – when it would have been so much easier to just give up – what excuse do I have not to do the same? How can I allow myself to give up when there are others who would die to give me the chance to live? Even when I use and mistreat and almost kill them?"

She looked to where Fairinelle lay on his back. "I include neglect among my methods of killing," she finished.

"Change it, then," he responded. "You've just shown you can change already. If you really are sorry for what happened, go home to him."

"I can't. I can't be what he needs."

Fairinelle studied her. "Perhaps I see it clearly now…I hated you because I thought you didn't care about what you'd done – that you drank and ran wild because you had forgotten him. But I think I see now, you did it because you *couldn't* forget. Because you did care…too much."

"But not for him. I hate what I did, but what's worse is that it didn't change what I felt for him. I ought to have loved him after he saved me, but I don't. I should have been happy to spend my life tending to him, but I'm not. I could go back and make myself stay, but he would know I didn't mean it, and I can't put him through that after everything else. I can't make myself feel what I should towards him, and without that, I have no way to make up for what I've done."

Renn listened to her speak, and without all her usual haughtiness, he could finally hear the notes of regret that must have been in her voice all along. She regretted that she wasn't who she thought she should be. But Renn had had plenty of experience with that.

"Before I went to Gaul," he said. I thought I had to hate all of you, but the truth is so far from what I thought I *should* do. It doesn't make me any less of a Wend to love you all, and it doesn't make me any less of a Gaul to love the people here, but I never would have known it if I had just stayed where I always was. So maybe you'll find the truth isn't what you thought, either. I don't think it makes your regret any less meaningful even if you don't love him. Maybe it won't even bother him so much if you don't, but you'll never know if you just stay where you are. You have to try to face him."

"Just so," Fairinelle said quietly, sounding a little distant. He shifted to look up at the ceiling.

"Celine," he continued. "Perhaps you were not the only one who acted...ignobly. I didn't want you to die, but I didn't make it easy for you to want to live."

"You both – " she started, and rose from her cot. A stray beam sunlight streamed in from a crack in the ceiling planks and illuminated her face. She took two steps further, and vomited all over the packed dirt floor.

"Ach, have a drink this once if it makes you feel better," said Emile, but Celine shook her head.

"I'm done with that," she panted with an expression as determined as ever. "I have to try to face things now."

CHAPTER 36
All Grief to Refrain

They were going to have to go, and soon. That much was becoming clear with each day. Linderic and the other houndsmen were still patrolling the perimeter of the barracks to keep them safe, but this safety meant they were stuck inside, bored, restless, and ill.

Emile was healing fast, much faster than he had at Angel's Arrow. He was soon able to sit up, and even began trying to get back on his feet within a few days.

Fairinelle was slower in recovering, but he was conscious for the most part, which was better than Jean-Marien had been after the same type of attack, and Fairinelle's face still kept its long, straight lines. His elegant features were scratched and bruised, but had not been shredded as his mentor's had been, and the bones were not broken, for he'd had someone to call off the dog this time, and he'd been under the care of Linderic, who knew exactly how to heal the wounds his dogs dealt out.

Fairinelle's legs, protected up to the knee by the black leather of his boots, had stayed intact. The boots were in a sad state, ripped and useless now, but they had kept him from needing the kind of wheeled chair Jean-Marien used in Faubourg. He would walk and dance again, and run, if wanted.

But to where? Renn wondered. He'd spent all his life running. Where would he go now, when this was over?

Celine was the least injured of the three, but she had less

luck in escaping the illness she'd brought on herself with her drinking, and although Linderic tried his best to keep things clean, working with Keno and a few of the other houndsmen whose curiosity had overcome their native distrust enough to venture into the foreigners' territory, nobody could pretend the smell didn't linger when the doors were always shut for Gauls' protection.

Nobody could pretend they didn't hear her retching at any moment of the day or night. for Linderic refused to let any of them outside without an escort, for their own protection, but Celine refused to ask for one when she was going to be sick, for the only thing worse than humiliating yourself in front of people you knew was doing it in front of people you didn't, and doing it in front of people you had hated as enemies up until they cleaned your own vomit for you was worst of all.

Even Emile's easy smile was strained by the second week of being captive witness to her struggles, and though he continually encouraged Renn not to dwell on it, one day he simply muttered "At least on the St. Juste, we could get out into the air!", rose and hobbled to the door, and attempted to push it open.

He didn't get very far. For one thing, his bad arm was still not strong enough, and the door was too heavy to push with only hand. For another, as soon as the door moved even a little, Linderic appeared on the other side, pulling Emile by his good arm back to his cot, and scolding him in a flurry of words that left Emile looking helplessly up at him.

"Just trying to get some sun on my face, boss," he answered apologetically. "I haven't felt this cooped up since I was behind bars waiting to go to the St. Juste."

"Is it very bad out there, Linde?" Renn asked. "Are the people very angry at us?"

"It's not so terrible," Linderic reassured him. "At best, they're curious. At worst, they're only afraid. But better to keep everyone protected in here than be sorry later. It's best not to tempt a dog to the hunt, remember?"

"But what about the warriors? I know there's no way they'd be afraid of three sick and hurt Gauls."

"The warriors are learning to deal with it," said Linderic, and his jaw tightened.

"But it would be safer, for you and everybody, if they didn't have to learn to deal with it." said Renn, switching to Wendish so that Emile wouldn't hear what he had to say next. He knew Emile would protest, and it was hard enough to have to say it already. "We need to get my friends out of here."

"You could order that they be given safe passage out," said Linderic carefully, in the same tongue. "If you claimed the title of chief."

Renn had been avoiding the subject all this time, for he couldn't bear the possibility that he might not go with them, but it was becoming clear now that he was going to have make the choice, especially if the others' safety depended on it.

"I don't…"

"I've told you since the beginning that you were ready to be a warrior," Linderic reassured him. "You used to think so, too. Remember all that time you spent trying to convince Hagen of it? You have what it takes to lead. You never would have taken Hagen on by yourself if you didn't."

"I know you're right, but…I'm afraid to do it."

It was the first time he had admitted such a thing out loud since before his father had died. Ever since he had gotten over his first frightening to introduction to Barenhohle five years ago, almost every moment had been spent trying to prove he was *not* afraid of the world around him. To prove that he had what it took to be a warrior, a Wend, and then, a Gaul. Now he would have to be a chief, and though he knew he *could* do it, he was afraid of what he would have to do once he had. He came back to the question: What good was getting the others safe passage if he would just have to turn around and fight other Gauls after they were gone?

"Lean on me, I can help you," said Linderic, sounding so much like Emile it was startling.

Renn knew he ought to have been satisfied. Even if the others went away, Linderic was still here, whom he had loved, and who had always been enough for him before he'd left home. But it wasn't "before" any longer, and he no longer wanted just to be at Barenhohle as a warrior and a chief. He loved this place, but he loved Gaul now, too. How could he have them both?

He did not find the answer as he watched the others gaining strength every day, for with each new victory they gained – sitting up, standing, walking – Renn could only think of how it brought them closer to walking away from him.

When he was well enough, Linderic took Renn out at intervals, to walk again amongst the people who would now be his subjects. It was silly, really, to have to have an escort, just as if he were ten years old again. These were people he had known for years, much longer than he had known the three in the barracks, but at times it almost felt like they were strangers again.

He looked into their faces, searching for signs of familiarity, acceptance of "the boy who'd been left behind" who had returned as their leader, and he wondered whether the caution, the wariness he felt when their gazes met, was on their side, or his. But Linderic, who had some experience in leading men, was constantly muttering in his ear, instructing him on what to do, what to say, how to react.

In the days that followed, Renn tried to learn as much as much as he could, to fill his head with that helpful voice to drown out the knowledge of what was coming.

What was coming was a sunny morning when the barracks were clean, and the wind blew fresh through the open doors, and the three Gauls were each finally strong enough to walk out of them.

It felt like the morning in Angel's Arrow, when he and Fairinelle had helped Emile navigate his way out of the inn where he'd healed from his concussion. But then, Renn had been pleased and proud to consider them his newly-made friends, and now he was sending them out as his soon-to-be former friends.

Linderic had suggested leaving under the cover of darkness to avoid potential trouble, but Renn had refused.

"No, we won't hide," he'd said. "If I'm to be the chief, then the people have to learn to respect my decision. These are my guests, and my friends, and they'll be treated that way."

As they walked, he, Linderic, Emile, Fairinelle, and Celine, some of the Cimbri gathered outside to watch the strange visitors. Many of them had never seen a Gaul before. Some looked in wonder, others sulked, but none made a move until Meinhardt, a young warrior who had been one of Jungbern's friends, stepped forward from the crowd.

"Stand back," Linderic commanded, his voice and his face hard as stone, and stared Meinhardt down until the other lowered his eyes and melted back into the crowd.

Renn saw Cressido of the bright, fierce eyes appear, clamping his hand sternly on Meinhard's shoulder as the group passed on.

They trod the same paths Renn had walked with Willow and Badger until they reached the river, the group somber and silent most of the way. Emile kept making small attempts at conversation, and Renn tried his very best to respond, remembering what Emile had told him when he'd been left for dead with a bullet in his side. But he was afraid to say too much lest Emile hear the tremble in his voice, and his responses defeat the purpose.

When they had at last ferried the group across to the nearest remnant of a landing on the Gallic side of the border, Emile turned and took his hands.

"If you need anything, let me know. You remember what I told you about how the post works, right? And you've got the address I gave you?"

Renn nodded, closing his fist around the scrap of

paper he'd squirreled away in his pocket, not trusting it not to get lost if he left it out in the barracks.

"I don't suppose you've got a post office here, but try and make it back to the tavern at Plainte if you can, and send it from there."

Renn wasn't sure how well the people in Plainte would take the arrival of a Cimbrian chief at their village, but it was pointless to say that, for Emile would insist no matter what Renn said. He always had, whether it came to getting Renn injury leave on the St. Juste, or taking double watches in the night, or even breaking rank in the middle of a firefight. If it meant the chance to take care of someone, Emile would not be talked out of it, and for that, Renn would always be grateful.

"If you ever need me," Emile said. "I promise I'll find a way to come to you, even if we're on two sides of the border. But you've got to let me know, yeah? You have to give me your promise, too."

"I promise. And I'll write you, too, Mr. Fairinelle," Renn turned to him. Emile had made each of the departing three write down a place where they could be reached on that paper.

"I should be glad to hear from you." Fairinelle nodded, his mouth a tight line, and extended his hand. Renn shook it gratefully.

"And me?" Celine asked, her tone not demanding, but rather meek, and even – amazingly – hopeful.

"Of course, you."

Nothing about this felt right. He'd already had to say goodbye to his friends once, and now he had to do it all over again. He didn't want to have to send them letters. He wanted to talk to them himself, as he'd been used to.

"Well, then," Celine said, turning, and, to Renn's amazement, dipping a curtsey to Linderic who waited silently behind them. Proud Celine Lauvin, who had hated all the world and especially Wends, was now bowing before a man she would previously have spat on, and whom she had come all this way to collect money to kill.

"Oh, Celine, wait!" said Renn, searching about for anything of value on his person, and settling on the beaver-fur cloak Linderic had given him to wear. It was the sign of the lords of Barenhohle, signifying that its wearer was ruler over the Cimbrian Woods. Linderic had made him this one in the weeks since Hagen had ceased to need his.

Renn slipped it off and pressed it towards Celine.

"You forgot to take something back for your bounty. This is something you couldn't get anywhere else, and it'll show that you've been here."

"Keep it," she said. "I didn't earn any bounty. You did."

So now he was a chief, and a Butcher, and a bounty hunter, too. It was more than he'd dreamed when all he wanted was glory for himself, but it was amazing what you could do when your goal had changed to protect someone else.

"You know I'm in no position to collect it!" said Renn in exasperation. "You have to take it in my place."

"You'll have to come visit me sometime, then, to claim what's rightfully yours," she said, her eyes slitted in that familiar way, but this time it was with amusement.

"Come see *all* of us, won't you?" Emile added. He grabbed Celine and Fairinelle by the sleeves and pulled them forward to surround Renn in a hug.

"Of course," said Renn, his face crushed against red wool and white cotton and brown leather. "Thank you all...for everything. I'll always remember..."

"I thank you for everything, as well. I learned much more from you than I ever expected," Fairinelle said as they broke apart, while Celine, unable to speak, took Renn's hand and nodded her agreement. It was the first time in either of their lives that she and Adrien Fairinelle had been of like mind.

"Remember to be happy, yeah?" Emile said, patting Renn on the back. "And I'll do the same."

"Will you go back to the army?"

"Nah, what if I do something crazy like help a Wend again?"

Renn laughed and Emile threw his arm around Renn's shoulder one more time.

When he finally extricated himself, the four of them stood and stared at each other for so long that Renn wondered if they might turn into statues, standing forever there as monuments to the fact that their two countries didn't have to hate each other.

But one by one, they turned, Fairinelle first, then Celine, followed by Emile, who looked back and waved more times than Renn could count, whistling to keep up his spirits. But their figures at last melted into the darkness and gloom of the trees – the same trees into which Renn had disappeared on that day when the dogs were howling and war was in the air – and now there was only Emile's lonely whistle, which, too, was fading, and Renn could not stop his tears.

With Linderic's arms around him, he cried and cried. It was dark before they returned to Barenhohle, for Renn was determined that the people should not see their chief showing signs of weakness in the telltale tracks of tears.

"But Renn," said Linderic, his own eyes wet as he held the boy. "Tears are not a weakness. Your uncle never understood it, but if a man can cry, he's got the most strength of all."

"I know," said Renn, and he remembered Celine who had chased away her tears with drink, Fairinelle who had chased his with hate, and Emile who had kept them at bay with love. It wasn't until all of them had finally been caught by their sadness that any of them had been healed. Could he ever teach the warring Wends to understand this?

"I know," he said again. "But we've got work ahead of us to teach the others. You'll help me, won't you?"

"Always," said Linderic.

Renn rubbed a hand across his eyes. "Let's go, then," he said.

*   *   *

"First things first. No more war parties."

Renn and Linderic sat across from each other in the barracks that seemed strangely empty, even after the rest of the Houndsmen had been allowed to move back in. Though he knew he would likely have to do it someday, Renn hadn't wanted to move into Hagen's quarters. It hadn't felt right; brought back too many bad memories. Plus, if he stayed in there, he would be alone. In here, at least, he had friends around him.

"We can't expect peace if we're constantly crossing into their lands...which we are, as I learned. Why didn't anyone tell me? I'd always heard it was the Gauls instigating things," he said.

"Sometimes they do. The day you left, for example. But your uncle loved to fight, and I think you've seen now that he wouldn't always let the truth keep him from doing it."

"That is not going to happen again," Renn said, his jaw sticking out in a manner that reminded Linderic of Celine.

"But what will you do if their armies do come to attack us?" he asked. "We can't let them just walk in, can we?"

Renn hadn't thought of that. It was true that he couldn't leave his people defenseless, but it made him sick to think that he would be ordering death down on people like his four friends if he ever gave permission to protect Barenhohle.

"You know so much more than me, Linde. Why can't you just be the chief?"

"*And let me go back to them*" he added silently. Even weeks after their departure, he still wondered about them. Had they made it home safely? Were their scars healing? How were they living and changing, casting off the shadows of their pasts?

It wasn't fair that he had seen the start of their journeys, and now he was unable to see the end of them. How could he go on forever wondering whether Celine had stayed sober, whether Fairinelle had let himself go back to the ship he hated and didn't deserve, and whether Emile had gotten settled in a new place where he wouldn't be known as a traitor.

Was Renn destined to spend all his life wishing he were somewhere other than where he was? Always wishing for someone to appear and lift him out of his situation? No. That was the old Renn. He used to *let* things happen to him, but he was Renn the warrior now, the chief. The brother and friend to soldiers and bounty hunters and butchers. The one who was a Butcher and a bounty hunter himself now. How could he expect the others to move forward if he wouldn't do it himself?

Fate had pulled him along once. It had pulled all of them along to places they hadn't wanted to be. But he would do the pulling now. He would show the others just how it was done.

Gauls and Wends had always hated each other. But then, up until this year, Fairinelle had always borne all the weight of his past on his shoulders, and Celine had always drowned hers in a bottle. Emile used to always be model soldier, and Renn had always been the boy who had left behind, who wasn't good enough to be a warrior.

What Renn had learned from all of this was: always didn't mean forever.

CHAPTER 37
You Were Alright

The sign with the painted sparrow swung in the breeze, but the door beneath it was closed. Two pedestrians hurried by the window, pulling their coats close as the wind picked up.

"Closed again," said one to the other. "Where's a person supposed to get their potions if the best shop in town is only open half the time these days?"

"Don't grumble, he only closes when he's got visitors, and we can't begrudge the man that."

"Is it the lady again?"

"Not today. It's a gentleman, a fine, tall man. Though he looked a bit banged up...his coat was awfully worn. Almost in tatters, really."

"Oh, that tall man? My brother says he used to live around here. He was one of the Circlars."

"Those Circlars get into an awful lot of trouble, if you ask me. *I* would never want to be one."

"Haha, you couldn't if you tried," said the other as they passed by the closed door.

Behind it, in the same room into which a Wendish boy once cautiously ventured, the man in the wheeled chair sat speaking to a friend, though it was not the weeping woman of before. The "fine, tall man" sat across from him, his arms in bandages, but he looked healthier than he had looked only a few weeks prior.

"Seems like medicine's advanced since the old days," said Jean-Marien with his half-smile. "You can't even see

257

any scars. And of course you're walking just fine, aren't you? You don't look any worse than if you'd had an extra long day on the hunt."

"I had the Wendish houndsmen themselves to help me. They know how heal the wounds their own animals cause. The Houndmaster himself tended to me...strange to speak of them as healers now, when the thought of them was always so painful before. I used to wonder how you stood it, when it happened to you, but I think I understand now."

"And what is it you understand?"

Fairinelle sighed. "I know there's a boy alive out there because of what I suffered. But then, I suppose I wouldn't be alive if it weren't for him, either. He killed the dog that attacked me, you know, and it was he who had the houndsmen care for me. They were his own people, as it turns out."

"Not that boy who was here with you and Celine last? But he was so polite and quiet. I never would have taken him for a Wend."

"There are many things I never would have taken for a Wend before," said Fairinelle.

"Well, it was good that he was what he was, in the end. I know it would've been hard if you'd ended up looking like me. You never could stand to see reminders of hard times, even before I met you. Even I, tucked away as I am, have heard stories of the Child Knight by now. Anyone else would have been lording that over all of us, but you've never talked about it. Then you ran away from here as soon as you could after the trouble with the dogs happened, though you'd always been so happy here before."

"I was," said Fairinelle wistfully. "I loved it here, and I didn't want to leave, but I couldn't stand what Celine had done to you, and worse, how she wouldn't take responsibility afterwards."

"That's what I mean. You never could bear to face hard things, so you run from them, carrying those bad feelings with you as you go. But trust me, as someone who's had no choice but to face them, they're easier to live with if you deal with them head-on, rather than trying to carry them all on your back."

"The key to being a Promethean is to make friends with the solitude," Fairinelle muttered, remembering Jean-Marien's first lesson with him when he was a new student recently arrived from Misère. "All these years, I threw myself at solitude, though I don't suppose I ever made friends with it. I wanted it to hurt. I ran, but I hated myself for running, so I ran harder, to punish myself for what I couldn't face. I loved my father and my home, but I ran from it because of what I'd done there. So I came here, where I thought to live as a poor, simple hunter. But it was wonderful here, too, and that was the problem, for once I began to think I could be happy here, it was broken all to pieces once more. Celine did to you what I had done to those Wends as a child, and I hated her for it the same way I hated myself. When I looked at you, I saw my own guilt following me."

"So you ran again."

Fairinelle nodded. "To a place where I thought I'd have no chance of hope at all, where it was only darkness and wretchedness, with no false expectations of anything else but the hard work and the pain."

"Your prison ship."

"And Celine wound up there, too, of all the places. But she hadn't forgotten, as much as she tried to pretend she had."

"No," agreed Jean-Marien quietly. "She tried to stay back then too, you know. You remember how wild she was to be out on the hunt, and she was willing to give it all up because she felt so bad over what happened. But I would've felt worse keeping her here. It would have been awful for her to stay cooped up with me when she didn't want to be, so I told her to go."

"But I thought…"

"It's true," Jean-Marien blushed even now. "I wouldn't complain if she chose to stay here forever, but she wouldn't be Celine if she didn't have her own passions to follow, and I'm not sure I would like her so much if she didn't. So even if she never does feel a certain way about me, I'm alright on my own, too. I always have been."

Jean-Marien held his breath, carefully watching Adrien's face. For so many years, his younger friend had nursed a wound regarding the girl who had come to Circle Promethio searching for glory. What would it do to poor, melancholy Adrien to know it was a wound which had never had to be there, in the midst of all the ones that had?

Fairinelle's eyes grew glassy. For a full half of his life, he had despised Celine for Jean-Marien's sake, but all that was for something Jean-Marien had already forgiven. He saw now that it was the same thing he'd always done; giving her hate where nonewas needed, just as he'd done to the child he'd once been. It another mark against him, another spot on an already failed life full of chances he had let go and guilt he had not.

But he had not gone to Cimbria for nothing.

It was there, in Cimbria, when this wasted life was almost spent, that he had learned to forgive. To forgive others, and himself. All of his hate had been a mistake, but he would not make it again. He wouldn't punish himself anymore for choices of the past.

"So it was only me, then, who wanted her to stay," he spoke quietly. "All this time, I tried to force her to make it up to you, when you didn't even want that for yourself."

"You didn't know," Jean-Marien tried to assure him.

"I think I did," said Adrien, rubbing his hand over his face. The skin over his knuckles bore faint marks of the kind Jean-Marien knew only too well, but they were healing.

"Neither of us quite learned how to deal with our demons. But somehow, that boy, Rennesson, he showed us the way. He showed me…" Fairinelle paused, fighting past the shame in admitting it. "He showed me how to be brave. Imagine! A little slave boy teaching a ship's first officer – a Butcher – what courage looks like. I thought I was taking care of him, but he was the one who took care of me, in the end. Of all of us."

"They'll do that," said Jean-Marien. "The children who come under your care."

"I wish he could have been there for you back then. I think he could have helped you. More than I did, at least."

"I thought you had decided not to hate yourself anymore," Jean-Marien prodded him.

"I have no Rennesson here to remind me," Fairinelle said. "But I know he would want me to learn to do it on my own."

"He's not the only one."

"I know."

"So what will you do now?"

"I think I need to go home – back to Misère. There are some things there which I've neglected for far too long, but I think I can face them now."

He ran his thumb over the spot on his sleeve which hid the kill marks of his youth, and it was the first time in fourteen years that the familiar twinge of regret did not come with it. He knew now that marks from the past were not just there to remind you of the troubles you had been through. They were there to show that you had survived them, learned from them, and come out stronger on the other side. That you were still here even after everything you'd been through, and you were alright.

CHAPTER 38
The River

Renn clutched the scrap of paper, re-reading it for what felt like the hundredth time. Fairinelle had offered to walk with him to the address written there, but Renn had wanted to try finding his way himself. He had already made it all the way from Cimbria to Misère and found Fairinelle Manor on his own, so he ought to be able to navigate the neat, orderly streets of the clean, well-kept city. And besides, it wasn't like before, when he'd been a stranger in the country. He belonged here now just as much as anyone else.

When he found the weapons shop with the sign of a horse and spear above the door, whose address matched the words on the paper, he poked his head inside, and with a passing remembrance of how unsure he'd felt in that first weapon shop by the sea with Celine, he stepped forward and boldly asked the man behind the counter if Emile was there.

"Sure, just around the back, polishing some new stock," said the man, gesturing him past the counter and into a small workroom.

Renn poked his head inside and, with a pang of joy, recognized the dark head bent over the wood, and the hands that had offered him so much comfort and friendship now carefully polishing the shaft that looked like so many he'd handled before, before tossing it hand over hand into a stack of similar poles on the ground next to him, and doing it so deftly that the wood barely made a noise.

"Which Badeau number is that?" Renn spoke up finally.

Emile went stiff, but his face was alight with hope as he slowly turned. When he saw Renn, he bolted up, and this time the poles did clatter as he knocked his chair over in his haste. But he didn't stop to catch them. He bounded forward and swept Renn into a hug so tight that it nearly knocked the wind from the boy's lungs.

Emile had hugged him the last time they saw each other, and Renn had cried then, too. They were doing both again now, but for entirely different reasons.

"What in blazes are you doing here?" Emile asked, stepping back and grabbing Renn's shoulders in a kind of disbelieving jubilation. "Aren't you supposed to be commanding your fine warriors back in Cimbria?"

"Not anymore," said Renn, smiling and brushing at his eyes. "Linderic's the leader now. A chief can give up his power if he wants to…and I wanted to."

"But won't they miss you? Can't tell you how strange it's been for me not to have you around here. I'd imagine it's the same for Linderic and all the rest."

"Fairinelle has some ideas for a solution to that. He wants to start using a boat service to get letters over the border once the treaty goes through."

"Ah, yeah, he told me about the treaty. I figured you'd have something to do with it, only I thought it would be from the other side of the border. So Wendland's on board this time; I wonder if our government will go for it again?"

"Please, with Fairinelle putting pressure on them? It'll be done in a month."

"Isn't that the truth," Emile agreed.

"So when that happens, he needs someone to take the letters up to Wendland. Someone who's worked on a boat before, and can be trusted to go there without trying to attack it."

Emile's face brightened even more. "Best of all if they can speak the language, right? I *told* you Fairinelle was your man if you needed to get a letter home, didn't I? Way back on the St. Juste?"

"But speaking of that," he went on with a suddenly-concerned look, "did you walk back here all by yourself? You didn't meet any more bounty hunters or kidnappers on the way, did you? Ah, listen to me," he paused. "Of course you'd be alright even if you *had* met them. You brought your lance, didn't you?"

Renn nodded. "Of course, though the only thing it might be good for on a boat is spear fishing."

"Then you can be a harpooneer, just like you used to want."

"I won't be the only one," Renn explained. From his sack he pulled a folded paper, a copy of the one the new vice-magistrate of Misère had sent off in the post, which bore the words *Recommendation of Pardon* at the top.

"Fairinelle thought you'd like to come with me," Renn finished. He didn't even have to ask what Emile's response would be. He'd already heard it once before, in their dark, shared room at the inn in this very city.

"It's a deal," said Emile, proving that remembered, too.

*   *   *

Celine looked around at the wood-panelled room, at the books on every shelf, and the curve-backed chairs Fairinelle motioned her towards before resuming his seat at the desk piled high with papers.

"So this is Fairinelle Manor," she said. "It's nice. You should have invited us all last time we were here."

"We all had other business to attend to then, if you recall. I did not even come here myself. And besides, even if I had asked, would you have come?" he asked, though not without the trace of a smile.

"No," she said simply, but she smiled back.

She looked to the stacks of papers. "You appear to have a lot of business here now."

"Treaty work, for the most part. Army generals,

government officials, there are so many different sectors to coordinate. I must confess this is one of the reasons I'd like the river postal service established. It will make things go much faster."

"I could never force myself to sit inside reading and writing like this all day," she said, picking up the nearest sheet, but only scanning it briefly before putting it back down. "Though I'll admit you've always been more disciplined than me. I never had the patience to work at anything for too long."

"Here's one I think you won't mind reading," he said, and handed her page filled on which she saw her own name written in a smooth, sloping hand, amongst many other words she knew she would never have read, words that would never have been written, if neither of them had gone to Cimbria. It was an official letter to Circle Promethio, from one of its own – a graduate of Deucalion rank and no less than a lord – recommending that Celine be re-admitted to its ranks, though she had not completed her training there.

"If you're going back, you may as well make full amends," Fairinelle explained, then added. "You don't have to use it if you don't wish to."

She looked up from the paper in disbelief.

"You could have mailed this to me. Why not use that new service of yours?" she asked with a waver in her voice.

"There's something to be said for doings things directly, face-to-face, isn't there?" he said.

She nodded, recalling the determined words she had spoken on the dirt floor of the houndsmen's barracks in Cimbria. "I have to face things now."

"I do expect to hear regular updates of your progress, which means you must spend at least a little time writing, or come here yourself now and then, to tell me how you are doing."

"I think I could find the patience for that," she agreed, for once not instinctively opposing him. Then, tentatively, she added, as she had done once before with Renn. "Do you think you could…find the time to send me updates on the treaty once in a while? I understand if you're too busy…"

It was the first time she had ever asked Fairinelle for a favor.

He smiled again, more broadly than before, and she fought the urge to think of a retort. It was an old habit, and she was so used to him mocking her, but this time she could feel there was no sting in it.

"Celine, if I could make time to walk the entire length of the river with you, I can certainly make time to write you a letter now and then. Isn't that what friends do?"

A friend. It was a far cry from how he would have described her before. It was far from what she had been worthy of before. But if they had gone to Cimbria looking for a bounty and came back with a treaty, perhaps it was only fitting that she had gone in with a mortal enemy and come out with a friend instead. Amongst all of the dangers that forest held, it also had the strangest power to heal.

*   *   *

"If it isn't my old hunting buddies!" the man with the spectacles called out, raising his hand to greet the two figures at the dock of Seven Wishes. "Have you two joined up to be sailors now?" he asked, eyeing the packet boat bobbing gently at the end of the boat ramp where Renn and Emile stood.

"Something like that," said Emile. "More like postmen, really. They're creating a new mail service carried by boat. It's supposed to be faster than taking it over land, so we're trying our hand at it."

"Hmm, I guess we've all got to find something else to do now that the army bounties are off for good. Did you all manage to get any before it was too late?"

The other two shook their heads.

"I told you that you were moving too slow," Rigobert

tapped Renn's arm lightly. "Though I suppose I was too, since I didn't get anything either. I knew I shouldn't have stayed with you all so long. It's a bit of a shame, as I wouldn't have minded the extra money, but I guess it's back to foxes and other creatures for me. They're probably easier to track, anyway. But what about you? What made you decide on going to sea...or river, as it were?"

Emile shrugged. "I've worked as a fisherman before," he said, leaving out the details.

"Hey, that reminds me," said Rigobert. "I saw a boat down at the coast getting forcibly dry docked by the authorities or something. They were unloading a whole ton of sharks, and the skipper or whoever he was kept shouting that he was running an honest government business and they could check his papers if they didn't believe him. I wasn't sure how 'honest' it could've been, as I'd noticed all his sailors looked pretty ratty, but when I asked around, it turns out he *was* actually running a government work program for prisoners."

"Really?" Emile asked with a look that was honestly surprised, but not for the reasons Rigobert thought. "I didn't know there was such a thing," he said, casting a glance at Renn.

"Sure enough, but it wasn't that which did him in. He'd apparently been selling the prisoners along with the sharks – the man was doing an illegal slave trade on the side. And then, get this; when they're taking him away in chains, he starts yelling "Find that Mr. Fairinelle and he'll tell you!' Then the people taking him away say 'You mean Vice-Magistrate Fairinelle? He's the one who sent us.'"

Rigobert's eyes sparkled with excitement behind his glasses. "Can you imagine! Fairinelle, of all people, and somehow now he's in government service? Is there anything the man can't do? First he cleans up threats at the border when he's just a kid, then strikes a peace deal with them when he's grown, and now he's even cleaning up messes inside our own country...anyway, my point is make sure you don't get mistaken for doing the same thing as that warden. Being thrown in jail doesn't sound like a day at the beach."

"Yeah, seems like it'd be an awful time," Emile said with careful innocence.

Renn watched to see if this exchange would turn as tense as the last one they'd had with Rigobert, but when Rigobert glanced away, Emile turned to Renn and pulled such a laughing face at him that Renn had to duck his head to hide his smile.

"You want me to tell Fairinelle what you're doing, so he knows not to arrest you?" Rigobert asked companionably, turning back to them. "I'm travelling back up that way soon, and I could go see him for you."

"Thanks," said Emile, coughing to hide a chuckle. "But we'll see him when we go up. We'll probably get there before you if we're travelling by water – that's the point of the new post service. Besides, he's the one who commissioned us, so we'll be alright."

"Are you kidding me?" Rigobert shoulders slumped in disbelief. "He's making the post run faster now, too? I need to get in on his job. I'd asked myself why he would give up the hunting life, but maybe now I know. Legislation sounds boring, but it seems like there's opportunity in it."

"Maybe so," Emile said, still working to keep a smile off his face.

"Really, though, this peace stuff docs sound like a better deal. Get a bounty on someone and that's a one-time reward, but strike up a trade with them and that's a lasting source of business, see? We should have thought of this years ago."

"Absolutely," Renn said. The last time they'd met, Rigobert's analytical mind had brought him too close to an uncomfortable truth. But this time, it had led him into a wonderful one. But that didn't surprise him. It wasn't the first time something that had once seemed frightening had turned out to be beautiful in the end.

"Right on, mate," Rigobert pointed at him with a

cheerful click of his tongue. "Glad to hear you see it my way. You know, it's a shame you didn't go to work on one of those passenger boats or you could've given me a lift up. But of course, going by foot's not such a bad gig, either. You don't get to learn as much about a place by just slipping through it as you do when you stop and really look at the things and the people there."

Did Rigobert, who prided himself on having the best information, even know how truly he was speaking now? Renn's plan had always been to slip out of Gaul as fast as possible, but he was ever so glad now that he'd been forced to walk through it, and thus learn to love it, one step at a time.

"And anyway," Rigobert went on, "If I walk, I might catch some marks on the way…only animals of course," he added with a resigned smile. "I'm not looking to get thrown in prison either."

"Sounds like a plan," Emile nodded. They were almost the same words as he'd spoken to send Rigobert away in Misère and stop him from asking too many questions, but Emile's tone had been falsely bright then, and it was truly bright now, for this time, he truly meant it.

"Sure is, friends. See you again somewhere along the route?"

"I'll look forward to it," said Renn, and Emile nodded his agreement.

When they'd shaken hands and said their goodbyes, Emile turned to Renn, bouncing on his toes, and both of them finally let out the laughter they'd choked down.

"If that isn't the best news he's ever had to tell!" Emile cried. "Bossy Buron finally getting a taste of his own medicine!"

"Fairinelle didn't even tell us!" Renn added incredulously. The officer had always had a talent for moving quietly, and for surprising everyone with a laugh at the most convenient times. Even as a vice-magistrate now, he hadn't changed in that regard. But Rigobert was right – a Butcher as a ship's officer and a bounty hunter was fearful, but one in the role of vice-magistrate, with a longer reach and more power behind him, was incredible.

"Though what'll happen to the others onboard, do you think?" Emile looked out over the water. "After all this time, there's some as I wouldn't mind seeing again. I hope they're alright."

"Dumoulin wasn't so bad," Renn agreed. "I'd bet Fairinelle would know what happened to him. Let's ask him next time we go."

"Now you're talking sense, friend," said Emile, imitating Rigobert's voice. "Let's get to it."

*   *   *

"That's all our deliveries for the day," Renn explained. "Here's what's headed out." He dropped the canvas sacks he'd been carrying at the feet of the man on the dock, who looked vaguely uncomfortable without a harpoon in his hand.

"You can have the first pick of them, *Skipper* Dumoulin," Emile said to the man, and gave a little bow.

"Oh, go on with you," Dumoulin grumbled. "Just call me by own name. It's only too bad Mr. Fairinelle himself couldn't be the captain. It would've been a real classy ship then."

"For what it's worth, you were a first-rate head of us harpooneers. Fairinelle wouldn't have given you this commission if you hadn't been," Emile encouraged him.

"Tch, and it was a time trying to keep everyone in line without Fairinelle there, let me tell you. You two went off and had all the fun, meanwhile I had to be the one stand up to Buron for all of us left behind on the old St. Juste."

"But I'm sure he knew you could do it, or else he wouldn't have left you there. And you managed it, didn't you? Well enough to get the rest of your time cut off instead of being reassigned like most of the others. So of course you can manage such an easy boat as this one," said Emile.

"The only blessing was that Buron was so jumpy all the time, ever since that woman who took you off threatened him about the provost. Plus he was convinced Fairinelle was in on it somehow, since you all left at the same time. He kept saying he'd do us all in if the provost ever actually came – as if *we* were the ones who told Fairinelle to go. Lot of good the threats did him, though, since the provost came for him anyway. Maybe Fairinelle and whoever she was really *were* working together."

"Not exactly," smiled Renn. "It was just the opposite for a long time. But you can ask them both when we go. Faubourg's our next stop, and that's where she is. Her name is Celine, by the way."

"Oh, Renn, that reminds me, don't let me forget to give Jean-Marien that new package of harpooneer's secret when we get there," Emile said, and Renn nodded before continuing to explain the route to Dumoulin.

"After that it's Fairinelle in Misère, and then Cimbria, before we turn around and come back."

"You all really sure about that place?" Dumoulin asked. "You sure they won't try something underhanded when we get there?"

"As long as you leave them alone, they'll leave you alone, I promise. You *will* leave them alone, right?"

"You think I lasted on the St. Juste as long as I did by picking fights that weren't needed?" he asked, straightening with pride despite his assertions just moments earlier that he wasn't fit for his new job.

"I know you didn't," said Renn. "I remember you were better at stopping them. I never said thank you for that – for helping me like you did with Xavier. It meant a lot."

Dumoulin blinked down at him, his rough face softening, if only just a shade. Renn wondered just how long he'd been on the St. Juste, and whether anyone had thanked him for anything in all that time.

"Go on with you," he said again, throwing one of the

mail bags over his shoulder and moving toward the ramp. But he stopped, still facing the water, and added "But I suppose you're right. If it's a choice between that dirty old boat and Cimbria, Cimbria's probably the better option. Couldn't be any worse, anyway."

Oh no, it definitely would not be worse, though Renn. He looked at the boat bobbing at the dock, with the name *THERMIDOR* painted on the side, in letters that were so much cleaner and brighter than the name that had been on the hull of their last ship.

"You ready to get back on?" Emile asked, throwing a bag over his own shoulder.

The first time Renn had gotten on a boat like this, it had meant being taken away from everything that he knew and loved, and no one had asked him what he thought about it. When he'd first crossed the river, on that the day when the dogs howled for war, he was afraid it meant he would never go home, never see the people he loved again. But now it was a boat and the river that would help him do just that, and all the better for he had so many more people to love now. He would cross the waters between Wendland and Gaul now as his father had done once before, but this time he would not stay only on one side.

He followed Emile onboard, imagining that this was how Celine must have felt when she went back to Circle Promethio with Fairinelle's letter in her hand, or how that man himself must have felt when he walked back into his place as the Knight of Misère. He was proud to share in the feeling.

"Let's heave her up then," said Dumoulin when they had stowed their cargo below deck, and bent over one side of the windlass which held the anchor rope. Emile and Renn took the other side, but after a minute of cranking, the line stopped snaking up from water, no matter how hard any of them pushed.

"Hang on, it's caught," said Renn, spotting how it had knotted itself just before the opening in the thick metal pipe it was supposed to slide up through. He ran to free it, picking the knot loose with hands that had been hurt by a similar rope before, and giving it a tug to get it running smoothly again as the other two cranked.

It wasn't the first time he'd hauled a burden up from the depths, but this time he knew how to hold the weight. Not so tightly that the line couldn't move, but neither so loosely that everything important slipped away with it.

This time, he did not lose what he was carrying. This time, the rope did not burn his hands.